# PRAISE FOR FURY

Clear your calendars! Delete the to-do-list! Lock the doors! Hang the do-not-disturb sign because there is a new Ronie Kendig and Steffani Webb release! Once you start reading the world fades away and you are immersed in Davis, Hollyn, and Fury's fight for their lives! But rest assured while the story is filled with nonstop action, adventure galore, eat-your-heart-out-romance, tears flowing drama, and faith-nuggets dispersed throughout.

CARLIEN, GOODREADS

Wish I could give this more than 5 stars! Exciting, heart stopping story! Loved the relationship with the RMWD and his handler. And the romance was also sweet.

NOELLE, GOODREADS

*Fury* has intrigue, romance, a dog, and an exotic location with an undercurrent of faith. What more can you ask for in a good read?!

ALISON, GOODREADS

I love this series. I love the relationship between the military working dogs and their handlers. *Fury* is a thrill ride from start to finish. I loved the twists and turns and the relationships that developed throughout the book. I am looking forward to the next book.

JULIE, GOODREADS

# FURY

## A BREED APART: LEGACY | BOOK 4

## RONIE KENDIG

## STEFFANI WEBB

Sunrise PUBLISHING

Fury
A Breed Apart: Legacy, Book 4
Published by Sunrise Media Group LLC
Copyright © 2024 Sunrise Media Group LLC
Print ISBN: 978-1-963372-26-7
Large Print ISBN: 978-1-963372-39-7
Ebook ISBN: 978-1-963372-19-9



For more information about Ronie Kendig please access the author's website at roniekendig.com.

Published in the United States of America.
Cover Design: Kirk DouPonce

*For You*

I have set the Lord always before me; because He is
at my right hand, I will not be shaken.
Psalm 16:8

# PROLOGUE



*UNDISCLOSED LOCATION, AFGHANISTAN*

Drool ran down the back of his hand.

"Knock it off, you goon," Davis Ledger muttered to his military working dog. He swiped at the liquid. Shifted his prone position on the rocky ground so he wasn't in the slobber LZ. "Down," he commanded the sable German shepherd.

Panting, Fury conceded, lowering his muscular frame. Like the wretch he was, he licked Davis's cheek, hot breath puffing against Davis's skin.

When the wet snout hit his ear, Davis jerked his head away. It reminded him of the wet willies his childhood best friend used to give him. He'd hated it then. Hated it now.

Fury yawned, clearly happy with himself, as suppressed chuckles from the rest of the nearby team filtered over. Davis shot a glare at his partner through the dusk slowly seeping into darkness. Resumed his patient watch of the mud-brown area below.

The compound was tucked between the craggy hills that were surrounded by parched, cracked dirt. Dust, dust, and more dust. That's all this part of the region was. A cluster of guards relaxed by the faded blue gate, smoking, AKs slung over their shoulders. Davis could have sworn the same company made the security gates for every Third World country he'd been to. They all looked the same. But it also meant they were familiar and easy to breach when you'd done it a few dozen times.

"Trouble in paradise, honey?" His friend Luke Ross razzed him. They'd been buddies ever since clawing their way through Basic. The guy was solid as they came but never missed a chance to joke around. Even from a few feet away, Luke's bright white smile was visible. It'd earned him the name Pearly.

"That's all he's got," his team leader, Shaw, chimed in.

"Yeah, but what a way to go." Luke again. The inflection in his tone drew another round of quiet chuckles. "When's the last time you took a girl out? Second grade?"

Davis shook his head. Not everyone found the love of their life on the first day of school like Luke and his wife, Jana. Davis admired their relationship. It resembled only one other that he'd seen. They were more devoted to each other than any of the relationship examples his mom had shown him growing up. Gave him hope that someday he might find the same thing.

Thought he'd found it once. He'd been wrong.

Least, that's what he told himself.

Wind started picking up, and Davis heard Luke's MWD, Reza, shift in her down position. She and Fury were two of the best electronic detection dogs in the military. They could find a mini USB in a sandstorm. Which was why they were both on the mission to acquire a USB drive with missile codes that intel claimed some fool had decided to sell to a warlord with ties to Al-Qaeda. Namely, the warlord camped out in the compound below.

Fury held up a giant paw. Swung it in the air in Reza's direction. She ignored him completely.

"Hey," Davis whispered loudly to his partner. "Pull yourself together. No flirting on missions."

Luke smirked at Reza. "Tell him he can flirt all he wants." He ran a hand down the Malinois's neck. "It'll just prove how much more dedicated you are to the job when you find the USB first because lover boy can't see straight."

"Yeah, we'll see who finds it."

"Loser buys?" Luke held out a fist.

"You're on." Davis leaned over and tapped his gloved hand to his friend's.

"VT6. Seller approaching the compound," came the gravelly voice of their team sniper, Rafkin, who was perched uphill, farther behind the team. Ten yards to their left, Zaid and Niles were set up and waiting for the signal to move in.

Fatigue poking his neck from the prone position he'd been in, Davis narrowed his eyes at the faint dust trail marking the progress of a small approaching convoy. The quasi-uniformed guards at the gate straightened their caps and unlatched the main gate. Swung it wide as three meticulous HiLuxes pulled into the courtyard.

"Buyer's coming out to meet him." Rafkin's calm voice could've been announcing sports scores. "Identity confirmed. It's Hardy."

After shifting his scope to the middle truck in the convoy, Davis watched a man in a suit step out of the vehicle, leather briefcase in hand.

"Confirmed seller onsite. Laurel." Rafkin again.

"Cleared to engage," came the order from VT6.

Shaw's voice nearly stepped on Command's transmission. "Lock and load."

With a flick of his right thumb, Davis rotated the selector switch on his M4 from SAFE to SEMI.

Just outside the front door of the main compound building, Laurel and Hardy—the code names for the warlord and seller—greeted each other. The lead truck in the convoy crept ahead a few feet before stopping again.

Rafkin growled over the comms. "No joy," he hissed.

Laurel and Hardy disappeared inside with five personal

security as gate guards returned to their posts—and two lit cigarettes. Clearly not expecting trouble.

Happy to disappoint, gents.

Davis glanced sideways at Fury.

The lug met him eye to eye, eager for the signal to work.

Time dragged by as they waited for Shaw to make the call. The hills around them turned purple-gray and finally disappeared into the night.

Still, they waited. It was above Davis's pay grade to know the ins and outs of why. All he and Fury were there for was to ensure mission success.

Compound lights winked out.

"Go, go, go." Shaw's voice broke the extended quiet.

Sliding backward to avoid silhouetting himself above the horizon, Davis pushed off the dirt and trekked stealthily toward the compound. Fury padded at his side, his NVGs breaking up the moonlit outline of his head. Davis paused at the expanse between the hills and building. Crouched, M4 tucked to his shoulder, he hid behind a cluster of scrub bushes ten yards from the gate to his right. Grasped Fury's harness. He didn't need to look around to know the rest of his team had moved into position as well.

*Crack!*

The sound from Rafkin's sniper rifle rippled through the night a few seconds after the bullet's impact threw one of the guards back. Davis took out the second gate guard even as the guy's startled companions brought up their weapons, looking around.

*Crack! Crack!*

Stalking forward, Shaw and Niles took out the remaining guards.

"Gate clear!" Luke shouted.

"Moving." Davis crouch-ran for the gate. "Fury, let's go." The green cast from his NVGs gave him a haphazard line of sight as he hustled forward. Slipped past the iron entry, attention trained on his highly skilled MWD. Over fifty-thousand dollars had gone into training this four-legged warrior, and Davis had learned to trust the dog.

Fury slightly ahead and sniffing, Davis also depended on the team to do their jobs, which allowed the MWD handlers to focus on the dogs. Luke and Reza swept the left side of the area.

Gaze locked down the barrel of his weapon, Davis continued his visual sweep along the left wall. The courtyard was empty from what he could see. Tail up, Fury continued to seek. Didn't alert to the presence of any explosives. Guess they wouldn't be blown to kingdom come just yet.

Skirting around the north edge, they came up to the front door. Luke gave him a thumbs-up.

"Courtyard clear," Davis affirmed.

Like water through a sieve, the team filtered past the iron entrance.

The first level of the building still sat dark and quiet in the ominous night. "Fury, *fuss*." Suspicious, nerves buzzing, he waited, weapon trained on the metal door the warlord and buyer had disappeared behind hours earlier.

No response fire greeted them. He hustled back a few steps with Fury to take cover as Niles picked the lock. Luke and Reza stood ready opposite him. They'd search for the USB containing missile codes after he and Fury cleared the rooms for any explosives. Reza wasn't cross-trained for that.

Fury jerked like he was trying to go behind Davis. "Easy," he hissed in a whisper, firmly gripping the handle on the dog's tac vest. Fury always got amped up before a search. His one downfall. "Stay."

The MWD whined but complied.

"On your six." His squad leader's low words over the comms warned him before the man melted from the shadows, M4 at the ready.

Niles shoved the unlocked door open, and Shaw breached first, quickly dispatching two tangos with brutal efficiency. The house was silent as Davis slipped inside, pulse thrumming, eyes out.

"Fury, seek-seek!" Muscles tense, finger against the trigger well, Davis stalked forward with his MWD into the combined dining and lounge area.

No alerts, nothing out of the ordinary. Various other rooms, all clear. No bedrooms on the lower level.

Clicking his tongue, Davis drew Fury toward the stairs. M4 firmed, he carefully ascended the rickety steps. Sweat trickled down his back under his personal protective equipment as he continued, breathing a sigh of relief when Fury reached the top, glanced around without alerting. Shadows hung on every inch of the walls, the air heavy with the stagnant smell of body odor and old smoke. But he saw no one through his NVGs.

Luke and Reza reached the landing. "Go, go."

He moved forward.

The door to the first bedroom hung slightly ajar. Davis reached for it. Shoved it open with the muzzle of his M4. Glanced around the room. Faint moonlight fell through the window onto a man lying in bed. His frame was similar to the seller Rafkin had ID'd earlier. Fury trotted over to the bed and sniffed.

Tense for a reaction, Davis eased closer for a better look, M4 trained on the guy. Something felt off.

Adrenaline spiked. He closed the gap. Saw blank eyes staring up. Mouth agape. Davis shoved the muzzle of his weapon against the guy's sternum a couple times. No response. Davis keyed his mic. "Laurel's dead," he said tersely. His gaze stalled on an open plastic container—empty—on the nightstand. "Looks like they didn't trust the guy." He indicated to the table. "Fury, seek."

The sable GSD glided from his side, searching the room quickly. Efficiently.

Luke and Reza entered and went to work. The Malinois sniffed swiftly back and forth, snout tracking.

Davis felt his adrenaline ratchet another notch as he watched. Waited. The MWD made her way across the room. Thrust her sensitive nose into every corner and crevice.

Nothing.

Fury growled softly, shoving past them back into the hallway.

Taking the cue, Davis followed, weapon up, expecting trouble. Saw that sable tail vanish into a second room. Checked it. Still nothing except a bleary-eyed man, who stumbled and brandished a weapon.

Davis neutralized the threat as Reza and Fury headed to the last bedroom, single-minded in their efforts. Under the empty bed. In the wardrobe. Around the nightstand. Frustration coiled and he keyed his mic at—again—coming up short. "Target and buyer rabbited." Made sure his tone didn't betray the irritation they all felt. "Likely together. Don't let him leave the compound."

The team copied.

"Movement at the front," Rafkin's voice warned from his nest on the hill.

Davis bit back a curse.

Fury was still sniffing around. Intensity in the GSD's body language ramped up. He was lead team. Should be the one heading outside first, but if he had something . . .

Davis turned to Luke. "I'll finish here. Go."

Luke nodded. Double-patted his leg, recalling Reza, and they raced down the stairs.

Fury turned to Davis. Wagged his tail. *False alarm.* "Let's go."

They retraced their steps to the lower level. Hustled to the front.

"Nonlethal measures!" Shaw growled into the comms. "We need him to talk."

*Crack! Crack!*

Gunfire outside snatched Davis's attention as his boot hit the bottom step. He booked it to the front door. Paused to clear it before hurrying into the courtyard. Saw Luke engaging Hardy, who seemed to be impervious to the bullets flying at him. Davis drew down on the warlord. Hit his leg and the guy pitched forward. Tumbled. Came up running toward the parked convoy.

Luke slipped the lead off of Reza. "Get him!"

Through the green oculars, Davis watched the Mal charge off with Luke close behind. Hardy lifted a fist near the truck he was closing in on.

What was he holding?

*Whoosh!*

Even as the fireball erupted, Davis felt himself punched backward amid the bright flash that lit the night. His NVGs were shoved out of place. Black spots dotted his vision.

*Boom!*

Vibration from the blast shook around him before he collided with a plaster wall. Hot pain tore through his shoulder despite his PPE. He bounced against the ground. Rolled. Came to a stop face up. He opened his mouth. Gasped for air.

His lungs refused the request.

He tried again. Oxygen rushed in, thick with gasoline and smoke from the fully engulfed HiLux. Coughing, gagging, ears ringing, head bombarded by warbled voices he couldn't place, Davis scrambled but got nowhere. Blinked through the haze. Where was Fury? He couldn't move. Was pinned to the ground. By what? His shoulder screamed at him, and he felt like a truck was lodged in his ribs.

Gingerly, Davis looked down the length of his body. Spotted jagged metal sticking out of his side. It'd managed to lodge itself between the cracks of his PPE. That was gonna leave a mark.

He groaned. Choked on another wave of pain dragging him toward unconsciousness.

Gotta stay awake. Get Fury.

Wait. Fury. Where was he?

Davis looked around, not caring about the pain it caused.

Ears still ringing, he saw flames from the truck coiling and twisting upward. They snapped at the night sky. Then he saw.

Fury. Lying a few yards away.

"Fur—" He coughed—which sent shards of pain through his chest. "Fury!" His diaphragm seized, and fear clutched his chest. Squeezed tight as he strained through the dust and smoke hanging in the air.

The big lug wasn't moving. Davis twisted to look over his shoulder. Call for help. Nausea rose in his throat.

Luke. Or what was left of him.

Davis cursed.

In the light from the fire, he saw his friend's body lying in a heap, cut nearly in half by a chunk of the pickup, eyes open and unseeing. Reza, a few feet beyond her handler. She was—

Davis retched.

No, no.

A guttural half yell spilled from him. He tried to scoot closer. Tried to get to his friend, but the metal in his side held him fast. Pain had him seeing black spots. The contents of his stomach nearly made another appearance.

"Luke!" The yell vibrated in his chest. His head.

"Ledger. Keep still." Shaw appeared. Dropped at his side, combat lifesaver kit open. "Pearly's gone." He shook his head and went to work on Davis. He activated the quick-releases on Davis's vest, then carefully ran his fingers around the edges before checking for a clear airway and moving on to extremities. Expression hard, Shaw finally began packing field dressings around the metal object projecting from Davis's side.

Pain ripped through him.

"Reza . . . " Davis could feel himself teetering on the edge of blacking out.

Shaw shook his head somberly. "Medevac is three mikes out."

What had he done? Had Hardy been outside the whole time?

Was that what Fury'd been trying to tell him before they entered the home?

Luke. He'd gotten his friend killed. Should have been him out the door first.

"Whoa! Fury, out!"

Davis blinked. Looked for the source of the shout. Fury was up—*alive!*—and trotting around the truck. Looking. Searching. For Davis? For his furry friend? He wouldn't be working any more missions with her. The landshark snapped at Niles, who jumped back, gripping his rifle.

"Quit, man!" Niles screeched.

"Fury, here!" Davis gruffed, the pain excruciating at the effort of calling his dog off.

The GSD's large head whipped in his direction and he charged. Shaw leaned back slightly as Fury came in hot. The lug's wet tongue was all over Davis's face the second he got close. He dug his fingers in his dog's hairy coat.

"Hey, buddy." He chuckled, distracted for a split second from the agony. "You okay, then? Just wanted to give me a heart attack?" He did his best not to look at Luke's body. Tried not to think about Jana and the notification she'd be getting.

The sable German shepherd lay down beside him and set his head on Davis's good shoulder.

The *thwump-thwump-thwump* of chopper blades whirling in the sky preceded the CH-47 Chinook that soon hovered over the compound. Dust swirled around as it lowered.

As combat medics raced over with a stretcher, Davis felt his head swimming. His side and shoulder were on fire. His hearing was hollow. Vision graying . . .

"Boss . . . " His words were lost in the thunderous sound of the helo.

Shaw turned just as Davis felt his body go slack.

# 1



*ABU DHABI, UNITED ARAB EMIRATES*

HOLLYN REINHARDT'S STOMACH WAS A BALL OF NERVOUS ENERGY AS the Rolls Royce pulled closer to the Eve Whitlock Gala. The prestigious event was held annually to honor those in the tech industry responsible for advancements in science. And tonight, *she* was receiving recognition. But not just any kind. It was the Polaris Achievement Award. Still didn't feel real.

Across from her on the rear-facing seat, Hollyn's parents spoke quietly to each other. She smiled at the way Mum's British accent contrasted with Dad's Swiss—something she'd loved from the first time she met them.

Running a hand down her emerald-green silk dress, Hollyn could hardly believe this was her life now. It was a far cry from the ten-year-old foster child dressed in ragged castoffs nearly two decades ago. *Grateful* didn't begin to express how she felt about Ansel and Lydia Reinhardt adopting her. Her life had changed drastically after that day. Her new parents had integrated her into their life seamlessly and without reservation. Not to say she hadn't done her fair share of testing them for a while, making sure they weren't going to dump her.

Eighteen years later, she sometimes forgot she wasn't their biological daughter. Rarely, but it happened.

Resting her hand on the door armrest, Hollyn's auburn-blonde hair fell over her shoulder as she leaned to peer up at their destination. "Is it just me, or does the place look bigger at night?" she asked.

Abu Dhabi was a gorgeous place to live, and the Conrad Abu Dhabi Etihad Towers were an even more breathtaking sight at night. Seventy-four floors of pure luxury shining like a jewel in the sky. Not even the surrounding city could dim its shimmer. Five years living here, and she still got blown away every time she saw it.

"I can't believe this . . . "

Dad reached over and took her hand as their driver, Bongani, slowed the car behind a line of others waiting to drop off gala attendees. "You're going to do great, hon."

His blue eyes, set off against white hair and age lines in his cheeks, shone as bright as his cheery smile—the one that lifted her spirits and encouraged her on the especially hard days.

She'd almost given up on this project so many times, but something Dad had always said growing up would pop into her mind: *"You can quit anytime. Just not on a bad day."* The quote had cemented itself in her heart.

"I hope I don't stumble over my words." Hollyn pinched a section of her dress between her thumb and finger. She looked down at Dad's warm hand still gripping hers.

His weathered skin spoke of a life well lived and countless hours in the lab, working on the next technological breakthrough. He had a drawer full of awards identical to the one she was about to receive. Never would he display them. She, on the other hand, had every intention of hanging the plaque on the wall behind her desk. Maybe even getting a spotlight for it. Who knew if she'd ever get another.

"You've practiced your speech dozens of times, darling,"

Mum said. "You'll be brilliant." She leaned forward to adjust Hollyn's jeweled clip, holding her hair at the temple.

Hollyn tried to put on a confident smile, though really she just felt like throwing up. She belonged in a lab, not in front of a thousand of the biggest names in tech, giving a speech.

*What do I know? I'm . . . nobody!*

"Here we are." Bongani pulled up to the portico and put the car in Park.

Dozens of camera flashes bombarded the car on either side of a red velvet carpet, as if this were a movie premier.

"Deep breath, now," Mum said with a wink.

Hollyn drew in air as an attendant opened the back door. She took the man's gloved hand and stepped out, praying she wouldn't trip in the heels she almost never wore. Waiting as Mum and Dad emerged behind her only made black spots dot her eyes as the photographers snapped away. Walking inside was going to be interesting.

Like a knight in shining armor, Dad held out his free arm, and Hollyn took it, relief flooding her.

"Look at me." His boastful voice was quiet as he led her and Mum toward the double doors ahead. He smiled for the paparazzi like he'd been born for this life. "Just an old coot, and I've got the two prettiest girls on my arms."

Hollyn and her mum laughed.

"Lucky, I suppose, dear," Mum joked.

Hollyn loved listening to her parents. Married forty-four years and still as in love as ever. She wanted that someday. Too bad the only person she'd ever pictured it with was halfway across the world. Probably even married now. They hadn't spoken in, what . . . eight years? That's right. At the café in Venice.

Anxiety soon shoved thoughts of a certain six-foot-three hunk from her mind as they were greeted by guests and thrown into full-on mingling. Hollyn had never been good at small talk. Once, at a banquet, she'd asked an Italian delegate if he and his mother were having a good time sightseeing. It'd been the guy's wife. Cue her wishing she could melt into the floor.

Blessedly, tonight she was spared most of the chitchat, as her good friends Leila Pierce and Archie Durand found her soon after she stepped into the Grand Ballroom.

"So proud of you, Hollyn!" Leila wrapped her up in a tight embrace before pulling away and brushing back her dark hair with a lace-gloved hand. Flawless, tanned skin from countless beach days, wide green eyes, and a figure that said she spent hours in the gym—which was absolutely untrue—set the woman apart as probably the most stunning person Hollyn knew. She always felt like a nun in comparison.

Tonight was no exception. Leila wore a black evening gown that brushed the carpeted floor and sparkled under the ballroom chandeliers. It hugged curves Hollyn could only wish for. Her friend looked like a princess . . . if you ignored the dress's side slit, which ran dangerously high up her toned thigh. That was Leila, though. Always pushing the limits.

It was a wonder Leila had even befriended her a year ago.

Archie slid his hands in his pockets. "You really deserve this, Hol."

He and Hollyn worked closely in the lab, and he was one of her biggest supporters. Always encouraging her. Always ready to step in when she was stumped. He flashed a wide grin, the black glasses he wore tonight matching equally dark hair that somehow managed to simultaneously be long and curly yet perfectly styled atop his head. Hollyn also noted that, while he'd donned a tux, he hadn't abandoned his trademark Converse. What she wouldn't give for a pair those now.

"Thanks, guys. I feel like such a fraud, though."

"Okay, well, we're not listening to talk like that." Leila winked at a passing waiter even as she spoke to Hollyn.

"Tonight, everyone finds out what we've known for a long time," Archie interjected, gaze locked on her. "You're incredible."

Hollyn didn't deserve friends like them. Though she'd suspected for a little while that Archie's intentions leaned more toward the romantic side of the aisle, he hadn't made a move yet. Which was okay. Very okay. She didn't feel that way about him.

"Come on. I need a drink." Leila took Hollyn's hand and sashayed toward the bar, catching just about every male eye in the place.

Caught up in conversation with her friends, Hollyn lost track of time. Before she knew it, she was standing offstage as Dad introduced her—with not a little bragging—to the crowd. Once he swung an arm her way, Hollyn strode forward. Shaking like a leaf, she couldn't bring herself to look at the clapping people at dozens of cocktail-style tables, so she focused on Dad.

Just get to the podium and you'll have something to hang on to.

Forget the podium. Once she was near enough, he gathered her in a firm hug she wished she could stay in. "Knock 'em dead, kiddo."

"Thanks," she whispered.

When he pulled back, he knuckled away a tear.

That single thing sparked her own. She wiped at the rogue drop as he bypassed the gold plaque she was very familiar with in favor of a small, velvet box also on the glass stand.

Hollyn's curiosity was officially piqued. "What . . . "

"First things first." Dad's voice was amplified by the mic as everyone settled. "I know tonight is about the Polaris my daughter has earned with her incredible research and advancement in the field of artificial intelligence, but a dad can't pass up an opportunity to do something special for his Sparrow."

The use of the nickname only he used for her nearly sent Hollyn's tears over the edge. Already it was hard to see him through watery eyes. The crowd's collective "aww" didn't help things.

Hollyn opened the box. An elegant gold necklace rested inside. She lifted it out. At the middle of the delicate chain, there was a small gold globe, and slightly off-center from it was the silhouette of a flying sparrow. Like the bird was flying to the world. Or *around* the world.

These had been her dreams for the longest time—make a serious advancement in the world of tech and see as many countries as she could. She was up to a whopping four so far.

"I'm so proud of you." Dad's steady gaze was fixed on her like she was the only one in the room. "The hard work and countless hours you've spent honing your craft and making leaps and bounds in your area of expertise are wonderful, of course. No one can deny that you're a prodigy. But more, I'm proud of the woman you've become and the daughter that your mother and I got"—he looked at his watch, and she caught a glimpse of the number tattoo the three of them shared— "eighteen years, five months, and three days—almost four— ago."

He'd been counting that, exactly? Hollyn couldn't hold back the tears anymore. They fell hot along her cheeks. Her makeup was as good as wrecked, but she didn't care.

"You have a strong moral character. You know what you want and you go after it. You're kind, loving, and you're beautiful, not only on the outside but more importantly"—he placed a hand on his heart—"here. Never forget how proud your mother and I are of *who* you are. And never forget, the *world* is at your fingertips."

The crowd erupted into applause once more as Dad secured the necklace around her neck. He placed his hands on the sides of her face momentarily before picking up the plaque.

The rest of the ceremony was a blur.

When she strode into the cool evening air with her parents a couple hours later, Hollyn couldn't remember a word of what she'd said in her speech. Could only hope she'd made some kind of sense up on the stage. But the feel of the evening, the slightest breeze in the air—she never wanted to forget. Hollyn was happier than ever that it was February. She loved the chillier months here, even though they were still technically warm. But they were better than August, when she wanted to melt into the ground.

She fanned herself with her hand. The Grand Ballroom had been at capacity tonight, and the heat that came with so many bodies in one room was no joke.

The Royce pulled up and an attendant held open the door. She noticed Bongani wasn't driving. Instead, Isayus was behind the wheel. He was their secondary driver, but . . . strange to have them switch on the same night.

"Where's Bongani?" she asked, situating herself on the seat beside her parents.

Isayus's gaze lifted to the rearview mirror. "Started feeling ill and called for a replacement driver."

"Oh, I see."

"Poor thing," Mum cooed. "I do hope it's short-lived."

Hollyn's body swayed as Isayus started to pull away from the Etihad out onto the curved driveway toward the main road. Drained from the evening, Hollyn allowed herself to slump in her seat as she looked out the window.

Suddenly, Leila stepped off the curb, waving her hand. The headlights washed over her, and Isayus had to slam on the brakes to avoid an accident. Several people in the crowd around the outside of the building instinctively drew back in surprise.

"Oh!" Mum gasped as they lurched forward with the momentum.

Isayus made no attempt to hide his irritation as Hollyn's friend walked around the car and rapped on the window.

"Leila." Hollyn shook her head as she lowered the glass. "What're you trying to do? Get killed?"

"Aww, come on." Her model-esque friend flashed a teasing grin toward their driver. "You know Bongani wouldn't hit me.

Oh, oops. Not Bongani." She shrugged. "I blame the tinted windows. Hello, Isayus." She jokingly winked.

Their driver murmured something under his breath.

Leila laughed, completely unfazed.

"Did you need something, sweetie?" Mum asked gently. "We're blocking traffic."

Hollyn looked out the back window. A line was forming behind their stopped car, unable to go around due to the candy-red Drako GTE parked next to them.

Leila's.

"I tried to catch you before you left," Leila said, her eyes bright with mischief. "I had a brilliant idea."

Oh no. Those were never good.

"I've come to whisk you away on a weekend ski trip. The Swiss Alps are calling!"

"*What*? Right now?"

"No time like the present, right? Archie's coming too, and some of the others."

By *others*, Leila could only mean her posse of equally extravagant friends. Hollyn was already conjuring a dozen reasons she couldn't go. "I can't. There's still a lot of work to do."

"You mean on the project you already finished and got recognized for tonight?"

Hollyn sighed. There was no denying she'd love to go. But she couldn't just leave spur of the moment. She was a planner. Last-minute things made her anxious. Plus, she could be getting a really solid jump on her next project.

"The lab will always be there," Dad unnecessarily pointed out. "And Switzerland *is* the most beautiful country, if I do say so myself."

Hollyn was aware. They'd vacationed in Dad's hometown several times over the years. But that wasn't the point. She tried to send him a look that conveyed she'd rather stay behind, but it only earned a grin from him.

"See? He gets it. Come on!" Leila looked at her for an answer.

Hollyn thought. No use saying she didn't have her passport with her. The tiny booklet was tucked away in her jeweled clutch. Dad had drilled it into her to carry the document at all times, and Leila knew it.

*"You never know when you'll need to get out of the country quickly,"* he always told her.

"I don't have any extra clothes with me."

Leila put her perfectly manicured hands on her hips. Her smooth, dark-brown hair swished with each shake of her head. "What you don't have is a good excuse. Besides, that's what shopping is for. So . . . " She dragged out the word, one eyebrow arching. "You've been locked away in that lab for at least a year having no fun."

Hollyn heard Dad trying to suppress a laugh. She couldn't expect Leila to understand that the lab *was* fun for her. Her friend preferred partying in a new destination every night and racking up massive spa bills and shopping sprees, which her billion-dollar family trust paid for. Jetting off to tropical islands or snowcapped ski lodges on a whim was typical for her.

But she *had* made a good point. Hollyn hadn't taken a night off in . . . well, she'd just call it a long time.

Still . . .

"I don't know." She played with the necklace Dad had just given her, finger brushing the gold silhouette on the side.

"Go on, Sparrow," Dad said. "Your mother has been bugging me for a weekend in the Caribbean for years."

"Years?" Mum scoffed. "Try decades."

Their laughter was interrupted by the Mercedes behind them honking long and loud. Clearly fed up with the delay.

Leila threw up her hands at the driver. "Hey! She's making a decision, okay? Keep your pants on!" When she turned her attention back to Hollyn, her scowl was instantly replaced by a sweet smile. "I've got plenty of clothes waiting on the jet. You can change into something until we get to Switzerland."

"Yeah." Hollyn huffed a laugh. "You forget I've seen the kind of things you wear when you're not at a gala."

Their senses of style couldn't be more different. The one-shouldered, glitzy number was mild compared to the revealing outfits Leila normally donned.

Leila rolled her eyes. She swung the car door wide and practically yanked Hollyn out. "You can buy an *I Love the Swiss Alps* T-shirt to cover up, okay? Let's go." Leila shoved her toward the sports car, turning back last minute to wave at Hollyn's parents. "I'll take good care of her."

"We expect nothing less." Though Mum's voice was lighthearted, the undercurrent in her tone warned she was also serious.

"I love you guys," Hollyn called and waved as she was pushed toward her friend's sports car.

"Love you," her parents replied in unison.

Leila whipped her Drako in front of another car after Isayus pulled away. She sped onto Corniche Street in the midst of honking horns like it was the Indy 500.

This was going to be an adventure.

So why did Hollyn have a gnawing in the pit of her stomach?

# 2



## USAG BAVARIA GRAFENWÖHR, GERMANY

*"We're sorry. The board recommends a medical separation."*

Davis shook his head, remembering the words of the physician from the Medical Evaluation Board meeting. He stormed down the corridor of the USAG building, replaying the meeting where they'd just deep-sixed his career. He punched open the double doors. They hit the wall with force. Earned him a couple hard looks from soldiers walking by.

In a single moment, his poor judgment call had destroyed years of blood, sweat, and hard work. Worse, killed his best friend. Blood that would always be on his hands. He couldn't even honor Luke's memory by trying to salvage his career and do better. Four months of pushing himself to the limit in rehab hadn't made a difference—evidence that decisions had lasting consequences. But he deserved this.

Davis jammed his cover back on his head.

What was left for him now? Luke, dead. Reza, dead. His career, dead. Fury—

He whirled and drove his fist into the brick wall of the building. Pain ricocheted through his knuckles all the way up to his bum shoulder. But the pain felt good. Better that than the numbness that kept creeping over him. Dragging him under.

No use taking it easy on his arm now.

*"Please accept our thanks for your service."*

Anger surged as he recalled the brush-off. He clenched his jaw. Stalked toward the parking lot.

The hearing that ended his career—and any hope for his future—had been insultingly quick. In and out. Tossed aside like years of his service meant nothing. Just another name on the docket. It hurt. More than he wanted to admit. More than the shrapnel ever had.

And he knew there was worse still to come.

## *LACKLAND AFB, SAN ANTONIO, TX*

*Should have left earlier.*

Tapping his steering wheel with his thumb, Davis drove up the dirt road as quickly as he dared on his way to the MWD kennels on base. Didn't want a run-in with the MPs, but he was also about three seconds away from being late for his meeting with Crew Gatlin.

He pulled his truck to a stop and hopped out onto the grassy area near the metal kennel buildings. The meeting with Crew would decide the fate of Davis's former four-legged partner, and being late wasn't going to start things out on the right foot. He jogged toward the structure they were supposed to meet at.

No doubt Crew was already waiting to discuss Fury.

Thoughts of the shepherd sent a pang of guilt through his chest. If he'd just paid attention.

Fury had healed up from his injuries but now refused to work with any other handler. The kennel master reported aggression as well. Couldn't have that, so they'd given Davis two options: adopt Fury, or it was the end of the line for the RMWD. Adoption was the only option here.

But not by him.

Not permanently, at least. Fury had too many workable years left. Years he could spend doing important jobs. Davis couldn't give him that. Didn't know if he even had it in him anymore.

He just prayed Crew would go for this idea.

Just before he stepped into the building, the cell in his pocket buzzed. He slid it out. No caller ID. Whoever this was kept calling but wouldn't leave a message. He declined the call.

Rounding the entrance, he swallowed and took a deep breath to ward off the emotion pressing against his ribs. Crew had a keen eye, and Davis didn't want to invite questions. As predicted, Crew was already standing near one of the training fields, arms crossed, watching some of the handlers work a Dutchie.

The six-two operator turned. Nodded to him. "Davis."

He extended a hand. "Thanks for meeting me."

"Couldn't pass up seeing what retirement looks like."

Defensiveness instantly flared. Davis did his best to shove it down.

*Easy.*

Crew frowned. "A joke. Remember those? Or have you forgotten how to laugh?"

Didn't feel much like laughing these days. "Something like that."

Crew assessed him for a moment. "Seriously, man." Crew tracked his every move. Likely read the truth about the last few months with uncanny ability. "How you holding up?"

A complicated question. The answers lay in a minefield best avoided. Davis roughed a hand down his neck. "Just peachy," he said dryly.

*Dude, seriously. Pull it together before he walks and takes Fury's only chance with him.*

"Sorry. Know it's not what you wanted. Doesn't have to be

the end either, though." Crew folded his arms. "I know everything's gone to pieces, but there's a handler spot open at ABA if you want it."

A handler? For Crew? The idea sparked, but just as quickly, he doused it. Didn't deserve to take care of Fury anymore. Davis just needed to find the boy a job. Be on his way.

Speaking of the ninety-pound lug, he trotted onto the field with the kennel master just then. Fury jumped and twisted his large frame away from the guy's side. Snapped at the air several times. Ignored a firm command entirely—Fury's behavior didn't change. The kennel master tried a lead correction, but Fury went right back to trying to break free.

"I see he's picked up your friendly disposition," Crew joked. "Thought you said he was ABA material."

Leave it to Fury to, within the first five minutes, screw up Davis's best chance at getting the beast back to work. He could be so stubborn.

*Come on, bud. Pull it together. This is your chance.*

"He's the best electronic detection dog I've ever seen." Davis frowned at the German shepherd. "Also an incredible landshark. His grips are solid."

"Doesn't matter if he won't work for anyone."

"He'll work."

The kennel master motioned to Davis. Without another thought, he strode toward his former partner.

When Fury saw him, he acted like a switch had been thrown. Instant calm and focus. Panting as he watched Davis.

"He's all yours." The kennel master handed off the lead and a roped KONG. Thankfully, Fury had already been dispo'd for retirement, and Davis had signed the papers taking ownership of him. All with the understanding that ABA would take the thick-skulled shepherd. He tucked the toy in his pocket.

Fury heeled without being asked to. Knew where he was supposed to be.

*Why won't you do that for anyone else?*

"Ready to work?"

Ridiculous question. These dogs were always ready to work. Least, until life beat it out of them. Just like their human counterparts.

Flashbacks of that night shot through Davis's head. He muscled them back.

He just had to do this one more time. Prove Fury would work.

He gave the signal for the decoy to come out. The guy waddled toward the middle of the field in a full bite suit.

As soon as he saw the guy, Fury was all bark. Gripping the tac vest, Davis straddled the RMWD, who surged. Begged to be freed.

"Ready?" he asked the decoy.

"Yup," the soldier said with a grin. He waved one of his padded arms, taunting Fury. Shifted to the side to receive the bite. Being a decoy was more than just standing there while a dog flung itself at you. It took a lot of training to ensure the safety of both human and RMWD.

Davis unclipped the lead. "Get 'im." He released his hold on the canvas handle.

Fury took off like a bullet. He shot through the steps like the pro he was. They moved through several other demonstrations with ease. Maintaining guard position. Searching for an enemy. Detecting explosives, hard drives, USBs.

If only he'd behave himself this well for other handlers.

After Fury completed the last exercise, Davis tossed the KONG out, keeping hold of the rope.

The shepherd snagged it from the air effortlessly before he was lured into a game of tug.

"Good boy." Davis ruffled Fury's ears instinctively, and the landshark leaned against his leg. His tongue lolled out the side of his mouth, around the KONG he refused to surrender.

They walked over to Crew.

"Joints?"

"Cleared on his last exam two days ago," Davis confirmed, rapping a hand against Fury's side a few times.

Crew watched Fury for a while.

"What'd ya think?"

"We'll take him. On one condition."

Relief chugged through his veins, confident they could work out any terms ABA might have. "Which is?"

"If he refuses to work with any of my handlers, you step in." Crew's expression dared him to challenge.

"I . . . " Half shaking his head, Davis fought the urge to argue. "If he won't work, I'll step in"—what're you doing?—"to *train* someone to work with him. I'm confident it can be done."

It was dangerous blowing smoke around someone like the ABA procurement officer, but Davis knew for sure he wasn't taking the handler position. Those days were over. The rest he'd figure out.

"We'll see."

Why did that sound a lot like an ambush? "So we have a deal?"

Fury lay down, happily chewing on his KONG, his teeth squeaking against the hard rubber toy.

Crew nodded. "We have an arrangement, and I expect you to uphold your end. I'm heading out on a buy trip, so I won't be able to take him for a couple weeks. He's your responsibility till then."

Great. What was he supposed to do with him? Davis's cell buzzed again. He yanked it out.

Same caller.

"I'll let you handle that. Try and work on the attitude."

"He'll do better."

Crew walked away. "Wasn't talking about the dog."

Davis accepted the call, shaking his head. "Okay, who is this, and why do you keep bothering me?"

"Mr. Ledger?"

"Speaking."

"This is Randall Cooper. I've been trying to reach you. I'm the attorney for Mr. and Mrs. Reinhardt."

Yanked hard into the past, he struggled to understand why their lawyer would be calling him. He frowned. "Okay. Why do you keep calling? Is something wrong?" *Please . . .* Hadn't he had enough bad news for one month?

"I'm sorry to inform you, but there was an accident a couple days ago."

His mind instantly went one place. "Is Hollyn okay?"

"We're still trying to reach her."

What did *that* mean?

"But I'm sorry to have to tell you that Mr. and Mrs. Reinhardt passed away."

What? His gut churned. No. The guy had to be mistaken. "They . . . " He couldn't repeat the words. Ran a hand through his short hair. A hot breeze whipped around him. "Are you sure?"

"Uh . . . quite. I'm calling because you're named in the will. As soon as we're able to locate Hollyn, I can let you know when the funeral is. If at all possible, I need you here for the reading. Otherwise, arrangements will have to be made."

Davis's mind was reeling. The Reinhardts—the closest thing to parents that he'd had—gone. Dead.

" . . . be here?"

He fought the fog clogging his thoughts. "I'm sorry, what?"

"I said, can you be here? For the funeral."

"Yes." Of course he would. His focus dropped to Fury, and he bit back a curse. He'd have to figure that out too, since the landshark was his for the time being.

"It's here in Abu Dhabi." Cooper rattled off an address that Davis filed away before ending the call. Immediately, he tapped Hollyn's number in his contacts. Straight to voicemail. He hung up.

Fury stared at him. Tilted his head to the side.

Forget waiting.

"Looks like we're going to Abu Dhabi."

## *ABU DHABI, UNITED ARAB EMIRATES*

Her head was splitting in two. Alcohol intolerance was no joke.

"You sure you're okay?" Leila asked, swaying to the left as the limo transporting them turned the corner to Hollyn's home.

"Here." Archie leaned forward and rested a hand on the seat, too close to Hollyn's thigh. He gave her a tissue before sitting back, and she blew her nose.

It felt like the five hundredth time. She didn't even want to see what her face looked like right now. Likely something akin to a firetruck. "I'm good. It's just going to take a while to wear off."

She'd been through this once before. On her twenty-first birthday, she'd had a brandy with Dad. An extreme reaction and hospital trip later, she'd found out she was allergic to any and all *spirits*, as Dad liked to refer to them.

She'd never had another drink in her life. Till now. In the chaos of Leila's friends and their drink orders on the private jet back to Abu Dhabi, there'd been a mix-up. The glass Hollyn had been given had had no Shirley and *definitely* no Temple. She should have caught that it was a different drink, but sleep deprivation from the long night before had already been playing tricks on her mind. All she'd wanted was her bed and about twelve hours of sleep.

"So sorry, girl." Leila's velvety tone was sincere. "Things were just nuts up there."

Hollyn waved off her friend's concern. Blew her nose again. Her head swam and stomach twisted. She considered telling the driver to pull over because she was about to be sick, but they were less than a block from her parents' villa—and her attached apartment.

*Hold on, stomach.*

She could *not* get sick in Leila's limo.

"You look a little green," Archie observed with a slight wince.

Oh good. Red and green. She was just ten months early for Christmas.

Her stomach coiled and heartbeat picked up as Leila's driver slowed to a stop in front of the modern, two-story mansion she'd called home for the last handful of years. White, with several tall windows, a four-car garage, and a small, highly manicured lawn, it was expansive. Contemporary. Much more stark than the log home back in America, where she'd spent her formative years.

Hollyn gripped the door handle. Told herself all she had to do was get inside and lie down. With probably one stop before the lying down part to visit the porcelain throne. She stepped outside, followed by Leila and Archie, and the driver removed her recently purchased bag of clothes.

Archie gave her a hug. For someone with such a thin frame, he constantly surprised her with his strength. "If you need anything, just call me, okay?"

"Will do." Hollyn gave him a weak smile. Turned. She was about two seconds from losing control over her stomach but didn't want to be rude. "Thanks for a fun weekend, Lei." She went to hug her friend, but Leila was staring at the front porch, mouth agape.

"Who is *that* tall glass of water?" Her friend slid her sunglasses down the bridge of her nose, making no effort to hide her interest.

Hollyn frowned. Looked to see who Leila was talking about. Froze.

Tall. Dark. Handsome as ever. Was that . . .

It was. Here. At her home. But why?

"Davis?" Maybe she was hallucinating. Was that a sign of an alcohol allergy and sleepiness too? She felt the world sway and wasn't sure it had anything to do with her bad reaction to alcohol.

He pushed his broad shoulder off the smooth plaster wall he'd been leaning against. A scowl clouded his handsome features beneath his baseball cap. Tree-like arms folded across his chest as he stood next to a huge duffel bag. And—she squinted, stumbled forward—was that a *dog*?

Definitely had to be hallucinating.

Holograph Davis started to talk to her, but the words came out like something from a Charlie Brown movie. Her stomach had had enough waiting. She felt the contents rising and lurched forward, throwing up in the bushes lining the stone path.

Mid retch, two thoughts sloshed around her mind. When was the ground going to stop swaying? And *why* had Davis chosen the most humiliating of moments to come waltzing back into her life?

# 3



*ABU DHABI, UNITED ARAB EMIRATES*

"HOLLYN! OH, SHEESH!" THE WOMAN—LEI, HE WÁS PRETTY SURE he'd heard—grabbed one of Hollyn's arms. Stood tiptoe in high heels. Leaned forward, trying to keep her dress away from Hollyn's vomit. Looked like she might lose it too.

Davis stalked down the path. Fury trotted at his side.

The guy with glasses too large for his face held back Hollyn's hair that had swept forward. Handed her a tissue when she stood. He eyed Davis. Angled in slightly when Davis approached, so that Hollyn was behind him.

Oh please, twerp.

The skinny nerd was hardly the threat he tried to be.

Hollyn moaned and wiped the napkin across her mouth. Stumbled to the side.

So this was the woman she'd become. Going out and getting wasted just days after her parents had died?

Not the person he once knew. Not even close.

"Davis?" she slurred.

"Yeah," he said coldly.

He kicked himself for having been worried about Hollyn. For

praying she was still alive. A phone call to the lawyer right before the military hop over had confirmed no one had found her at the crash site. Or heard from her. He'd been imagining her lying in a ditch somewhere. Bleeding out. Not in a limo, clearly partying it up while her parents lay in the morgue.

Given her past, it was especially surprising.

Davis shook his head. "Why haven't you been answering your cell?"

"And she answers to you because?" Twerp demanded.

Davis didn't dignify that with a response. Didn't even pan a look in the guy's direction. Side pressed to Davis's leg, Fury growled low. Davis gripped the lead tighter, just in case. Though, here was one instance he'd be fine with the lug teaching some respect.

Hollyn looked confused. "My cell? I accidentally left it here the night of the gala."

"I'd answer my cell if you called," Lei teased with an arched eyebrow.

Davis ignored her. Pinned Hollyn with a hard look. "Ski trip? Are you serious?"

Hollyn shouldered her bag. Fury reached his nose toward it. Sniffed.

Did she have something in there?

"Wait." She held up a shaky hand. Looked like death warmed over. "Why are you here?"

Heat flared up his neck. Why was he here? "Why *wouldn't* I be?" They were essentially parents to him too.

"Okay, well." Lei stepped back, tugging at the twerp, who hadn't stopped sizing Davis up. "You two clearly have business, so we'll leave. But, uh . . . " Her heavy-lashed gaze seared its way up his frame. "Call me if you want a personal tour of the city."

Not on her life.

She slipped into the limo behind Twerp, and the vehicle drove off.

"Who's the dog?" Hollyn reached toward Fury.

"Don't." With lightning-fast reflexes, he grabbed her wrist. Though, it surprised him that Fury hadn't growled at her. "He's a military working dog. Not a pet."

She wrinkled her nose. Yanked her arm away. "My, my," she said dramatically. Then bypassed him for the front door. Drifted side to side as her unsteady gait carried her.

Drunk.

Mr. Reinhardt would roll over in his grave. Davis clenched his jaw. Moved to help her with her keys. No need. Didn't have any. Instead, she pressed her thumb to a pad above the door handle. The lock disengaged.

"Why fingerprint access?" He couldn't stop the words, even though irritation bit through them.

"Locks are easy to figure out. Biometric authentication is much harder." She shot him a small grin that reminded him of the girl he used to know. Even this close, her different colored eyes could almost be missed.

One blue. One green.

Davis remembered the first time he'd been suspended from school for punching someone making fun of her heterochromia.

When Hollyn sauntered inside, he grabbed his ruck and followed. Tried to keep his anger in check.

Gonna lose that battle.

*Whack!*

Davis bit down on a curse when his leg rammed an awkwardly placed entry table he hadn't paid attention to.

Fury stepped forward like *she* was suddenly his handler.

"Hey," Davis warned. Rubbed his leg less as a recall than to rid himself of the thrumming pain. "*Fuss.*"

With a spin, the RMWD complied and pressed up against his leg, soulful brown eyes on him. Davis roughed a hand over his furry neck.

"Dad? Mum?" Hollyn looked around.

Whoa. Hold up.

His heart thudded—did she seriously not know? Another curse rattled through him. Didn't want to be the one to tell her. But he also couldn't stand here and say nothing. He cleared his throat. Set his ruck down. "Hol."

She pressed a hand to her forehead like she had a headache. "You didn't have to wait out on the porch, you know. All you had to do was knock. Dad loves you—he would've let you in."

"Hol." He tried again.

Her bag dropped to the floor, and she sank onto the living room couch, face contorted. "I'm actually surprised they didn't see you on the cameras and come out."

"Hollyn." He spoke more firmly.

"What?" Head whipping his direction, she glared at him. Squeezed her eyes closed momentarily. "Sorry, I'm just . . . " She waggled her hands like she couldn't come up with the words.

How was he supposed to do this?

Davis sat in one of the white chairs, while Fury decided to have a look around the room. "Uh . . . " He ran a hand down his face. Time to man up. "There was an accident."

She frowned. "Accident? What are you talking about?"

"It's your parents. There . . . was a car crash."

Panic rose in her eyes. She leaned forward. "W-what are you saying?"

"Just that your parents—they . . . " Was there even a way to soften this?

"No." Her voice was barely above a whisper. Trembled in a way that had his gut twisting.

He balled a fist on the padded armrest. "They're gone, Hollyn."

Her eyes widened, pooled. Hand flew to her mouth. But she didn't make a sound.

"I'm so sorry."

She just sat there for a minute. Then her head was shaking. "No," she snapped. "No. You're wrong." Hollyn stood. Swayed.

He was up and trying to steady her before he knew it. "I'm sorry," he said again.

"No!" A shout this time. She shoved.

He let her push him back.

Fury growled. Barked a warning. Davis motioned for him to stop.

"Dad! Mum!" She turned. All but ran down the wide hall connecting to the living room.

"Fury, here." Davis sent the firm command to the RMWD before the dog's training kicked in and he tore off after her.

It didn't escape his notice that he never had to question if Fury would obey. Almost made him wish he was keeping the big guy.

Almost.

Gutted, Davis watched Hollyn check the rooms knowing what she would find—emptiness. In more ways than one. The way she kept calling for her parents, voice growing more erratic with each second, gouged a deep line through his chest.

No one would be answering her yells.

Hollyn raced down a flight of stairs—without falling face-first, amazingly enough—and through a door at the bottom. He followed with Fury. They stepped into a connecting apartment that Davis assumed was Hollyn's. She snatched a cell off the coffee table in her living room, hands shaking so badly it dropped with a thud.

A small sob broke free as she clawed for it again. The glow of the screen lit her face. Highlighted her tortured expression. She clapped a hand over her mouth. Sank onto the couch. "Seventeen calls from Randall," she breathed, tears sliding down her flushed cheeks.

Davis felt like he should do something. Didn't know what. He sat next to her as she tapped the first voicemail. By the time she was on the fifth, Randall's recording had moved on to asking if she was alive.

Fury's head tilted to the side as he looked at the device, focus pinned to the voice without a body.

"Hollyn, it's absolutely imperative that I get ahold of you regarding your parents. There's been an accident. We haven't found you at the crash site, so I'm choosing to believe you're okay."

"No," Hollyn cried, grief-stricken eyes colliding with his. "They were f-fine when I left with Leila and Archie. I-I don't believe it."

Next to him, Fury watched her intently.

Davis wished he could take away this pain. Wished he could hold her. But they weren't in that place anymore. Hadn't been for a long time. Instead, he put an awkward hand on her back. She felt so frail beneath his palm. "It's true, Hol."

She shook her head. Tapped Cooper's number and put the phone on speaker.

"Miss Reinhardt?" The guy sounded hopeful.

"Is it true?" Hollyn cut straight to the chase.

Why did it bug Davis that she wanted confirmation from someone else?

For a moment, Cooper was silent on the other end. "I'm . . . afraid so."

Hollyn's whole body was shaking. Tears ran down her cheeks. Davis had always been terrible with tears. Especially hers. Felt water pricking his own eyes. Swallowed the lump in his throat at seeing her this way.

The cell jiggled in her hands. Dropped to her lap. She let out a strangled cry.

"Hollyn?" Cooper asked. "Hollyn!"

Davis retrieved the phone, then hesitated as he glanced at Hollyn. Decided to step in—at least he could do this for her. He took the phone off speaker. Put it to his ear. "Uh, Davis Ledger here."

"Ah, very good," Cooper said. "I'm glad someone is with her. Did she say where she was? Is she okay? Injured?"

Hollyn stood. Walked around the side of the couch.

"She's shaken by the news, of course, but otherwise fine." He lifted his gaze and visually trailed her across the room. "So, Cooper—what's the next step here?"

"I can come to the house and go over the necessary details with her. The Reinhardts were specific on how they wanted the funeral handled, so there isn't much for Hollyn to worry about. Are you staying with her?"

He eyed Hollyn. Hadn't planned to stay, but he couldn't imagine leaving her like this. Debated his answer for a minute. "For now." He rubbed his neck. Tried to stretch the muscles leading to his bum shoulder. It was time for more pain meds. He turned to check on Hollyn, but she wasn't in the room anymore. Neither was Fury.

Great.

Davis punched to his feet. Started searching the apartment.

"Good, good. I'll come by tomorrow morning around ten, if that suits?"

"That's fine." He ended the call without waiting for a response as he hunted for her. Bedrooms were empty. Hollyn and Fury weren't on the staircase either. He took the steps two at a time to the first level of the main house. Back down the hallway, clearing more bedrooms as he went. Nothing.

His pulse ticked up. If Hollyn accidentally made the wrong move—

Davis whistled. "Fury, here!" he called.

They weren't in the living room or kitchen. He stalked around the massive island.

Where the blazes had they gone?

Soft sobs drew him up short in front of another doorway.

A bedroom—Ansel and Lydia's? It was definitely the primary suite. Much larger than the others.

Hollyn sat on the end of the bed, crying as she clung to a dress shirt with one hand. The other . . . ran mindlessly over the four-legged hero's thick sable neck.

Holy fluff . . . she had no idea how close she was to danger, to losing a digit or two.

Fury had posted himself at her side. Leaning against the comforter, his muzzle rested on her leg.

The RMWD watched Davis but didn't move. Looked relaxed. That didn't do anything for the tension radiating through Davis's body, though. It only took a split second for things to go wrong with a working dog. And Fury wasn't that stable to begin with these days.

He needed to get control of the GSD. Slid the leash out of his pocket and stepped forward. He'd rather be dropped into a war zone than try to navigate a crying woman. Of course this was where he'd find himself: trying to keep Hollyn calm while securing the shepherd who was capable of inflicting more pain than she could imagine.

"Hollyn." Davis's voice broke into her thoughts.

She kept running her hand down the dog's warm neck. His fur was both coarse and smooth, if that was even possible. She wasn't really a dog person, but something about his presence was comforting. The weight of his head on her leg grounded her in this painful, agonizing moment. Somehow made it more bearable.

"Don't make any sudden moves." Davis's voice was closer.

She barely registered his words.

"Good boy." His hand broke the plane of her lowered gaze as he casually clipped a lead onto the dog's collar. "I told you—Fury's not a pet."

Fury. What kind of name was that for such a sweet animal?

Hollyn sniffed repeatedly. Wiped at her puffy eyes as her stomach continued its irritated churning from before. Her headache still lingered but had dulled to a mild throb. A photograph of her with her parents a few years ago sat on the dresser across from where she sat. Tears pooled on top of each other. She needed a tissue. Or ten.

How could they be gone? How could she be on her own . . . again?

Another wave of sadness washed over her. Pressed in hard and tumultuous. She wrapped her arms around Dad's shirt. The fabric was soft. The scent of his cologne still lingered within the threads. Crumbling into another round of sobs, she squeezed her eyes closed.

Why them? Why had God taken away the family she'd prayed for and finally found? Just when she'd dropped her guard and felt like she was whole again. Like the scars of the past couldn't touch her.

She should've known.

The Grim Reaper was never far away. It stalked her no matter how much distance she tried to put between them, carrying behind it a thick chain linking them together. The happier she was, the closer it got. She would never be free.

The bed sagged beneath Davis's intrusion into her grief. His arm brushed hers. She remembered how many times he'd sat with her during those first few years they'd been friends. He hadn't had the brightest childhood either, yet somehow he'd always made her feel better. Like she wasn't alone. He'd been her best friend.

*I was going to marry him.* And they'd been going to have two kids and three cats and live in a house by the ocean. She'd had it all planned out. Then . . . he'd left.

"I wish I could change this for you, Hol." His tone was warm. Genuine.

"I should have been in the car with them." Her voice wobbled as she held back another flood of tears. "*I* was. But then—" She wiped at her eyes. Shook her head. She never should've gone with her friends.

Fury whined and pressed his weight into her leg. She went to reach for his head but stopped herself when Davis's warning about him not being a pet flashed to mind. To avoid disaster, she kept her hands to herself.

Davis wrapped an arm around her shoulders, and Hollyn sank into his embrace. She buried her face in his shoulder. Thought she felt him tense for a moment before his other arm came around her. He held her close. Didn't say a word as she cried. He didn't need to. Just like countless times before, his presence alone softened the blows of the world and gave her a safe place to fall.

Hollyn didn't know what to do now. She felt so lost. So alone. All she knew for sure was that it felt like her heart had been ripped from her chest and shredded to pieces. She cried until sleep finally enveloped her.

Eyes feeling puffy, throat raw, Hollyn forced herself out from under the weight of slumber. Her teal floral comforter lay on top of her, the fabric cool to the touch. She reached up to manipulate the necklace Dad had given her. It rested in the hollow of her throat. She tugged the globe back down below her collarbone.

When had she made it to her room? The last thing she remembered—

Davis.

Hollyn propped herself up on her elbows and looked around the dark room. He wasn't there. Did she really expect that he would be?

The house was silent.

"Davis?" she called out.

Silence was her only reply. Had she dreamt that he'd come? Dreamt all of it? Hope flared. She reached out for her phone on the nightstand. Tapped open the voicemails. All eighteen from

Randall glared back at her. Her chin quivered. That part, to her dismay, was true, then.

Dad and Mum. Gone. Forever.

Drawing on the last ounce of strength she had left, Hollyn shoved the blankets back and got out of bed. Turned on the light. She couldn't remember the last time she'd fallen asleep in jeans. It was really uncomfortable. Before heading out to her living room, Hollyn changed into sweatpants.

Despair permeated her bones.

"Davis?" She called once more, even as her brain told her that part *wasn't* true. The combined living-dining room showed no sign he'd ever been there, proving the lie her mind was trying to pass off as truth. Probably just the imaginings born of desperation. The mind was a powerful thing. She knew that.

Through the giant glass doors that led to the lower level of the backyard, all she could see was pitch black. Hollyn just stood there next to her couch, unsure what to do. Eat? She didn't feel like it. Call Leila? Archie? And say what? *Hello, my parents are dead*?

Her chin quivered even as the sound of rustling paperwork upstairs caught her attention.

*Dad!*

But reality scaled her heart almost as soon as the thought popped into her head. No. It wasn't him. Wouldn't be ever again.

Davis, then?

She flung herself at the short staircase to her parents' living room. The upper floor was dark. Not a single light on. Yet she continued to hear someone in Dad's office. "Davis? Is that . . . "

Keen familiarity with the home's layout made it easy to maneuver despite the lack of light. Even the moon wasn't shining brightly tonight. Hollyn trod along the runner behind the couch, turned the corner to the left, heading toward the study.

Why didn't he have any lights on?

Before she could reach the switches, the sound of drawers slamming shut preceded shoes running. A figure barreled into her. Collided. Threw her back. She screamed as the heavy force of the person hauled her off her feet. Fear surged. Her legs flew up as a strong arm wrapped around her waist and rammed her into the floor. The back of her head smacked against the hardwoods.

"Agh!" She reached toward her head.

Panic lit through her.

A hand squeezed her throat as air whooshed from her lungs. She could feel a hard knee pressed into her stomach. The intruder held one of Hollyn's hands up by her head. Crushed her knuckles against the hard surface.

Hollyn flailed. Tried to scream for dear life, but air—she couldn't get any. She thrashed. Pounded her free hand against his wrist. It didn't help. The guy didn't even budge. Terror rose as oxygen drained.

She was going to die!

"Give it to me!" the man demanded. His voice was hard. Gravelly. He leaned into her throat.

Hollyn coughed around the hand. Frantically tried to press it back a little so she could breathe, but he squeezed harder. Her muscles shook with fear and fatigue. She could feel pressure building in her face the longer she went without air. Pins started pricking her vision.

"You know where it is! Give it to me now or I'll kill you."

What was he talking about?

Her vision faded.

Faintly, the barking of a dog filtered into the back of her consciousness. At the sound of shattering glass and the alarm blaring, the grip on her neck released. The intruder swore and bolted away from her seconds before the barking grew louder. A dog shot past her in the darkness as she rolled to the side, gasping for oxygen.

"Hollyn!"

A hand clasped onto her shoulder.

Hollyn screamed and threw out a fist. It collided with flesh.

"Freakin—" The guy grabbed her wrist to stop the blows. "Hollyn, it's me!" She froze.

That voice.

"Davis." Hollyn's breaths came short and fast.

In the dark, it was hard to tell.

"Yeah. Here." He spoke loudly over the alarm. With quick motions, he helped her sit up. "Was he alone? Are you okay?"

Outside, Fury was barking like crazy.

"I'm fine. I think he was the only one." She coughed again. Her heart raced so hard she thought it might beat right out of her chest. She rubbed her tender neck.

"Stay here." Davis was gone in the next instant.

Hollyn stood and rushed to the keypad on the wall to stop the shrieking sound. Flipped on the light. Relief filled her when she saw it was nothing that couldn't be undone. Wearily, she glanced out the wall of windows facing the backyard. Could kind of see Davis with Fury. Carefully working around the glass littering the entryway, she moved in for a better look while still keeping herself hidden behind the solid part of the wall. The dog was trying to scale the nine-foot fence. Again and again, he jumped.

What she didn't see was her attacker. Was he hiding? Should she turn on the porch lights? Go out there and help?

*Yeah, right, Hollyn. You'd be a big help.*

She was all but cemented to her hiding spot anyway. Arms wrapped around her middle, she curled into herself. Her neck was on fire. Nightmares from this new trauma would plague her for a long time. Add it to the list of others.

Piercing sirens grew louder as police cars approached.

She felt a strange, intangible weight lifted from her shoulders when Davis and Fury stepped back inside. How many times could her life be turned upside down in the span of twenty-four hours? Was it even safe to ask that question? Had she just jinxed herself?

The gnawing in the pit of her stomach warned that even thinking the question was akin to playing with fire . . . an inferno that would consume her life.

# 4



*ABU DHABI, UAE*

". . . SO AS YOU SEE, THE DEATH CERTIFICATES SHOULD BE TAKEN care of in a matter of days." Randall's voice sounded more monotone than not as he went over the necessary details he'd come to discuss. "My connections here are helping speed the process along. Your parents had no outstanding debts either, so that helps as well. And of course, the funeral will be held three days from today. I know you're aware of that, but still."

Sitting here in the living room, Hollyn felt numb. She burrowed back against the soft sofa, staring at the vanilla candle she'd lit on the end table. The small flame flickered and danced, and every now and then gave a small pop.

Weariness pressed down on her. She and Davis had been listening to Randall for the last hour about how he was working on taking care of all the paperwork related to her parents' deaths. And she was thankful. Really was. But she couldn't handle much more of this. On top of everything else, she was still shaken up from the attack the night before.

After the break-in, the local police had said they'd find whoever was responsible, but it hadn't stopped her mind from reeling at every sound during the night. She felt so vulnerable. Even running a virtual screen through the house security system hadn't turned up answers as to how the guy had gotten into the house without triggering the alarm.

At Davis's feet, Fury lay, looking relaxed. But his keen gaze roamed over Hollyn and Randall. Watching. Waiting. Seeing if they were friend or foe?

"Thanks, Cooper." Davis's voice broke the silence that had fallen over the room.

Hollyn slid her gaze to him.

A mixture of concern and frustration clouded his face. He hadn't changed much since she'd last seen him. Except maybe filled out a little. The dark stubble on his jaw added another layer of striking good looks to him. Still, his ring finger sat glaringly empty. Why?

Davis cleared his throat, and she realized she'd been staring.

What would Dad say? He'd probably smile knowingly and see how things played out. He'd never made his hopes that the two of them would end up together a secret.

*Oh, Dad . . .*

Back then, Hollyn had been caught up in her crush on Davis. How many times had she scrawled *Hollyn Ledger* in her notebooks? An embarrassing number.

Hollyn rubbed her forehead as she nearly lost her grip on precarious emotions. Her limbs each weighed a thousand pounds. People weren't lying when they said grief was heavy. "I'm sorry. You were saying?"

Randall, ever the gentleman, let her lapse in focus slide. "Just that the police have almost finished processing your parents' things that were in the car and should be releasing them this afternoon. I can pick everything up and bring it here. You should also be aware that there was a break-in at the lab the night of the gala."

"There was?" Hollyn's heart clenched.

Another violation of her personal space, since the lab had

practically been a second home to her. The one place she could relax and be herself. Archie'd told her many times that he felt the same way. While Leila was Hollyn's closest friend, she and Archie were most alike. Both lifelong geeks and still good-standing members of the Socially Awkward Club.

"They reported nothing stolen, and repairs are underway," Randall went on. "But we thought it was important for you to know."

Hollyn's brow furrowed. What was *happening*? Break-in at the lab. Break-in at her home. The world was no safer as an adult than as a child.

"Thanks for letting us know," Davis said.

In control and unshakeable. Just as he'd always been. She admired his calmness. Craved the stability of it.

"Of course." Randall reached for his leather briefcase.

"Is Isayus dead too?" Hollyn was well aware how callous that sounded, but she didn't have the strength to ask in a more tactful way.

"He is."

Numb still, she nodded. "And have you heard from Bongani?" He and Isayus had been close friends. He must be devastated too.

"Not at this time," Randall said. "Do you want me to reach out?"

"That's okay." She'd call him herself.

Davis looked to her. "Who are they?"

Hollyn was getting wearier by the minute. "Bongani is our driver—um, *my* driver"—the metaphorical dagger in her heart cut deeper—"and Isayus would fill in on Bongani's days off or under special circumstances."

He seemed to mull that over. "But Bongani wasn't driving that night? Why?"

"He drove us there, but then came down sick during the gala."

The muscle in his jaw flexed. What did that mean? She was

desperate for the closeness they used to share. But Davis had clearly been through things that had changed him. He still cared, she could tell that much, but he seemed to be holding her at arm's length, which confused her.

A strained moment of silence passed between the three before Randall broke in. "As the executor of the estate, you will have various paperwork you'll need to sign along the way, Hollyn. I can bring it here, or you're welcome to come to my office."

"Thank you." Did she look as drained as she felt? Why did she even care right now anyway?

"As we discussed this morning, I brought the will with me," Randall said. "You two are the only named parties, so it's really a simple situation." He looked between her and Davis. "Unless you'd prefer another time."

Biting her lip, pressure rising in her chest, Hollyn couldn't help but think that the reading of the will seemed so final. As if there was still hope if it remained unread. She jiggled the gold globe on her necklace back and forth and lifted her gaze to Davis, willing him to step in. Give her guidance or something.

"Up to you," he replied to her silent plea.

Right. Under the weight of both men's focus, Hollyn could feel the room getting smaller. She could say she wasn't feeling up to it. That was certainly true. They'd understand. Probably wouldn't even question it.

The thought of hearing things her parents had planned out before their death made her queasy, but there was no sense in putting this off. It wouldn't be easier tomorrow. Or the next day. Better to just get it over with.

"Okay, let's get this done." Her chin quivered and she took in a slow breath. She didn't want to break down again. She'd cried more in the last twenty-four hours than all her high-school years combined. She wanted to be strong.

*Ha! That's a pipe dream, Hollyn. You're not strong.*

Randall gave her a practiced smile and pulled a folder from his briefcase. "All right."

Hollyn sank back against the fluffy couch as Randall began.

"Davis." He handed over a piece of paper. "To you, the Reinhardts left their cabin on the Minlan, Tennessee, property and ten acres surrounding it. They owned it free and clear and created a stipend to cover the annual costs such as property tax and upkeep."

Hollyn managed a small grin. She knew how much that would mean to Davis. From the time they'd become friends in fifth grade all the way through to high-school graduation, the cabin built in the early 1800s near the lake had been his favorite spot on their property. On more than one occasion, he'd said it was the only place he felt at home. His family life had been broken at best, much like hers before getting adopted.

Turned out Dad had listened and stored that information away. So like him. Generous and kindhearted.

A pang of sadness nearly took her down, but she fought to recover.

"You'll also see listed the financial portion of the inheritance as well as the stocks and bonds they wished transferred to you. Ansel was also insistent that you take possession of the 1948 Willys Jeep. It's been stored in an enclosure at the cabin."

Davis's knee bobbed rapidly up and down. The corded muscles in his forearm flexed, but his facial expression remained unchanged. Stoic and somber.

So . . . not happy, then? Or was she simply unable to read his poker face?

"Hollyn." Randall handed her a piece of paper as well. "Everything else has been entrusted to you, including your father's controlling interest in Reinhardt Tech."

"What?" she breathed. She'd assumed that if anything ever happened to Dad, the company shares would be divvied up between the other funding members of the company. But this . . . . She was only a couple years past being an intern. Now she had a place at the table where all the decisions were made? It was too much pressure! The board would not be happy about this.

*Dad, what were you thinking?*

Randall moved on. "This villa, I'm sure you know, is under a seven-year lease. There are two years remaining. If you want to stay after that time, we can renegotiate a new lease. Or there are the options of simply living here until the end of the contract or terminating the lease early. The home in Tennessee is currently rented out."

Hollyn's head was spinning. She dropped her gaze to her hands, clasped so tightly in her lap they were hurting. There was a dry patch of skin on her first finger. She scraped it over and over with her thumbnail. Tried to buy herself a second to soak all of this in, but her mind was racing.

Davis reached over and gave her wrist a soft squeeze before settling back, not looking at her. There he went again. Giving just enough to reel her in before he put the wall back up between them. Despite herself, she instantly missed his touch. There was something reassuring about it. As if everything would be okay.

But it wasn't going to be okay. Not ever again.

Hollyn heard Randall rummaging around in his briefcase. Looked up.

"Ansel made a video for you, Davis. And instructed me to give you this letter." He spoke the last to Hollyn, holding out a folded piece of paper to her. The wax seal with an embellished R in the middle reminded her of all the times she'd sealed letters with the same stamp as a kid. She'd felt so grown up.

Gingerly, she took the letter but knew there was no way she could read it. At least, not . . . yet. She tried not to be upset that her parents had recorded a video message for Davis but not her. They always had a reason for the things they did.

The German shepherd's head popped up, and he nosed the drive Davis was handed.

"Easy," Davis murmured to Fury.

"I'll leave you to it, then." Randall and Davis stood. Hollyn slowly followed suit. "If you need anything at all, let me know."

She nodded. "Thank you, Randall. For everything."

He shot her a tight grin before Davis walked him out. She watched the men make their way out into the foyer and stared after them, heart and thoughts heavy. A weight pressed against her leg, and she glanced down to find Fury sitting, his muscular shoulder leaning on her thigh.

A gust of warm air brushed through the open door, making her very glad they'd been able to get a window repairman out first thing this morning to replace the glass Davis had shattered to save her.

Hollyn's legs gave out and she dropped back onto the couch. A few rogue tears trailed down her cheeks. This couldn't be her life now. She sensed Davis come back into the room.

Even without making a sound, he had a presence that demanded notice. "How about some food? I can make you something."

Why was his voice so . . . peaceful?

Hollyn shook her head. "I'm not hungry."

"Come on, Hol." Concern edged into his tone. "You didn't have breakfast."

But she didn't care if she ever ate again. Food was the absolute last thing on her mind right now. "I'm fine." She didn't dare look up at him, because she knew she'd cave.

He was quiet for a while before whistling to Fury. "Come on, bud."

When she heard his door close down the hall, Hollyn finally stood. Walked into Dad's study. The walls were lined with mahogany bookshelves, filled to the brim with books on everything from classics to theology to tech. The section of classics was actually a secret door that hid a large safe.

Grabbing the afghan off Dad's reading chair, Hollyn sank onto the carpeted floor—letter still clutched in her hand. The strength to read it evaded her. She was curious what her parents had recorded for Davis. Wondered what their last thoughts were. What they'd deemed important enough to record for this moment. She wished more than anything they were still here. There was nothing she wouldn't give to have them back for even an hour. Not getting to say goodbye to them had reopened a deep wound.

Hollyn's chin quivered as she slid the remote off the side table. She hit the button to close the blinds. The room slowly descended into darkness and took with it any chance that she'd find happiness again.

Turning the USB drive in his fingers, Davis paced his room. He ran a hand over the stubble on his cheek before finally dropping onto the desk chair and sliding the USB drive into his laptop. No time like the present to find out what Ansel had put onto the device.

Even through the closed window beside him, he could faintly hear the midday *adhan* being recited from mosque loudspeakers in the distance. Fury panted next to him, tail swishing across the wooden floor, thinking he was about to get a scruff on the head. Davis obliged.

When Ansel appeared on screen, Davis steeled himself against sadness at seeing the familiar face again, and his hand went reflexively to the shepherd's head.

Fury nudged his knee a couple times. The RMWD was going to go nuts cooped up in this house without a job to do. A solid reminder that their time together was temporary. He cast a glance out the window. Drew in a steadying breath as his gaze scanned the local vegetation and palm trees lining the property. It had surprised him how pristine Abu Dhabi properties were, at least in the Reinhardts' neighborhood, compared to the ghetto he'd grown up in.

Davis turned back to the computer, effectively closing the

door on memories of his volatile childhood. Opened the lone file on the drive. The fact he'd been named in the will—not to mention the things bestowed on him—was like salt in a gaping wound. Guilt at the distance he'd put between them piled on thick. How many years had it been since he'd met in person with the man who'd been like a dad to him? Too many. He should've done better. Should have made the effort to visit while on leave.

Didn't feel right keeping the money from the inheritance. Maybe he should donate it to ABA. Give him some leverage behind not wanting to join their team.

Too bad he couldn't use this to strong-arm the med board into reversing their decision.

One blow after another lately.

"All right, let's see what he says," Davis said to Fury when he hit play. He roughed up the RMWD's ears. Thumped a hand on the dog's shoulder a few times.

Fury pressed into him. Put a paw on his knee.

"Davis." Ansel's voice drew his attention to the screen.

In his usual solid-colored button-up shirt, the man who'd been like a father to him wasn't massive by any means but still took up almost the whole frame. For a guy in tech, Hollyn's dad had never quite mastered recordings of himself. Davis had seen plenty of home videos with half of Ansel's face or an angle with more of the underside of his chin than anything else.

White hair. Familiar grin. Steady gaze. Seeing Ansel now took Davis back to a simpler time.

"If you're seeing this, then things . . . turned out differently than I'd planned." A pensive expression passed over the man's face. "You were always like a son to me and Lydia."

Hearing that was a knife to the gut.

Yeah, a son that'd abandoned the people who cared about him most.

"Remember near the cabin, you and Hollyn found that nest with sparrow eggs that had fallen to the ground?"

Davis frowned. It was a strange memory to bring up.

"Hollyn was so upset and you comforted her. Stayed with her. We got the incubator, and you two checked on the eggs constantly until the day the nestlings hatched. Then fed them every day till it was time for the birds to fly away."

Davis remembered. It had been the first summer he'd spent most of his days with the Reinhardts. He'd been eleven, still unsure if he should even be there. It'd been about a year after the accident. But Hollyn had been sure enough for the both of them.

Why was Ansel talking about this?

A serious expression came over Ansel. "Protect the sparrow, Davis."

Davis paused the video. Sparrow? Did he mean Hollyn? Had to be. It was the nickname Ansel had used for his daughter.

"... *things ... turned out differently than I'd planned ...* "

Davis's mind drifted to last night's break-in. To the lab incident Randall had just told them about. Man, if a knot wasn't forming in his gut right now. Were they connected? Seemed too coincidental not to be.

Video resumed, he rested his forearms on his knees. Shoulders taut. Hands fisted. Willed Ansel to tell him to stand down. That he was overreacting.

Instead, warning ...

"It's of the utmost importance now. Be watchful. Trust is earned, not given. First boy who was paired with Hollyn at the sixth-grade science fair, five eight."

Do what? Davis paused the video. Ran it back and listened again. Okay, so he hadn't misheard it, but it sure as heck didn't make sense. He listened again. And again. A couple more times. What did *that* mean? Tried to figure out that last sentence. Almost sounded like a Bible reference.

He roughed a hand over his face.

All these riddles. Clear sign something wasn't right. Did the coded message mean he'd suspected it might fall into the wrong hands? Randall was the only one with access. Didn't Ansel trust the guy? Or was he just being cautious?

Davis itched for a team to work this out with. Come up with a game plan—if that was needed. Maybe reach out to Chapel. With what evidence, though? At this point, all he had was a hunch.

Davis bounced his knee as he thought.

The video mentioned the science fair . . . He thought about sixth grade. Didn't remember much of it. Wasn't something he looked back on often. The face of Hollyn's lab partner came to mind, but the name was slipping him.

That last line in Ansel's video, and the way the last line sounded like a verse reference, stuck out to him. Hollyn's dad was known for quoting scripture at the drop of a hat. Seemed to have a verse for everything. It'd been so foreign to Davis at first, then started to get ingrained in him as the years went by. Somewhere along the way, since joining up, he'd stepped away from that way of thinking.

He repeated the line to himself, running through possibilities.

*Boy who was paired with Hollyn at the sixth-grade science fair* could be a book of the Bible if the verse theory was correct.

Paul? Not a book of the Bible. Timothy? Peter.

Bingo. Davis pulled up the verse on his phone—the first letter of Peter, since the second only had three chapters. Hoped he was on the right track.

*Couldn't have given me a little clearer direction, could you?*

*"Be sober-minded, be watchful. Your adversary the devil prowls around like a roaring lion, seeking someone to devour."*

He clenched his jaw. Any doubt in his mind about things not being connected was instantly incinerated. "Okay, Ansel." He tapped Play once more. "Message received."

"We want you to know how proud we are of you, Davis. Your commitment to God and country is extremely admirable."

Talk about a punch to the gut.

"We've been praying for you. For peace. For purpose."

He shook his head. Their prayers had apparently fallen on deaf ears, because here he was. Tossed out of the Army and wholly without purpose. The military had been his life. His identity. What did he have now but plans in ashes and a shoulder that kept him from doing what he loved?

Ansel went on for a while longer before the video cut out.

Arms crossed, Davis thought about what Hollyn's dad had said at the beginning. Wished he had a better idea of what was going on. But the mission was clear: protect Hollyn.

Davis leaned back in the chair. "What were you into, Ansel?"

# 5



THE NEXT MORNING, HOLLYN MADE HER WAY TO THE KITCHEN AFTER sending Davis the security footage of the break-in that he'd asked for. She wanted to think about something more pleasant than that night, and pancakes sounded good.

Archie would be here any minute, and he always wanted breakfast foods.

It was the first time since finding out about her parents that she felt like she had any kind of energy, and she wanted to take advantage of it. Passing through the living room, she eyed the overcast sky. Looked like rain was a possibility. Good  Sunshine would just feel like a slap in the face—besides, Mum loved the rain.

Tucking her hair behind her ears, she stopped in front of the kitchen sink to wash her hands before sending music through the speaker system via her phone. Christmas instrumentals. Her and Mum's favorite. She didn't care that it was long past the acceptable time to listen to them.

Through the kitchen window, she spied Davis in the microyard, working out—push-ups, sit-ups. He was definitely easy on the eyes and his presence a balm to her fears. And there was Fury, repeatedly dropping his funky, black rubber toy at Davis's feet. Both were working up an appetite, so maybe extra pancakes were in order. Not that she thought he would let his dog eat human food. But still.

Hollyn went for an apron from one of the drawers. Her hand stalled over the one Mum always used—it'd been her great-grandma's. It was white with hand-stitched floral embroidery and ruffled edging around the sides and bottom. Swallowing a sudden bout of misery, Hollyn scooped up the apron and put it on, feeling as if she had some loved ones back. Wrapped in their love. She then grabbed the recipe book from the cupboard. Not that she needed it. With as many times as she'd made pancakes with her parents over the years, she had it memorized. But taking the book out was part of a comforting pattern.

*Embrace the routine.*

Gathering the ingredients and measuring cups, Hollyn placed everything on the island. Last thing was a bowl. The large one that had also been Grana Mae's. She looked in the lower cabinets with no luck.

"Where did it go?" she murmured as she began opening the uppers, growing more frustrated with each dead end. When she opened the last cabinet, something slid off the top shelf. Flew at her.

"Augh!" In the split second that gravity flung it at her, she recognized it—Grana Mae's yellow glass bowl. Tried to catch the heirloom but slipped thanks to her socks, which provided no traction on the tile floor. She hit the floor just as the bowl did.

*Crash!*

Shards of the cherished bowl spread across the floor around her.

"No, no!" Hollyn pressed up and hissed when pain shot through her hand. When she reached out, she saw a large piece of the bowl embedded in her palm. It looked deep. Blood trailed from the wound onto the floor. Triggered by the sight, she swallowed the bile that leapt up her throat.

What had she done? Hollyn scootched back against the cabinets, clinging to her injured hand. Didn't care that she might be sitting on glass. Pain thrummed with the beat of her pulse. Teeth gritted in annoyance, she closed her eyes. But rather than tears of sadness, tears of anger burned in her eyes.

"Why?" she shouted to the ceiling. "Why them?"

She screamed her frustration. Pressed her head back against the cabinet.

The side door opened. "Christmas music? Really?" Davis called out.

She could hear Fury bouncing around.

Swallowing down the ball of ire heating her throat, Hollyn managed to look up just as they rounded the corner.

"There should be a law against—" The grin on Davis's face disappeared the second he saw her, replaced by a frown. "What happened?" He was suddenly all business as he rushed around the island toward her.

"Careful," she pushed the word out. "Glass."

Davis used a hand signal for Fury. "Down."

The RMWD instantly dropped and held position like a statue, watching his handler's every move. Davis brushed aside slivers of the bowl with his foot. He took a knee in front of Hollyn and reached for her. In gym shorts and a T-shirt that hugged tight around his muscular arms and chest, he looked much more casual than he had since he first got here.

His proximity was both unnerving and . . . something else she couldn't figure out.

Before he even touched her hand, Hollyn went rigid. "Wait." Jostling the injury was torture. If she held perfectly still, it helped.

"I need to see it, Hol." His calloused hand gently took hers. The warmth of it only mildly distracted her from the pain.

Slowly, he turned her palm to the side.

Hollyn sucked in a sharp breath. Instinct had her free hand jutting out to stop him.

"Easy," he soothed, even as he blocked her attempt to intervene. His gaze found hers.

Body stilling, breathing ragged, the world tunneled until the only thing in focus was him. She could feel beads of perspiration forming on her forehead and was keenly aware that her reaction was more than a little over the top for what had actually happened. Her brain told her to calm down, but her trauma response was fully engaged now.

"You're okay." He was the definition of calm. "Just hold still, all right?"

Hollyn mentally braced herself and nodded. Whatever came, it was nothing compared to what her parents must have felt. She clenched her teeth.

"Looks deep." Davis grabbed a dishtowel off the stove next to them and dabbed up the blood, doing a good job avoiding shifting the shard embedded in her skin. Still, it sent bolts of fire up and down her arm. "I'll take you to have it checked out."

"No!" The word was out before she could stop it. "No hospitals."

"Hollyn—"

"*No.*" There was no way on this earth.

There went the muscle in his jaw again. "Fine. Hold on." He stood and left the kitchen.

Hollyn looked over at Fury. The good boy hadn't moved an inch. "Think he's just gonna chop the whole thing off?" she joked. Ran her good arm across her forehead.

Fury's tail swished once and then he returned to his statuesque state. His only movement was panting, razor-sharp white teeth set off against his dark, sable fur. He could probably crush her arm if he wanted to.

For the first time, she noticed how intimidating he looked. Maybe it was because she was eye level with him now. Though, thankfully, he was on the other side of the kitchen. The way he tracked her was unnerving, to say the least.

Davis was back in a flash with a canvas pouch that he unzipped as he knelt. Took out a handful of packaged first-aid items and tweezers before holding her hand once more. "Looks like it should have missed the tendons."

Blood continued to ooze out. She'd never been good with the sight of it. Felt like she might pass out. Or throw up. Or both. It was nearly enough to make her reconsider the hospital option. But no. That was out of the question. Never again. Not after . .

A small moan escaped her.

"Look at something else," Davis told her while he readied the tweezers. Her fingers curled around his thumb as he kept her hand from closing into a fist. "Try not to tense up."

A strangled laugh bubbled out of her mouth. "Yeah, sure. This is basically a spa day." She looked up at the kitchen window.

His chuckle pulled a grin from her. "That's the spirit."

A bird flew up to the glass. Hovered just on the other side. The grin drained from her lips. It felt like God was rubbing salt in her wound as she watched the bird flit up and down in the sky without a care.

Dumb bird.

She made the mistake of glancing down as the tweezers neared. "Agh!" She threw a hand out. When the corded muscles of his arm tensed beneath her touch as he paused, she stilled.

Davis eyed her. "Good?"

Hollyn's heart pounded. For more than one reason. She released her hold. Closing her eyes, she nodded.

The glass being tugged from her palm was what she imagined having a knife blade run across her skin would be like. She hissed in pain. Tried to hold still, but her hand was shaking uncontrollably now.

Fury whined.

"Almost there," Davis told her.

Just when she was at her breaking point, the pressure was gone.

"Done." Davis grabbed some gauze and pressed it firmly into her palm.

Hollyn groaned and opened her eyes.

The doorbell chimed as he kept working on her hand. She slipped her phone from the apron pocket. Noticed the fabric covered with blood droplets. The corner of her lip curled in disgust.

*Perfect. You destroyed two heirlooms in one morning.*

A tap brought up the porch camera feed.

"It's Archie," Hollyn stated. Dread weighed her down. She didn't want to do this. Any of this. But she'd already told him she would.

"Leave him out there." Davis didn't look up as he readied a tube that read *liquid stitches* with one hand. He moved through the steps like he'd done it a thousand times.

Which he probably had, she realized.

"The fresh air will do him good."

"What's the deal with you two?" she breathed. "You spoke, like, five words to each other when you met."

"Five too many."

She shook her head. "I don't know why you two don't get along."

"I get along with everyone," he countered with a mischievous expression. Just as quickly, it was replaced by a look of disdain. "It's that—"

Hollyn arched an eyebrow even as pain continued pulsing in her palm.

"—*twerp*"—the stress he put on the word told her he had other names in mind for Archie—"that doesn't get along with me."

Maybe it was her fault. She'd mentioned Davis and his career to Archie a few times. Had she inadvertently said something that would put her friend on edge before he had a chance to ever get to know Davis?

On her phone, Hollyn tapped the button that unlocked the front door. "Yes, you do seem to have a very warm and inviting disposition when it comes to him. Much like a caged tiger looking for dinner?"

Davis smirked as the front door opened and closed. "One of my better features. Stay." His command stalled the shepherd's upward motion even as his wink sent Hollyn's heart fluttering.

How many different emotions could she feel in the span of a few minutes? It was dizzying.

Gaze dropping to his mouth, her vision tunneled. She'd always wondered what it would be like to kiss him.

"Hollyn." His voice was deep. Gravelly.

Their eyes met even as she felt frozen in place. Could he feel whatever this was between them too?

*You're playing with fire.*

Archie entered the room. Davis cleared his throat and started applying the bandages.

"Hollyn!"

Fury hopped up and let off a growl in the direction of her friend as he neared the kitchen. The fur along his spine rose.

"Down," Davis muttered like he didn't really want to call the dog off.

Archie's face blanched at the sight of the dog, whom he side-skirted, a laptop in hand. He was here for her help on a work project. When they'd talked early this morning, he'd let it slip that he was having trouble. At first, he'd refused her help because he didn't want to add to her plate, but she begged him to let her in on it. Now she was regretting that decision.

"Are you okay?" Archie asked her.

"I'm—"

Archie leveled a hard look at Davis. "What happened?"

Cradling her hand in his, Davis glanced at her friend. Did a double take when he realized *he* was the one Archie was targeting. "It's called an accident."

Archie jutted his chin. "You sure?"

"What's your problem?" Davis demanded.

"Hey, you're the one who has the problem," Archie countered.

Davis turned back to working on Hollyn's hand. "One I'd like to get rid of," he said under his breath.

"What's that?"

"Step off, Twerp." Davis scowled as he held Hollyn's wound closed while the liquid dried. It didn't escape her that her blood coated his skin.

Fury growled. It was enough to push Archie farther away from the dog.

Not enough, however, to stop him from more snarky comments. "Not happening, GI Joe."

Seriously! Why were these two always at each other's throats? "Okay!" She tried to stop them.

Davis placed a nonstick pad on the dried stitches and started covering her hand with self-adherent wrap. Softly, Hollyn noted. Even though he was upset—evidenced by the firm set of his jaw and twitch of his cheek muscle—he was still being gentle with her.

"You military types are all the same," Archie snapped. "Only thing you know how to do is shoot, kill, and injure."

"Archie!" Wow. Where had that come from?

He ignored her. "We're"—he motioned between himself and Hollyn—"trying to *help* humanity."

"What would the world do without you?" Davis's words were coated in thick sarcasm.

Hollyn nearly rolled her eyes. She'd never seen Archie act this way—or Davis, for that matter. "Guys, come on!"

Both men looked at her.

"Just—stop, okay?" Annoyed, she looked up at Archie. "A

bowl fell and a piece of it got stuck in my hand. Davis was helping me. Not hurting me."

Why was she even explaining this? They were acting like children. While Davis hadn't started this, he also hadn't let it go. Not that it surprised her.

When Davis slid an arm around Hollyn to help her up, she thought Archie might launch himself across the kitchen. She gripped Davis's solid shoulder with her good hand as he stood. Felt him tense. Didn't miss the way her heart fluttered again being pressed against him but quickly pushed the feeling away when he released her. Missed his touch when his hand slid from her waist.

No matter how much her heart still wished he were the one, he didn't feel that way about her. And even if he did, she was dangerous. The people she loved always ended up dead.

"Let's just go over the project, all right?" Hollyn hoped Archie could see the plea in her eyes for him to give it a rest.

He looked between her and Davis before his shoulders dropped and he nodded. "Yeah, okay. Sorry, Hollyn."

An apology for her. But not Davis.

She tugged at the loose apron knot at her back with one hand and set the garment on the counter. "I'm just going to clean this up first." She moved toward the pantry for the broom, but Davis caught her arm.

"I'll do it. You two . . . do what you need to." It looked like the words were physically painful for him to say.

If looks could kill, Archie would be dead a thousand ways already. Bandaged hand up against her chest to lessen the throbbing pain, Hollyn didn't waste time walking toward her friend. She needed to get him out of here before he started running his mouth again.

When Archie turned the corner toward Dad's office, Hollyn cast a glance back at Davis and found his primal gaze fixed on her. She bit her lip before stepping into the study.

If she weren't careful, these two would eventually engage in a battle she wouldn't be able to stop.

Irritation heated his neck as Davis flicked on the faucet to wash his hands.

Freaking twerp.

Gazing into the sink, he watched the blood mix with water and funnel down the drain. An unbidden flashback from that night shot to mind. Smoke in the air. In his lungs. Truck on fire. Loud shouts. Luke's body.

He gripped the edge of the countertop. Fought back the images.

He hadn't wanted to fix up Hollyn's hand. Didn't need anything else going wrong on his watch. But the way she'd begged him not to take her to the hospital . . . maybe he *should* have taken her. Wouldn't have had to deal with the twerp if he had. But there wasn't much he'd deny Hollyn.

From the office, the sound of muffled voices and the clacking of keyboards broke into his thoughts. He yanked some paper towels free. Dried his hands before finding the broom to sweep up the last of the glass. Sanitized the floor of the blood. Worked on getting the dark stains out of the apron.

Fury watched the office door like he didn't like the guy either.

Twerp was toeing the line of what Davis would deal with. And what was with him assuming Davis had hurt Hollyn?

That ticked him off more than anything. He'd never laid a hand on a woman. Ever. The punk calling his integrity into question had him seeing red.

Since he couldn't throw the guy out on his backside like he wanted to, Davis headed up to his guest room to get rid of his post-workout funk with a shower and clean clothes. Decided to go over the security footage Hollyn had sent him earlier. See what he could find.

When he stepped from the bathroom, Fury was sprawled out on the bed. His tail thumped down on the blankets. "Hey. You failed me down there. What good are those razor-sharp canines if you aren't going to eat his throat or at least take a chunk out of his smug butt?" Davis asked the lug. "Show him one of your trademark snarls?"

Fury sneezed.

"Whatever." He laughed, grabbing his laptop.

On the bed, he pulled up the recording. It wasn't easy seeing Hollyn attacked on camera, but on the fourth time, he realized something so glaringly obvious that he should've picked up on it on the first pass. Blame his preoccupation with the petite woman who still seemed to have a vise grip on his brain.

The burglar negotiated the house as if he'd been inside a hundred times. Seemed to know where every piece of furniture was and moved around it with ease even in the dark. Didn't bump into a single thing or trip on a rug.

Could've had the blueprints of the house memorized. But that wouldn't account for where furniture was. Davis still had a bruise where his leg had nailed the corner of that entry table.

In the office, the guy didn't mess around with the closest drawers. He went straight for the drawer farthest from the door.

Why?

Insider knowledge? Or . . . insider?

Davis closed the laptop and motioned to Fury with it. "Come on."

They walked down the hall to the study, and he opened the door. Didn't really care if he was interrupting the twerp. Hoped he *was*.

Behind the thick-rimmed BCGs on the bridge of his nose, Twerp balked. Was practically steaming.

Mission success.

"Hey, Davis." Hollyn greeted him with a small smile. Her

elbow was propped up on the desk, bandaged hand in the air. "What's up?"

"Can we talk?"

He had Twerp's full attention now.

"Alone." He dared Twerp to intervene.

"Uh . . ." Hollyn cast a sidelong glance at Twerp. "Sure. We were pretty much done here anyway, right, Archie?"

Mouth opening, Twerp grunted, then deflated.

Mission victory.

"Yeah. I think we're good." With more than a huff, he got his stuff together. Stood and hugged Hollyn—a little longer than necessary.

Fury let out a low rumble of objection.

*That's my boy.* Well, Crew's, but . . .

Chin up, Twerp skated Fury a nervous glance and scurried out the door. "See you 'round."

Davis bit back the retort on the edge of his tongue. Moved toward Hollyn. This close to her, his heart thundered in his chest. "How's the hand?"

She shrugged. "Not great but I'll live." Sliding her light auburn hair behind her ear, she smiled up at him. Those gorgeous eyes were going to get him in trouble one of these days. "Thanks for your help." Was she blushing?

The front door rattled when it closed with extra force.

Davis ignored the outburst. "Course."

Fury came up beside Hollyn and pressed his weight into her leg. She smiled. Reached for him, then pulled her hand back. "Is it okay?" She looked to Davis.

He considered the request. "Slowly."

Without missing a beat, she reached down to Fury's back. Ran her hand over his fur. The lug panted happily.

He wasn't sure what to make of the way the landshark acted with her.

"What did you need to talk about?" Hollyn sank quietly onto one of the large chairs near the windows. Pretzeled her legs under her like she always used to. Cradled her injured hand in her lap.

Though he didn't want to freak her out, they needed to get to the bottom of this, so he dropped into the other chair and rested his laptop on his knee. "I was going over the security footage"—he saw the confidence in her smile falter—"and I noticed that whoever broke in knew not only the layout but had an intimate knowledge of furniture and décor placement."

Davis opened the laptop and replayed the footage. Pointed when the burglar stepped around the entry table near the door to the study. "It's like he's been inside before."

The crease in her brow deepened. "Like he's broken in before and we didn't notice?" Hollyn looked scared.

Fix it.

"Whether he broke in or was let in"—he watched her absorb that information—"he's been here before. Does the way he moves look familiar?"

Touching her throat as she leaned in, she watched the video.

"Anything about him remind you of someone you know? What about your driver?"

Her gaze snapped back to him. "No! Bongani wouldn't do something like this. Please, just—shut it off." She locked away and he closed the laptop.

Davis was inching closer to losing her. Couldn't stop, though. Had to get her to think about the details while they were fresh in her mind. He was playing catch-up here. Didn't know the people in her life.

For a moment, he considered telling her about her dad's warning but shoved the idea away. He needed more intel first. If Ansel had wanted her to know, he would have addressed the message to them both. "Think about it . . . "

"I don't want to think about it!" Hollyn punched from the chair. "It was just a burglar, and the police will find him." Was she trying to convince him or herself? She paced back and forth.

"I don't appreciate you implying that Bongani could be to blame either."

Davis didn't say anything. It wouldn't help. She wasn't thinking logically.

"Of all the people here, he's been one of the kindest to our family."

Yeah, maybe in order to get close to whatever's here.

"These things just happen sometimes, you know?"

"Not this time, Hol." He worked to keep his tone even. "Think about it: your parents. The lab. The break-in here." He came to his feet. "Ian Fleming said, 'Once is happenstance. Twice is coincidence.'"

Hollyn stopped pacing, eyes wide, arms wrapped around her middle. "And three?—you mentioned three."

He held her gaze. "Enemy action." He exhaled heavily. "I do think we're beyond coincidence here, Hollyn. It's connected—your parents' murder—"

"*Murder?*"

"—the lab break-in, the break-in last night. To me, the pattern suggests someone close to the victim is responsible."

She spun on her heel. "The victim—you mean my dad!"

"Ansel, yes. I think he knew who killed him. The pattern suggests—"

"But not always. Right?"

*Come on, Hollyn.* Her piqued voice and frantic expression told him even she didn't believe what she was desperate for him to agree with.

"*Right*?" she asked with more force.

"Not always, but—"

"Then"—she flared her nostrils beneath the way she exclaimed that one word—"until we have some kind of hard evidence, I'm not going to be suspicious of the people closest to me." She touched her temples. "I just . . . can't. I can't live that way."

Davis frowned. Sighed. She was waist-deep in denial. "Fine."

Hollyn was going to continue to see the good in people. That's just who she was. Who she'd always been. He, on the other hand, had been around the block too many times and knew few people were really good. In fact, he recalled a Bible verse that said no one was good but God. That was a rule by which he approached life and ops.

Was that callous? Maybe. But he'd been tasked with ending too many snakes in this world to think differently.

Wouldn't stop her, though. If she was willing to stake her trust in them, so be it.

As far as he was concerned, the list of suspects numbered two, and he wouldn't stop till he narrowed it down to one.

# 6



*ABU DHABI, UAE*

Davis woke up in a foul mood the next morning. Arguing with Hollyn had always grated on him. Looked like that hadn't changed after years apart. Usually, he could keep things from getting to him, but for some reason, the aftermath of yesterday was messing with his head the second his eyes opened. It wasn't like he enjoyed saying her friends were suspects, but when the obvious was staring you down, it was moronic to look away.

Add that garbage to a shoulder he'd definitely slept on wrong, and he was about ready to punch something. Sitting on the side of the bed, he rubbed his deltoid. Gritted his teeth.

Was this thing ever going to heal? According to the docs, he shouldn't be in this much pain anymore.

"So much for that," he murmured to himself. Grabbed some meds from the nightstand and downed them dry. If his current luck held, things weren't going to get better.

The smell of fresh coffee filled the room. His stomach growled.

At the door, Fury stood ready. Tail wagging, tongue hanging out the side of his mouth. A very familiar look filled the shepherd's amber eyes. This guy didn't have the intensity of the Mals some of Davis's buddies worked with, but his drive was much higher than a non-working-line GSD nevertheless.

Always liked to be moving and was choosy with the people he liked.

"I'm coming." Davis shoved off the bed. He grabbed a T-shirt. Threaded his arms in and tugged it down before he strode out to the living room with Fury.

The RMWD trotted over to the couch where Hollyn was reading a book. Rested his head on her lap.

Well, call him a liar, then. Never, in all the years he'd worked with the lug, had Fury been one for just sitting down. Especially not with a civvy. But there was no denying the dog had a thing for Hollyn.

*Like I do?*

Frustrated with the thought, he rammed it away.

"Hey," Hollyn crooned to Fury. She looked drained. Gorgeous, but drained. Ran a hand down the shepherd's head before glancing up at Davis. Her eyes widened. "Why do I suddenly feel the need to drop and give you fifty so I don't get sent to the brig?"

Davis roughed a hand over his face. Tried to replace the scowl he could feel. Didn't work. He sank onto the couch adjacent her with a sigh. "Don't tempt me."

A weak grin tugged at the corner of her delicate lips. Ones he should stop staring at. Good grief, she was beautiful. Davis shifted his gaze to the windows overlooking the backyard. Crossed his arms.

"Still a grizzly in the morning, I see. Rough night?"

"Something like that."

"Want some coffee or pancakes?"

"Just coffee, thanks."

Hollyn slipped off the couch and returned a couple minutes later with a steaming cup of dark roast. "I figured you Army men take it straight, but I can add creamer or something if you want."

"This is fine."

Truth was, he wasn't a huge fan of the stuff in general. But he was counting on it changing his mood this morning.

She situated herself in the chair again. Crossed tan legs that were more than a little distracting in her lounge shorts. In his peripheral vision, he could see her slippered foot bouncing up and down as she went back to reading her book.

Noted that, though minutes passed by, she didn't turn the page.

For the thousandth time since high school, he mentally kicked himself for never having been man enough to ask her out. He'd come close but had always talked himself out of it. Dating meant the possibility of falling in love. Love meant marriage. Marriage meant responsibility he had no interest in. The day he'd left for bootcamp, he'd shut the door on all things relational and hadn't looked back. It figured she'd be the one to sink a crowbar into his resolve.

*Focus on the coffee.*

Piping hot liquid ran down his throat. The burn felt good.

Fury pressed into his leg now. Stared him down. That was his cue.

"Okay, come on," he said to the RMWD.

Fury snapped to attention, and Davis let the lug out into the backyard. Stood at the wall of windows, waiting.

Ansel's warning came to mind again. Davis mulled it over. Scanned the perimeter for anything unusual. He'd give his life to protect Hollyn. Didn't have to think twice about that. But could he find the person responsible for all of this before they hurt her?

He played the security footage through in his head. Had to be missing something. Anything that could point him in the right direction.

"You look like something's on your mind," Hollyn said.

Understatement of the year. "Just going over things."

"I've been doing that too. I didn't get much sleep last night. Or really any night this week."

No one would be able to guess that from the way she looked.

"How you holding up?" He was surprised. Usually he wasn't much for talking about feelings. Or talking at all. But Hollyn had a way of turning his world upside down. Probably didn't have a clue that she had that kind of power.

She peered over the top of her book. Gave a one-shouldered shrug. Played with the corner of the hardcover. 'I've been running through things in my head, but I still can't figure out how that guy got in the house. I've run security checks, and no tampering with the system was detected. It doesn't make any sense."

"The fingerprint scanner can't be hacked?"

Hollyn bit her lip. Shrugged. "Any piece of technology is technically hackable. But the locks use an optical scanner, not a capacitor, and the system uses AES 256-bit encryption "

She said that like it was supposed to mean something to him. "In other words—no?"

"In other words, only if they had a billion years on their hands or had the key code. And *that's* only up here." She tapped her temple. "Dad was meticulous with the details when setting up the system, so the code was only memorized, never written down."

Impressive, but it didn't surprise him that Ansel had been thorough.

"What about a 3D finger?"

Again she shook her head. "No. It's not as easy as just creating a mold. While the chances aren't zero, it's highly improbable. Systems these days are hard to fool with something like that." Her thumb brushed along the edge of the book. "Still. Whoever it was *did* get in. I just wish I knew how. And with the lab break-in on top of everything else"—he thought he saw her chin quiver—"it scares me."

Davis's hand fisted. When he found who'd broken in, the guy better pray his medical insurance was active.

Fury ran back to the door, and Davis let him in. Started back toward his spot on the couch. But instead of joining him, the RMWD bolted to Hollyn. Jumped forward. Hollyn yelped. Fear strangled her voice as Fury's paws pressed against her. He nosed her neck. Tail up. Intent.

Hollyn's eyes were wide as saucers.

"Don't move!" Panic that Fury would bite her if she hit at him surged in his gut. "Fury, no!" Davis launched forward, ready to throw his arm in the way if the GSD's strong jaws lunged forward.

He grabbed the dummy's collar and pulled him off a now-terrified Hollyn.

"You good?" he huffed out, pulse thrumming.

Fury continued to try to plow forward, though not aggressively, Davis noted.

Hollyn leaned her body as far away from the RMWD as she could. Eyes still wide, she lifted them to Davis. Her chest rose and fell rapidly. "I'm . . . yeah. I th-think so."

Without warning, Fury dropped his backside to the floor. What was with this dog lately? Maybe he'd been wrong to suggest that Crew take him on.

"Sorry." Davis shifted focus to Fury. "*Fuss.*" He tapped his side once, and the lug flew into position. Pressed against his leg. "*Af.*"

Fury lay down without hesitating. His body trembled and he looked up with an expression Davis had seen on nearly every mission they'd worked. He was happy with himself. Proud even.

Davis studied Hollyn, making doubly sure she was really okay. Forced his racing heart to slow down. She was fine. He lowered to the couch again.

"Reminds me of you back in high school, tackling everything on the field." Hollyn ran a hand along her shirt. Davis could practically see her telling herself to act like she wasn't rattled.

"Remember?" She forced a smirk that didn't reach her blue and green eyes.

He did, unfortunately.

"All the girls were so obsessed with you. Especially the cheerleaders."

Where was this going? He couldn't think of anything he wanted to get into less than his high-school days. But Hollyn seemed to be barreling down memory lane faster than a BrahMos missile.

"They were always trying to pump me for information on how they could catch your attention, because they knew we were close." She grinned.

No chance of that happening. Only girl he'd been interested in back then—and even now—was her.

"Remember the Asheville game?" Hollyn's grin was timid.

Davis had closed the door on that part of the past. Didn't really want to rehash things now.

Hollyn rubbed her hand. "Sophomore year, and it was the first game my parents didn't make it to. I was on top of the pyramid that night. I was so disappointed they couldn't make it. And then you—" She gasped. Clamped her mouth shut.

He swallowed. Knew what she'd been about to say.

He wasn't there.

"You were lucky to have them as parents." He tried to redirect the conversation. Didn't feel like hashing out why he hadn't made it to that game. "Better than a mom who didn't really care about anything her kid did."

Her expression went soft.

Perfect. He'd just exchanged one can of worms for another.

*Get your head together.*

"Davis, I'm sorry. I wasn't thinking."

He clenched his jaw for a second. "No sweat, Holly Hobbie."

The use of her childhood nickname tugged out a grin, but her eyes were pained.

Both of their pasts were littered with too many landmines to count, but even her biological parents had been a step above his mom. At least they'd cared about her. Had tried to be better. Then the Reinhardts had come along. No comparison there.

They'd been everything Davis had always wanted his mom to be. Had known she never could be.

Hollyn stood and walked over to him. Eyed Fury as she sank down on the couch at Davis's side. She rested a hand on his forearm. Heat burned between their skin.

*Don't move a muscle.*

If he did, knew what would happen. Disaster a thousand different ways.

"What happened that day? You never told me why you weren't at the game. Then suddenly you were off the team and basically enemies with everyone at school except me." She tilted her head.

Davis swallowed. Bounced his foot. Gave a half shrug. "Not much to tell."

Hollyn hmphed. One eye drew up like it always did when she wasn't going to let something go.

All right, fine.

Hollyn watched Davis closely. He ran a hand down the back of his neck, corded arm muscles flexing. The image was more than a little intrusive to thoughts she was trying to keep on track. She really *did* want to hear this story, though.

Looking back, it'd always felt like the beginning of the end for them. The one part of their story she constantly wished she could change—to be a better friend who wouldn't just let him shut down.

"Grady's folks were out of town. He spent the night at my place so he wouldn't miss the game. My mom was supposed to drive us to meet the bus the next morning. When we woke up, she wasn't around. We waited for an hour before she sent me a text saying she'd been asked out on a date and wouldn't make it."

"Davis," Hollyn murmured sorrowfully.

"By that point, it was too late to catch the bus or even drive to the game, and neither of us had our licenses. You know the rest. Second-string QB couldn't handle the pressure riding on the game and we lost."

"So . . . what? The team just placed all the blame on you? How is that fair?" She was getting upset now. It hurt that, as close as they'd been, he'd never told her about this. "It was your mom that bailed, not you!"

Davis shrugged. "Should have predicted that she couldn't be counted on."

"That's harsh."

"Is it? Holidays. Birthdays. Sports. She wasn't around for any of it. Always had a better offer."

"Still!" Hollyn balled her fist. "For the team to blame you and not her is just—"

When Davis smirked, it caught her off guard.

"This is funny to you?" She looked at him aghast.

"No," he said with a seriousness that set butterflies loose in her stomach. "But this"—he motioned a circle around her face—"is exactly why I never told you."

"I don't get it. All these years I thought *you* were the one unjustifiably angry with *them* and blowing things up so you didn't have to stick with something. You could have told me the truth."

He shook his head, features darkening in sunlight snuffed by clouds outside. "It took you a long time to make friends with other people, Hol." He rested an arm over the back of the couch. "I watched it every day. And some of your closest friends were cheerleaders. The team was ticked at me. If I'd told you, you would have taken my side and likely would have been dropped by them too. I wasn't gonna let that happen."

Breath whooshed from her lungs as tears pricked her eyes.

He'd only been thinking about how it was going to affect *her*? She knew full well how much being on the team had meant to him. It made this revelation even worse.

Suddenly, it registered that she was leaning in. Davis had gone silent and was staring . . . at her mouth. He was so close. Or was she? Maybe this was a bad idea. But like being locked in an invisible tractor beam, she felt herself drawn in.

Heart pounding, she swallowed. Davis was hardly more than a breath away.

*Is this really happening?*

Chest rising and falling swiftly, Davis cleared his throat and drew back, expression hardening. He shifted to the edge of the couch.

Spell broken.

Hollyn blinked. Recoiled into herself, feeling like a fool.

*Of* course *he wasn't going to kiss you! What were you thinking?*

Shoulders hunched, forearms on his knees, Davis sighed as he ran a hand over his face before shoving to his feet.

Emptiness flooded the space between them that anticipation had filled seconds earlier.

"Sorry. I . . . " But more words wouldn't form. What could she say? Sorry, Davis, my childhood crush on you has come roaring back, and I'm so weak I couldn't fight it?

"It's fine," he murmured.

She looked up at him, feeling like it was anything but. He wasn't even looking at her. Just continued staring out the large living-room windows. Rejection coursed through her. Embarrassment burned her cheeks. There were about a hundred reasons leaning in had been a bad idea. She could have chosen any one of them to ground herself in reality. But she hadn't. Thankfully, Davis had decided to act rationally and save her from humiliating herself more than she already had.

If only she could sink into the floor and disappear.

Likely sensing the change in tension, Fury popped up. Looked between them with a severity that made her nervous.

Davis turned. "I'll . . . be in the gym."

With that, he and Fury stalked toward the second story workout area, leaving Hollyn to wonder what had just happened. How could she have messed things up to *that* extent?

"Good job, Hollyn," she admonished herself.

How much was she going to put herself through before she got it into her skull that Davis was *not* interested in her?

*Stick to science. Romance is way out of your wheelhouse.*

She stood and snatched her book off the chair.

Dad's letter slipped from the pages she'd tucked it between. Fluttered to the ground. For a minute, she just stood there, staring at it like it was going to grow teeth and bite her. Then anger—at herself, at her parents' senseless and still unsolved deaths, at the ridiculous crush she still had on a man who returned her feelings in absolutely no way—bubbled up.

Hollyn grabbed the letter and stalked to her dad's office. Better to just get this over with. It was starting to haunt her nightmares, and now that she was in a terrible mood, things couldn't possibly get worse.

Opening the parchment for the first time was eerie. She broke the wax seal and tucked her feet up under herself in the corner chair. The letter was handwritten but oddly spaced. Hollyn read through the words, which repeated much of what he'd told her that night at the gala. The overwhelming urge to stop crashed against her. Tears pricked her eyes, and she could feel the floodgates about to break.

*Stay strong. For once in your life!*

Pressing on, she held her breath to stay the tears. When she finished the letter filled with sentiments of love for her and how much she meant to her parents, she just sat there. Reread it, willing the words to change. To tell her that this had all just been some kind of sick joke. That it wasn't real. On her third pass, the spacing between the lines was really starting to distract her. It was awkward, especially for Dad.

Wiping at her eyes, Hollyn frowned. Dad had a compulsion

for uniformity, and not once had she ever seen him write something with more than a single space between lines except—

She gasped. Quickly scanned the letter again. Chewed on her lip thinking. Was it . . .

Hollyn dashed for Dad's desk and pulled out a drawer. Shuffled the contents around before finding what she'd been after. A lighter. With shaking hands, she lit the flame and held it to the backside of the paper.

Hidden words appeared.

Hollyn bit her lip. Growing up, her parents had used notes like this as their hidden message system, and she used to think it was the coolest thing ever. Lips moving along with the words that appeared, Hollyn read:

*Sparrow*—even just reading the word was a punch to the gut—*I hope I'm wrong about my suspicions, but if you're reading this, then sadly, I wasn't. Get to Davis as soon as possible. You're in danger. He'll protect you. I've hidden what you're looking for where you'll find it. Never forget, we love you more than life itself.*

What she was looking for? What did that mean? All she wanted to know was who had broken into the house, but he wouldn't know that.

The gravelly voice of her attacker pierced her memory. *"You know where it is . . . "*

Her whole body shook with adrenaline now.

Could it be the same thing Dad was talking about here? And if so, what did it refer to? She didn't like this. Too many unknown variables were in play.

Spinning on her heel, she bolted for the stairs. "Davis!" she called out as she crested the landing. She dashed for the workout room, deciding she was going to put her schoolgirl foolishness behind her.

*Don't think about what almost happened. Don't. Think. About. It.*

Sliding through the door, her mind whirled with everything that had happened since her parents' death.

A loud clang of metal caught her attention as Davis replaced the dumbbell he'd been using. His gaze shot to her. "What's wrong?"

So much for forgetting.

*Just focus!*

Fury barked at her, and Hollyn froze as the menacing sound echoed off the hard surfaces of the walls and floor. Fear seized her chest. She didn't want the dog to misinterpret her rushed movements as her trying to go after his handler. She also couldn't tell whether his bark was friendly or not.

Yeah, his name definitely made sense now.

"*Leise*," Davis commanded firmly.

When the dog quieted, she took a couple tentative steps forward, watching for any sudden movement from the corner of her eye. She didn't want to add *being turned into mincemeat* to the list of other things going wrong. "I just read the letter Randall gave me from my dad. I . . . I think you're right. They *were* murdered."

Just saying that lifted bile to the back of her throat.

Davis reached for the letter, and she let him take it, careful not to brush his skin. She needed her mind sharp right now. Which, in reality, seemed laughable.

"Here." She lit the lighter.

For a second he frowned in confusion, then the words appeared in the margins once more. "What . . . " The rest of the sentence fell off as he read. His jaw flexed every few seconds as the silence grew unbearable. When he finished, he gave her a curt nod. "Ansel's video was a similarly coded message."

Really? Why hadn't he mentioned that?

"What do we do?" She looked up at him for answers. "Can you even stay, or do you need to get back to your base soon?" She didn't even know where he was stationed or in what country. So. Many. Questions.

A look she couldn't decipher hardened his features before he shook his head. "No. I can stay." He grabbed a hand towel from the nearby shelf and wiped at his face. Pain trickled over his expression when he rolled his shoulders. "I know someone I can reach out to. See if he can help us figure out what's going on."

*Relieved* didn't begin to cover what it was like knowing he wasn't going anywhere. She was safe as long as she was with him. That, she knew deep in her core. Though, looking at him was causing ten different levels of embarrassment right now.

Still, it was odd that he had the option to stay. Maybe he was on leave or something. That's what they called it right? Why hadn't she thought to ask him? She'd been so caught up in herself and her own grief this whole time that she hadn't really thought to ask him how *he* was feeling or about *his* life since they last saw each other.

Inwardly, she cringed. Was he dating? Married? After all, some guys didn't wear wedding rings. Was a relationship why he'd shoved her away downstairs? If she'd kissed a married man . . . The thought made her sick.

"Don't worry, Hol. We'll get to the bottom of this."

If only he could read her mind, he'd know just how far apart their trains of thought were in this moment. And how badly she wished they weren't.

# 7



*ABU DHABI, UAE*

GREAT. TWERP WAS BACK, AND HE'D BROUGHT THE MAN-EATER with him.

Leaning against the kitchen counter the next morning, Davis took a long sip of coffee. Was it possible for the stuff to grow on you after two days? He eyed Leila and Twerp, following Hollyn into the open-concept living-room-kitchen area.

While Twerp had the decency to hang back by the couches, arms crossed, Leila made no effort to hide the thoughts running through her mind as she detoured in Davis's direction. "Morning, soldier."

Davis hoped the look on his face matched the disgust in his head. She was barking up the wrong tree. "What are you two doing back here?" He added a heavy layer of annoyance to his words.

Posted up at his side, tac vest on because they had somewhere to go today, Fury growled.

Only then did the vixen halt her advance.

"Davis," Hollyn said softly. Came up next to her friend.

"Tsk, tsk, soldier boy." Leila grinned wide. "I don't bite."

"That makes one of us."

"Promise?" She quirked an eyebrow.

Davis's frown deepened. True, she was beautiful—knew it too—but she was an IED waiting to go off the second a wrong move was made. His phone vibrated in his pocket, and he slid it out. Checked the ID. The call he'd been waiting for. "I need to take this." He tapped his leg, and Fury heeled as they walked to the back door.

Why Hollyn was friends with that woman . . .

"Chapel." He answered the call when they stepped outside. A breeze swirled the scents of cypress and cardamom that infused the air around him.

Deciding he needed a little help, he'd texted a former Army buddy who ran private security and was currently in the area. Hadn't known if he'd get a response, but he needed someone to run things by and trusted the guy more than most.

"To what do I owe the *need to talk* text?" Chapel asked.

From his position, Davis kept an eye on Hollyn and her friends through the windows. "I've got a situation."

"You're in luck, then. Situations are what I do best. What's up?"

"Not over the phone." Davis roughed a hand down his neck. "Last I heard, team was in the Dhabi area. That still the case?"

"Might be."

"Able to meet in about an hour?"

"Sure do ask for some steep favors."

Davis chuckled. "Feel free to call them in at the most inconvenient time."

"Don't you worry about that." The line went silent for a minute. "All right, sure. Send me the location. I'll make it work."

They ended the call, and Davis shot off a text with coordinates for a place he'd picked out ahead of time. A place that couldn't be bugged if the conversation were being monitored. Which he doubted, but why take the chance?

Fury looked up at him expectantly. Pranced. Ready for action.

"Always could tell when we were about to head out." Davis grinned at the RMWD. "Let's go."

At the sound of the G-word, Fury barked and flung his solid body into heel position. They went back inside. The room fell suspiciously quiet as three sets of eyes swiveled to them.

"Everything okay?" Hollyn asked.

"Yeah. Gotta step out for a bit." The only reason he was even considering not taking her with him was that he knew she wouldn't come. He could drag her outside, but the neighbors would have the cops on him faster than he could say "get in." He still thought of Leila and Twerp as suspects, but he didn't have any evidence to support that. So—for now—he'd have to take a chance that Hollyn was right and he was wrong.

Still. It felt like gambling with the thing he cherished the most. He'd been dangerously close to giving in and kissing her the other day. But this wasn't the time for it. Not in the middle of grieving, when she might regret things later. He'd have to man up and make sure they didn't have another close call. Even if that was the last thing he wanted to do.

Davis glowered at Leila and the twerp. Prayed that if his suspicions were right, God would give him some kind of sign. All he got was silence. He didn't really think he'd get an answer after ignoring God for years, did he?

"Think you'll be okay?" he asked Hollyn.

"She's got us, doesn't she?" Twerp's chest almost visibly puffed up.

"Like I said," Davis stated.

Twerp's eyes narrowed. He got the message.

Hollyn looked between them.

Focus locked on the newcomers, Fury barked. Deep and loud.

"Holy." Twerp jumped in his seat. Swung an arm toward the RMWD. "Keep that animal under control."

Davis squared off. "If he wasn't under control, I'd be prying you from his jaws already."

Hollyn gave Davis a slight shake of her head. She wanted *him* to stand down?

Twerp's eyes widened.

Next to him Leila looked . . . impressed? "Better listen up, Archie."

Twerp scowled at the sultry woman.

"I'll be okay," Hollyn said.

"Good if I borrow a car?" He had no idea what was in the garage, but he stalked in that direction anyway. The sooner he left, the sooner he'd be back to keep an eye on Hollyn's *friends*.

Fury stuck close without being asked to.

"Of course. Take whichever one you want. Keys are in the lockbox to the left of the door. There's a thumbprint scanner. It'll work for you since you're in the system now. Where are you going?" she called after him.

But he was already slipping through the garage door with Fury. "Be back in a couple hours."

A row of four vehicles greeted him as the door closed, but one in particular caught his attention.

Cobalt blue Chevy Chevelle SS. A 1970, if he were to hazard a guess.

He found the corresponding key in the lockbox and let Fury in the backseat. Issued up a short prayer for forgiveness for letting the landshark on the pristine leather. At least the derp was clean. He'd dirtied up plenty of Humvees over his career.

Tapping the garage door opener hooked to the visor, he turned the ignition, and the muscle car roared to life. The engine vibration rumbled through his chest.

"Always did have great taste in cars, Ansel," Davis murmured with a smirk.

Half an hour later, they pulled up to their destination: a beach off of the north shore near the Al Khalidiyah district.

Davis parked. Led Fury down the beach and took up position on a wooden bench. Waited for Chapel.

At his side, the RMWD lay in the sand. Head up. Eyes alert. Ready to take care of any trouble that came. A strong breeze ruffled his fur. Wearing his tac vest, the shepherd got more than a few wary looks from people out for a walk.

A few yards down, Chapel materialized from behind a group of passersby. Dressed in black tac pants and tee, the giant operator stood out from the crowd of people wearing long white kanduras. He slipped around the crowd toward Davis

"Ledger."

"Chapel."

Chapel glanced down at Fury. Back to Davis. "New development? Didn't think he was out too."

"Med boarded and retired for aggressive behavior."

Chapel smirked. Spoke to Fury. "Hope you feel better soon, bud."

Davis shook his head. "Yeah, yeah."

"What's with all the smoke and mirrors?" Chapel sat on the bench.

"Had to be sure no one else had ears on this." Davis kept an eye out. "Heard anything on the dark web about a hit on someone named Ansel Reinhardt recently?"

Chapel thought. "There's been chatter. Why?"

"I'm staying with his daughter, and there was a break-in at her home as well as the lab she works at. Led me to believe her parents' deaths might not have been the accident everyone seems to think it was."

Arms folded, Chapel nodded. "That would track."

"I don't have the connections you do anymore. Thought you might be able to point me in the right direction."

Fury watched a woman walk by with a yappy little dog. Didn't even flinch when the mutt lost its mind. The woman apologized. Tugged the dog away as Davis and Chapel stared her down.

"We've got eyes on a few people," Chapel said. "We're working in cooperation with local authorities to bring down an arms dealer who has significant value to both sides. Only reason we've been allowed to operate in-country. And it's . . . possible your guy is involved. We'd need to compare notes."

"I have video of the break-in." Davis brought up the footage. Handed over the phone.

Chapel watched in silence as waves continued crashing onto the beach. He paused the footage. "Can't really see the guy's face, but looks to me like it's Braum Germaine. He's in deep with the group we're after. That the daughter he attacked?"

Davis nodded. Didn't have to see the video for the images to flash across his mind. When he found the guy . . .

Chapel pulled out his own phone. Tapped the screen a couple times. Held it up to the image that he had paused on Davis's phone.

Davis examined the two images.

"He was good at keeping his face away from the cameras," Chapel said. "Like he knew where they were."

"Noticed that too." Davis bobbed his leg. "Same with the furniture. First time I walked into the entry, I jammed my leg into the corner of that table. This guy sidestepped it like he'd been in the house more than once before."

Chapel smirked. "Maybe you're just not as agile as you once were. Retirement setting in hard?"

Davis fought the knee-jerk instinct to come up with a retort. Chest tightened. Heat flared up his neck. Getting kicked out wasn't retirement.

*Easy, Ledger.*

Chapel knew that. Was just giving him a hard time.

Fury watched him. Tilted his head.

*Let it go.*

Great. Now that stupid kid song Rafkin's daughter used to sing to her dad via webcam while they were deployed was going to be stuck in his head.

Chapel cleared his throat. Nodded to the photos. "The daughter didn't recognize anything familiar about this guy?"

"It was hard for her to watch. Given her parents' recent deaths, she's not in the best frame of mind. Didn't think she knew him."

"Ever hear her mention the name Germaine?"

"Not since I've been here. But it's only been a few days. I'll ask her about him."

Chapel nodded. "I'll dig deeper. See if I can find anything that connects Germaine to the family."

"Thanks, man." Davis shifted his stiff shoulder. Pain pulsed deep into the muscles. "Okay if you send me that photo? It might jog something for her."

Chapel airdropped it. "If she recognizes him, you've got trouble."

Had he expected anything else? Seemed par for the course these days. "That's about all I've got."

"Yeah. But you don't want him added to the mix." Chapel's warning was just the cherry on top of this dumpster fire of a week. "Germaine is serious business. We've been trying to make something stick to him for a while now so we could take him down. He's slippery, though, and if he kept Reinhardt alive, there's a reason for it. We know he has an affinity for running hits himself and doesn't leave loose ends. Has an unfortunate talent for getting his hands dirty, if you catch my drift."

"Copy."

Time to get back to the house. Back to Hollyn He'd been gone too long.

They stood. Shook hands.

"Thanks for your help."

"Anytime." Chapel's gaze dropped to Fury. "Take care of him, bud."

Fury wagged his tail as the operator walked off.

On the way back to Hollyn's, Davis tried calling her. Rapped his thumbs on the steering wheel. The phone rang several times before her voicemail started. He hung up. Dropped the phone in his lap. Shifted down when traffic slowed. Something in his gut told him to call again. He'd learned long ago not to ignore that feeling.

When she didn't pick up the second time, the knot in his stomach twisted.

Davis clenched his teeth. Checked his rearview mirror. Fury's head obstructed half the view. "She might be in the middle of something."

Fury barked his reply.

Pulling onto another street, Davis sped up as GPS guided him. Tried Hollyn again. Left a message this time.

"Hol, it's me. Give me a call as soon as you get this."

He was less than five minutes from the house now. Gunned the engine and made it in two. The cherry-red sports car that'd been outside when he left wasn't there now.

Davis locked the Chevelle. Jogged up the front path with Fury instead of waiting for the garage door to open.

"Hollyn?" he called when he and Fury stalked through the entry.

The house was quiet. Too quiet.

Empty.

## *ABU DHABI, UAE, EARLIER THAT DAY*

"Oh my word! That's frightening!" Leila exclaimed after Hollyn had finished telling them both about how her parents' deaths might not have been an accident.

Davis was wrong about them, she could feel it in her bones. Not to mention the fact that the man who'd attacked her had been much larger than Archie. And it felt good to talk everything—well, almost everything—out with her friends. Already, she was emotionally lighter than she'd been in days.

"You sure you're okay here? Alone with him?" Archie asked, protectiveness edging his voice. "You said yourself that he hasn't been in your life for years."

Hollyn didn't like what that implied about Davis's character. "Archie, really. You two have *got* to start getting along. And yes. I'm positive that I'm safe with him."

"What about Bongani? Could it have been him?" Leila postulated.

"Lei, no!" What in the world was happening? First Davis, now them with these unfounded hypotheses.

Hearing Bongani's name reminded her that she still hadn't reached out to him, though.

"What do you think the burglar was after?" Archie interjected. He shot a hard look at Leila.

"All I know is that it has something to do with my dad's work. But that could be any number of things. Even we"—she motioned between Archie and herself—"didn't know about everything he was in the middle of. I've been so busy with my AI project." She shrugged helplessly. Once again, she should have paid attention to someone besides herself.

"What can we do, Hollyn?" Leila asked. She reached out and grasped Hollyn's hand. "I know I'm no lab tech, but is there anything I can do to help you figure this out?" She sat up straight. Tucked her brunette hair behind her ears. "You know what? I can have Daddy's security team station people here."

See? Hollyn truly didn't deserve her friends. They were so kind to her at every turn. "It's okay, Lei. Really. Davis has things under control." She heard Archie mumble something under his breath but didn't catch what. "Plus, I've already bulked up the security protocols for the house system."

"But you just said that the guy somehow got in here without tripping the alarm." Leila looked horrified. "Even we don't have access to your place," she said, referring to herself and Archie. "That really worries me. How is it even possible to do that without fingerprint access?"

Hollyn had to admit she'd constantly been thinking the same question since that night.

Leila's phone went off, playing "Girls Just Want To Have Fun" loudly. She slipped it from her Vuitton and rolled her eyes. "It's my agent. I forgot about the modeling campaign I was supposed to shoot today." A torn look marred her perfect features.

"It's okay, Lei. You should go."

"But you'll be here alone. And Archie said he's got a deadline coming up on something at work."

"What?" Archie looked like he'd been caught daydreaming. He cleared his throat. "Oh yeah, right." He looked to Hollyn and shrugged. "It's the Robison. I really should get the last of the paperwork finished up."

"Of course." She knew the project well. It was the one she'd helped him on the other day. "I promise I'm good, you guys. Davis said he'd only be gone a couple hours."

Leila and Archie exchanged tentative glances before Leila nodded. "Okay. But I'll have my phone with me. If you need *anything*, you call me."

"Same," Archie echoed. He stood. Paused like he was going to say something, but didn't.

What was going on with him lately? The animosity toward Davis. Needing help with work. It wasn't like him. At all.

Hollyn shoved the worries aside and hugged her friends goodbye. Soon the silence in the house was nearly deafening. It caused her mind to wander, and where it landed . . . was Bongani.

It was time.

Seeing him wouldn't be any less traumatic next week or the week after, and he was probably grieving just like she was.

Without another thought, she locked the house and trotted to the garage before she changed her mind.

Hollyn didn't take risks. Truly. She calculated all the dangers of every situation and made plans accordingly. So how was it that she found herself parked in front of Bongani's apartment? Alone. Knowing full well that there was a guy out there actively trying to get to her.

At least she'd made it here in one piece, though. She'd only driven herself around the city a handful of times in the last few years, and it wasn't for the faint of heart.

"This was stupid," she mumbled.

What was Davis going to say if he got back before she did? Nothing good, that was for sure.

She should go. Right now.

"Hollyn?" a familiar voice asked from the passenger side of the car.

Surprise threw her heart into her throat, but it was Bongani, not a random killer, who waved to her from the sidewalk. He was holding fabric grocery bags. Likely full of fresh produce from nearby Al Mina Fruit and Vegetable Souk.

"Uh, hey." She waved back and got out of the car. Locked it as she walked to Bongani.

"What are you doing here?" he asked, confusion all over his face. His Hindi accent was instant balm to her grief. Familiar and warm.

Really should have at least called him first instead of showing up randomly.

He towered over her, and she had to crane her neck to look up at him. "I'm sorry. I just wanted to see . . . how you were doing since—" She couldn't even say the words.

Awareness tugged up Bongani's eyebrows and he nodded. "Please, come in."

Hollyn followed him up the stairs and into the apartment building.

"I should have called you first," she apologized as they ascended stairs to the second floor.

"It's okay." He smiled graciously. "How are you?" He unlocked the door, and they stepped inside.

"I'm . . . " She shrugged. Sighed. "As good as I can be, I suppose."

His apartment was small and minimalistic, but she got the impression she could eat off the floor if she needed to. The place was spotless.

Bongani placed the bags on the counter and started putting things in his fridge. She caught him eyeing her. Probably wondering why she'd come over just to stand mute in his kitchen. Hollyn felt like such an intruder right now. She shouldn't be here.

"Is there anything specific you wished to talk about?" he probed.

"Isayus." The word was out before her next breath, and it surprised her.

Bongani's hand stalled over the carton of milk. "Yes." He was quiet for a moment. "I will miss my friend. But I take comfort in the fact that he is with Heavenly Father now."

She'd always admired Bongani's unwavering faith. He'd actually been the one to invite her family to the church they all attended now. Their belief was something they had in common, but if she were honest with herself, God had taken a backseat in her life the last couple of years.

That should change.

"You're not mad?" she asked.

"Mad? No." He shook his head. "I decided long ago that anger only hurts me. It does nothing to the one who did me wrong."

Hollyn nodded and slumped down on one of the bar stools around the peninsula.

"But *you* are mad?" Bongani closed the fridge.

"I'm trying not to be, but I can feel it getting stronger. The more we find out about the accident and that it likely *wasn't* an accident . . . it just"—she balled her bandaged hand—"makes me so angry. And terrified. And . . . fragile."

Entirely too close to how she'd felt the day she'd been taken from her childhood home and placed in foster care.

"It was not an accident?" Bongani repeated.

Hollyn watched him. "We don't think so."

He was still for a moment. Sighed. "I will pray for whoever is responsible."

"What?" Hollyn seethed in shock. The idea instantly ignited a lividity that had her shaking. He couldn't be serious. "Pray for them? To be caught and prosecuted, right?"

"To turn themselves in. To find redemption in Heavenly Father."

She was on her feet in the next second. Deep-seated anger flared. "*Redemption*?" She couldn't be hearing him correctly. "How about pray they're taken off this earth before they have a *chance* at redemption!"

Sadness rested in his dark eyes. "I cannot pray for that. And neither can you."

The nerve

"You know what?" She stalked toward the door. "This was a mistake."

"Hollyn."

"Forget it!" Hollyn closed the door on his next words and shot down the stairs.

She could hardly see straight. Pray for the people who'd murdered her parents?

Not happening. Ever.

"Agh!" She raged to no one but herself as she shoved out the front door.

People passing by on the sidewalk frowned at her and picked up their pace as she neared.

Somewhere close, a car alarm was blaring, loud and obnoxious. It mixed with the angry monologue in her head. Then awareness dawned and she froze. Glass shards littered the ground at the passenger side of her BMW.

Her car. *Her* alarm.

"No," she breathed as she jogged over. She shut off the alarm with her key fob. "No, no . . . "

The window had been smashed into a million tiny pieces. In the sun, flecks of glass glinted against the dark interior of the car.

Hollyn leaned through the window, shoes crunching on the glass that covered the ground. Her purse—why had she been foolish enough to leave it behind?—was still there. Frantically glancing around, she dug through the bag, careful to avoid the sharp shards protruding from the doorframe. Relief sparked when her fingers brushed her passport and phone.

*So lucky, Hol. Maybe use your head next time.*

The feeling of being watched intensified. She stood. Looked around. Several parked cars lined the road, but even squinting into the glare of the sun's rays, she couldn't tell if people were in them.

But that feeling. It grew more ominous.

*Get out of here. Now.*

Hollyn dropped her purse down on the passenger seat. Raced to the driver's side, furiously pressing the unlock button, and jumped in. With shaking hands, she rammed the key into the ignition and peeled away from the apartment building. She tried once, twice, to get her seatbelt in place and had just felt it click when she caught sight of an SUV pulling out of the row of vehicles. Jerky moves of the black vehicle told her the driver was in a hurry.

Gaze darting from the road to the rearview mirror and back, Hollyn could feel her whole body trembling. She pressed the accelerator to put more distance between herself and the SUV.

It sped up.

Hollyn cried out. She saw a road coming up. Took it. Her tires chirped in protest at her lack of deceleration, but she maintained control. Both hands gripping the steering wheel, heart solidly in her throat, she kept checking behind her and almost sighed when she didn't see the SUV turn down the road.

Then it appeared.

And bore down on her at a speed that said she was about to be in serious trouble.

# 8



*ABU DHABI, UAE*

Davis was officially worried.

Something wasn't right. He'd called Hollyn several times since arriving back at her place, and it still kept going to voicemail. Gripping the counter, he ran through his options. Should have insisted that she share her location with him.

To his right, Fury barked. Looked at the front door.

"I know," Davis bit out. "But where do we start looking? Not like this town is small. She's a needle in a haystack out there!"

Irritation warmed his neck. Puffed his chest.

What did he know about Hollyn? What she liked to do. Where she liked to go. He didn't even know how to reach Leila and the twerp. Good thing, because he'd wring their necks.

If they'd taken Hollyn . . .

Like he'd summoned her with his mind, her face lit up his screen with an incoming call. Davis snatched the phone off the kitchen island. Swiped it open.

"Where are you?" he growled. "Didn't you see—"

"Help!" Her frantic voice silenced his dressing-down. Made his blood run cold.

Davis could hear her crying and car noise in the background. His pulse thundered. "Did they take you? Do you know where you are?"

"I'm driving," Hollyn cried into the phone. "Someone's after me!"

He listened to the background noise. "Are you on speaker? Bluetooth?"

Please say yes.

He didn't need her driving one-handed in the middle of a car chase.

"Speaker."

Hands-free. Hopefully. That was good. "Tell me where you are and I'll—"

"They won't stop following me! I—agh!"

Her yelp gutted him. "Who? Who's following you?" Davis grabbed the car keys he'd set on the counter. Tapped his leg on the way to the foyer.

Fury reached the door before him.

Hollyn sobbed. "I don't know, but I think they're trying to run me off the road. Is it them?"

Davis slammed the front door behind him. Hoofed it down the front path to the Chevelle.

God, please not her.

Why hadn't she stayed at the house? Or at least waited for him.

He heard the tires squeal. "Hollyn!" he snapped.

"I'm here." He hated the way terror clung to every syllable. "I think it is them. It has to be, right? I'm gonna die!" The last word held a tremor.

"You're not gonna die," Davis stated firmly. Willed it to be the truth. He couldn't lose her.

In the backseat, Fury panted, amped up, ready for action.

The engine of the SS roared to life when he turned the key. "Where are you?" he asked again, voice tight. Without a twenty on her, he'd just be driving around wasting time. Putting her life in more danger.

"I—I don't know. We were in town and then—" Her cry-moan cut off her sentence. "He's getting closer!"

Davis rammed a fist against the steering wheel. "Baby, give me something." He didn't have time to wonder where the intimate moniker came from. "Anything. A landmark. A freaking piece of trash on the ground!" Did she really not know a single road name after living here so long?

"I'm . . . I'm . . . " Her voice sounded distracted. "I'm driving along the ocean."

Better than nothing, but he still needed more.

"Going which direction?"

"I don't know!"

Davis shoved down his irritation. She was doing the best she could. "Is the ocean on your left or right?"

"Right."

Heading south.

"I don't see a road name. The last sign I saw was Al Mahdar Street, but then the road turned and I couldn't stop in time, so I went straight. It's a dirt road." She finished the sentence words on top of each other.

Dirt? Not good. Davis clamped down on a curse as he thumbed the map on his phone. None of the cars from the garage were made for off-roading. He found Al Mahdar. Switched to satellite view to get a sense of the terrain. Zoomed in. "Any city buildings around you?"

"Only industrial. Most of them are behind me now. There's something up ahead."

Out of town then. Check.

"Found it," he told her. "I'm on my way."

The constant, muffled sound of the soft road beneath her tires coming through the speaker was both assuring and unnerving. If she lost control or hit some kind of hole . . .

Davis pulled away from the house. Hurried down side streets till he made it onto the main road.

"Davis!" Hollyn cried out.

"I'm coming, Hol." A lump formed in his throat. He slammed a fist down on the middle console. Swallowed his emotion as he maneuvered around cars. They honked at him. Didn't care. He'd lead a twenty-car police chase if that's what it came down to. Wasn't slowing down or stopping. "If you—"

"Agh!" Hollyn's scream pierced him before the line went dead.

Davis pressed the accelerator for all it was worth. Willed himself to find her before it was too late.

Hollyn grappled for the phone, but it flew out of her hand when her car jerked to the left. The line of communication to Davis tumbled onto the passenger floorboard as the back end of her BMW swung out at an unnatural angle. Doing her best to hold in another scream, she gripped the steering wheel, body on fire with adrenaline. Tried to remember what she'd been taught about turning into a fishtail. She pumped the brakes a second before she saw a flash of the black SUV coming up on her bumper.

Regaining control, she gunned the engine. This close, she could almost make out the driver. All she knew for sure was that it was a male—or a very short-haired woman—wearing a hat. Almost every time Hollyn glanced into the rearview mirror, the person lifted their wrist to their mouth, like they were talking into a smartwatch or something.

Or were they covering their face?

She didn't have a whole lot of time to think about it. Not crashing was taking up more than a little of her focus.

The road veered precariously near a drop-off toward the ocean below as both cars sped farther outside of the city. A shipping yard—or so she assumed—grew larger the closer she got. Hollyn squinted. She couldn't tell which way the road went. Then suddenly it curved and disappeared inside the gates of a massive shipping yard. Straight ahead was just wide open field. No roads.

Dead end.

Hollyn didn't have time to think or to stop to find another way around. She hit the brakes and drove her car through the opening, praying there was another way out on the other side. Otherwise, she'd just signed her death warrant.

"I don't want to die!" she shouted to God. "Please, help me!"

Had her parents said a similar prayer?

*Focus or you'll be able to ask them yourself!*

Inside the gates were stacks of shipping containers. She took the widest path between them, grateful there weren't many people inside. Still, it was far from empty.

Her pursuer had slightly less luck with the turn, and it gave Hollyn a bit of a lead she hadn't had before. The healing injury on her palm screamed from holding the steering wheel so tightly, but she didn't dare relax her grip. Probably couldn't have even if she'd wanted to.

Blessedly, it was a Saturday, which meant there were fewer people working in the industrial facility than she'd anticipated. Still, she was given more than a few choice gestures as her car shot along a row of shipping containers. She pressed her horn with all her might in warning. The thought of someone unknowingly stepping out from behind the containers and walking into her path . . .

On the far side of the massive area was an opening in the fence. A way out. She accelerated toward it.

Hollyn drew in a deep, shaky breath. The SUV was about two car lengths behind now and closing in.

A forklift holding a smaller container started backing toward her path.

"No, no, no!" she yelled in vain.

She blared the horn over and over. Held her breath. It was going to be close if the guy driving the machine didn't hear her.

At the last second, the guy stopped. Yelled at her just as she sped out of the yard and back onto dirt. Her body jostled as she navigated the uneven terrain. The road curved back toward the ocean and was getting progressively bumpier. Hollyn wasn't sure how much road was left.

Please, let Davis be close!

It was getting harder to keep her car steady. The BMW definitely wasn't made for off-roading. White knuckled, she watched as the driver of the SUV came up beside her. Hollyn cast a quick glance at her blind spot. The black vehicle suddenly rammed the side of her trunk.

Hollyn screamed as her BMW twisted. It pitched off the side of the road, rear first over the embankment. Hollyn's hands pressed to the ceiling, and her backside lifted off her seat as earth gave way to sky in the windshield. Her seatbelt kept her from going too far, but weightlessness was instantly replaced by hard edges when the car hit something.

Her head whipped forward from the impact. Airbags deployed and hit her with brute force. Her ears rang, head throbbing as she flailed against the bags.

Adrenaline continued pulsing in her veins, but she could feel herself fading.

"Davis," she heard herself moan. Where was he?

Hollyn's vision swam and she slumped forward as consciousness teetered toward darkness.

# 9



A WHOLE NEW LEVEL OF TERROR SEIZED DAVIS WHEN HE SAW MORE than just the dirt road ahead.

Hollyn's BMW.

Crunched into an embankment, resting precariously in a grove of bushes just this side of falling into the ocean. Smoke billowed from the hood of the car.

Haunting memories of an equally smoky car in A-stan flashed across his mind. Of unseeing eyes. Bloodied faces. Shouting voices.

Singed fur and the acrid scent of burning gas hit his nose like no time had passed.

Davis's stomach pitched. Sound hollowed. Vision tunneled.

If he'd failed to protect her . . .

*Let me be in time.*

"Sir," the emergency operator prompted from the other end of speaker phone. "Are you still there? Police and ambulance en route."

Davis blinked. Shifted down as he approached. "I'm on scene. From what I can see, it's a single-vehicle crash." He rattled off the coordinates listed on the GPS. Slammed on the brakes. Shut down the Chevelle. "Checking on the driver."

He launched himself out of the driver's seat without a second thought.

Fury followed closely through the open door.

"Hollyn!" Davis raced toward her vehicle, but a plume of smoke billowed out, pushing him back a step.

In the distance, emergency sirens howled their response.

A figure stumbled through the smoke, hand on their head. Slunk his direction.

Instinctively, his hand swung to the SIG at his stomach. Drew down. Then recognition flared.

"Hollyn." Thank God! Davis holstered his weapon inside his waistband. He'd never been more grateful to see anyone in his life.

Fury shot past her in favor of searching the car as he shifted closer, assessing her physical condition. "You hurt?"

She neared. Grabbed his arm.

There was blood spatter on her shirt. Looked like it was dripping from her nose. That was concerning. He felt her head. Arms. Ribs. She didn't flinch, but that didn't mean much right now. Adrenaline was an expert at masking serious issues.

Hollyn squinted up at him, then shook her head. "No . . . I don't think so " She wiped at the trailing liquid with the back of her hand. Groaned. She swayed forward.

Davis's hands shot out to steady her. Where was the freaking ambulance? "What happened?"

Hollyn pinched the bridge of her nose. Winced. Her hand shook violently. Tears streamed down her cheeks. "I . . . I . . . " She was looking around, eyes wild.

Davis felt her head again, afraid he'd missed something. Concussion was at the forefront of his thoughts. "Do you remember losing consciousness?"

"H-he tried to kill me!" Her bloodied hand grabbed a fistful of his shirt. Continued the adrenaline shake Davis knew all too well.

Davis stilled. "He? You saw the driver?"

Germaine?

Her lids squeezed closed.

Davis clenched his jaw at the sight of her so visibly shaken. He thumbed her tears away. "What'd he look like?" he tried softly.

"I didn't g-get a close enough look." Anguish filled her blue and green eyes. "All I remember was he kept l-lifting his arm to his face like he was talking into a watch." She dug her fingers into her hair. Sobbed.

The sirens grew louder.

Davis looked over at Fury, heart launching in his throat at the sight of the shepherd sitting statue still, focus pinned to the back of her car. Was it explosives? Electronics? The RMWD was trained to find a lot of things.

He needed to check it out.

"Stay here, okay?" He gripped Hollyn's shoulders till she made eye contact. Nodded.

Davis hoofed it to the wreck. Thumped his hand against the shepherd's side a few times. Wished he had the landshark's tug for a reward. "Good job, buddy." He knelt. Carefully inspected what he could see of the back bumper.

Fury's tail swished back and forth in the sandy dirt. He didn't stand.

Waves of the Persian Gulf crashed against the shore below. From what Davis could tell, the BMW seemed secure, but it was hard to be positive. This kind of ground might give way at any time. He shot a glance over his shoulder at Hollyn. She watched him, arms wrapped around her middle. Loose hair swished in the breeze.

Attention back on the car, Davis ran his hand along the backside of the bumper. Could hear EMS coming up on scene, stopping not too far away. Emergency personnel rushed their way.

Davis frowned as he kept feeling around. Nothing seemed out of the ordinary, so—wait. His finger touched something small. Almost missed it.

Slowly, he ducked under the car for a better look. Prayed he wasn't about to get crushed or blown up.

"Ma'am! Are you all right?" an unknown female voice asked. "We got a call—"

The rest of the conversation faded when Davis saw what was attached to the car.

A tracking device. He'd seen ones like this before.

"Davis!"

He jerked at Hollyn's shrill tone. Forehead hit the underside of the car. "Freakin' . . . " he growled as he scooted out. Rubbed his head.

"Did you find something?" She had a small grey blanket around her shoulders now, and one of the EMTs was addressing her nose injury.

Uniformed police officers formed almost a barrier between him and Hollyn. He had their full attention.

"Found a tracking device." He nodded to the bumper.

But instead of coming closer, they solemnly watched Fury, hands on the weapons at their sides.

It was then Davis realized his partner was growling at them.

"Easy." He spoke calmly as he stood. "Fury, heel " With no sudden moves, he held up his hands to the officers. "It's okay. I'm the one who called this in. This is my retired military working dog, trained to detect explosives and EMDs. He alerted on the car."

"It's the truth," Hollyn interjected. "He isn't the one who ran me off the road."

The officers looked reluctant to believe them but finally dropped their hands from their sidearms. "We'll need statements from you both," one of the officers spoke up. Took a couple steps closer.

"Fair enough," Davis replied. But shoot his dog and they were gonna have a problem.

"Step away from the vehicle," the officer instructed. "Slowly."

Davis nodded. Did as they asked. Fury stuck to his side but made no effort to hide the way he scrutinized every move the officers made.

When he neared Hollyn, she wrapped her arms around his neck. Davis slid his arms around her waist. She clung to him like she had no intention of letting go. Fine with him. He'd stay like this as long as she wanted to.

"I'm so sorry." She cried quietly into his bum shoulder. "I never should have left the house."

Davis had royally screwed up by leaving Hollyn at the house. He wouldn't make that mistake again. She was going to get sick of how close an eye he was about to keep on her.

"Just glad you're safe," he said for her ears only.

Fury pawed his leg. Pushed his giant head between them.

Jealous much?

Davis reached down to pet the lug's head.

"Thank you for coming." Hollyn sniffed.

"Always."

The word was out before he even had time to examine it. But it was the truth. Didn't matter how much time or distance had come between them over the years. She was the one person he'd drop anything for. Always had been. Always would be.

*What're you doing, man?*

It felt too good to have her in his arms. This was dangerous ground. And not just physically.

Davis could see the officers checking Hollyn's car now. They motioned to each other, and one of them was radioing for something.

Slowly, Hollyn pulled back. Wiped at her eyes. Her other hand gripped his bicep.

Her brow furrowed. "They aren't going to stop, are they? Whoever's behind this. Not until I'm dead too."

The way her chin quivered was like a KA-BAR to the gut. But he refused to entertain the thought of her dying. Forced a grin. "Well, then, their mission is scrubbed. 'Cause they're gonna have to go through me from now on."

Hearing him say that made Hollyn's heart skip a beat. But just as quickly as the feeling came, she admonished herself. Davis was just being protective of her. Nothing more. It was how he was built and what he'd been trained to do for the last decade. He saved people. Protected people. It didn't mean he loved them or felt anything other than a sense of dedication to the mission.

She was just the most recent mission. She could *not* let herself be swept away by romantic frivolities based on feelings from their past. Her chest ached from an erratic heartbeat that hadn't stilled since the chase began. Now it was freaking out for a completely different reason. She rubbed her sternum. Willed the thumping to slow, but it didn't. Especially not with his close proximity.

"Ma'am, I need to take your statement." A tall officer nodded for her to join him. He didn't come too close, and Hollyn had an idea that it was likely due to the furry beast currently panting at her side.

Regretfully, Hollyn broke contact with Davis to step away with the officer. But even as she answered question after question, she couldn't stop her gaze from lifting over the guy's shoulder to Davis every few seconds. Each time she did, it confirmed that he hadn't taken his eyes off her. It was unnerving. Electrifying.

Tugging the blanket tighter around her body, Hollyn tried to focus on talking about the chain of events before her crash. A sneeze crept up, and she sucked in a sharp breath, trying to stop it. A sneeze would be murderous with her injured nose.

"Are you okay?" The officer looked concerned.

"Yeah," she replied, relieved when the urge to sneeze passed. "Just in a little pain."

That was an understatement. Her face was killing her right now—more like her whole *body* was killing her—and the thought of rattling it made her cringe. But at least whatever the EMT—who'd said it wasn't broken—had swabbed into her nostrils had stemmed the bleeding. Her shirt was history, though. Same with her car.

But she was alive.

Something she'd be thanking God about for the rest of her life.

"Can you describe the vehicle that was following you?" The officer's Middle Eastern accent was thick.

Hollyn's body trembled with subsiding adrenaline. She couldn't stop playing the last half hour over and over in her head. She was so stupid for driving to Bongani's alone.

"Ma'am?" the officer asked again. His dark eyes pinned her.

"Right. The car. It was . . . black." Hollyn pictured it in her mind. "An SUV. I don't know about the make or model." She rubbed her forehead. Images of the car getting closer in the rearview mirror sent chills down her spine. Panic started pricking her stomach. Then she recalled seeing circles on the grill . . . "Maybe an Audi?"

The officer jotted down some notes. "Any distinguishing characteristics? Dents or stickers?"

"It was *behind* me." Hollyn's brow furrowed, but she swallowed down her irritation. The guy was just doing his job. "No. I . . . don't think so. I'm sorry, it all happened so fast."

The officer nodded, the tan-colored beret on his head remaining securely in place. "That's okay." He tugged a business card from the chest pocket of his uniform. "If you think of anything else, even the smallest of details, this is my number."

The small card was cold in her hand.

"The EMTs will take you to the hospital to get checked out and—"

"No!" Her refusal was so instant, so intense, it surprised even her. She took it down a notch. Stepped back. "No, I'm fine. Thank you, but—"

"I'll take her." Davis and Fury stepped up to them. The hand he placed on her back was so unnerving she almost came out of her skin. "Come on."

Fury pressed into her leg like he was trying to herd her.

It was all too much. "No!" She jerked away from him. "I'm not going to the hospital."

Suspicion darkened the officer's eyes as he frowned at Davis. "Are you *sure* you're okay?" he asked Hollyn.

"*Yes*. I'm—everything is okay."

With one last assessing look at Davis, the officer stepped away to join the others still working the scene. No doubt he'd be keeping a close eye on them from a distance.

"Hol—"

"I'm *not* going, Davis. I'm fine."

"It's just to make sure—"

"No." Hollyn felt her resolve lock into place. She narrowed her eyes. "You will literally have to drag me kicking and screaming."

He scowled. "What's the deal with you and hospitals?"

She couldn't completely blame him. He didn't know her why. She'd kept that vulnerable piece of her past tucked away all these years.

"You were just in a car accident." Davis gripped her elbow through the blanket. His gaze was urgent. "Could be bleeding internally or any number of other things you can't feel yet because adrenaline is masking it."

Hollyn didn't back down on this. "No hospitals."

"Why?"

"Because!"

"*Why?*" he demanded.

"Because it's the last building I was in with my birth parents!" Hollyn spat. Her heart raced for an entirely different reason now. She was shocked the words had actually come out of her mouth this time.

Well, she was in this now. He wanted the truth? Fine.

"My parents had a lot of issues, but they always made me breakfast before I went off to school. One morning, I woke up and the house was just . . . still. I could feel something wasn't right. I raced out to the living room, and that's when I"—her chin quivered as the images beat her—"found them." She shook her head. Swallowed a lump in her throat. Didn't dare look up at Davis, or she'd lose her nerve.

Fury tilted his head as he watched her, amber eyes warm and almost caring.

"They were on the floor." Her voice cracked. Apparently, it didn't make a difference how far from that day she'd gotten. It was still a vivid scar in her psyche. "Almost like they were sleeping. But when I saw the bands wrapped around their arms, I knew—could feel it in my gut." Shame curtained her. Would he think less of her because of them? "They'd overdosed. I called for an ambulance, and they rushed us to the hospital. I sat alone in those plastic chairs for hours before anyone finally talked to me." Curse the man for making her think about this! The memories were going to crush her.

She felt Davis shift. He crossed his arms. Though she didn't look around, she could hear the police radios going off intermittently as they worked the scene. The ambulance drove away.

"A doctor came out and told me they'd done their best but my parents were dead." Hollyn could still picture the way the doctor's nametag had been clipped at a weird angle on his white lab jacket. How it'd kept tapping the side of the pen in his breast pocket every time he moved his arm. The metallic scent of blood had lingered on him despite having washed up, and strongly contrasted with the hypochlorite and peracetic acid used to keep the hospital clean.

This time Hollyn dared to meet his gaze and saw Davis's Adam's apple bob as he swallowed. "He said it so callously. Like . . . because I was nine, it somehow wouldn't hit me as hard as it would an adult, and I could just move on. Just get a new family, you know?" She shrugged. Gripped the blanket tighter. Her fingers brushed her necklace. "He acted like my parents' struggle with drugs made them less worthy of mourning or compassion somehow. But I didn't care about any of that. They were my parents! I just wanted them back!"

Davis shook his head, sympathy washing his handsome face. He ran a hand over his jaw in thought, chest rising and falling in a steady rhythm, but for the first time since he'd come here, he looked rattled.

A warm breeze tugged at the edges of the blanket currently trapped between her clenched fingers. It was filled with the salty scent of the Persian Gulf waters and rustled through nearby palms.

"I'm sorry, Hol."

"Then CPS came and took me to my first group home." She shook her head, tears welling. "I didn't even get to say goodbye to them. For months I was convinced that they weren't actually dead and would come get me."

Davis didn't say anything else. Just released a weighted breath and closed the distance between them. He gently slipped his arms around her.

When he pressed a kiss to her forehead, it was nearly her undoing.

Hollyn sank against him. Relished the way his strong arms were like a shield from the nightmares raining down on her For the first time in years, she allowed herself to relax. Her nose hurt where it pressed into his chest, so she turned her head to the side. Clung to his firm waist.

Maybe she should've told him this years ago.

Pfft. Right. Nobody had been ready for that back then, especially her. And though she hadn't planned on telling him at all, she was so thankful no secrets stood between them anymore. It was . . . freeing.

Fury pawed at her shoe and pressed his weight into her leg. She smiled at the pressure. The three of them felt like a family.

Wait, wait, wait. No!

Hollyn chided herself.

A hug and innocent kiss, and she'd been swept off her feet again without so much as a mild protest! Emotions couldn't be trusted! It was just the car accident messing with her. She wasn't thinking clearly. She thought she'd done a good job reining them in over the years. But Davis hadn't been in her everyday life then. Now, he was throwing her for a loop. She needed to snap out of it.

Seriously.

It was nothing more than a surge in endorphins from his comforting reaction to her story that had her hurtling down the path toward Happily-Ever-Afterville.

However, the moment her gaze met Davis's, an overwhelming surge of something—call it bravery or insanity—washed over her, and Hollyn threw caution to the wind. Forgot about emergency personnel still going over the crash. Ignored all the screaming warning bells blaring in her head and pressed up onto her tippy toes . . . and kissed him.

She, Hollyn Reinhardt, kissed Davis Ledger.

He went rigid beneath her hands as they slipped up and over his shoulders, then his arm came around her waist. Tugged her close as gloriously, shockingly, he returned the gesture. For a moment, all her starry-eyed dreams came to fruition. However incredible she'd imagined this would be, real life blew it out of the water. In the arms of the man she'd loved for so long, she felt perfectly at home, and he was drinking her in like she was water in the desert.

But then he pulled back. Held her at arm's length. "Hold up," he said breathlessly.

Hollyn slanted forward in the wake of pressure.

Davis's heavy gaze raked over her face, looking like he wanted to do anything but stop.

"I'm sorry," she heard herself say, suddenly very aware they had an audience. "I didn't mean . . . "

He just stared at her for seconds that seemed endless. "I can't," he finally replied. "*We* can't."

Right. She knew that. "Of course." She stepped back, gathering the blanket tighter. "I just . . . I was caught up and . . . adrenaline, you know?" Her excuse was weak. Even she could hear it.

Davis just gave a small nod, jaw muscle popping.

No. They'd never be a family.

"I'm sorry, Hol." His tone was quiet, and the way he was looking at her—like he thought he'd broken her—twisted her stomach.

Fury watched her with keen interest, tongue hanging out the side of his mouth. He almost looked like he was laughing at her.

She just wanted this day to be over already. "Let's just go home, okay?" she said to Davis.

Did he just stiffen?

*Her* home! She didn't mean *their*—she understood! They were two separate, *non-romantic* people who would never be together in that way. Inwardly, she groaned. Would she ever get this right?

"Sure thing." Davis released his hold. He lifted a hand to get an officer's attention. "Good if I take her home?"

"I just need your statement first," the tall officer said to Davis, who provided it in record time. "The car will be towed," the officer told them when Davis was done. He handed them a slip of paper. "You can make arrangements by calling this number."

Hollyn would worry about that later. All she wanted right now was a hot shower and sleep. As they pulled away from the crash site, Hollyn felt something buzz in her back pocket. Her phone. She shifted to the side to pull it out, thankful she'd thought to grab it as she escaped the wreck.

Fury poked his head out between the front seats. Slobber flicked off his tongue as he panted. Hollyn wrinkled her sore nose and scooted away from the droplets.

"Get back," Davis commanded the furry giant.

Fury disappeared into the backseat.

Hollyn looked down at her phone. A text from Leila lit up the screen:

LEI

SOS. They've got me and Archie. Don't know I have my phone.

Hollyn gasped. Her blood ran cold.

"What's wrong?" Davis asked firmly.

She stuttered but couldn't form actual words. Below the text, it showed Leila had shared her location. Hollyn quickly typed a reply.

HOLLYN

Who has you? Are you hurt?

LEI

. . .

She watched the dots bouncing on the screen. They disappeared but no text came through.

"Talk to me, Hollyn."

"They've got her!" She could hardly hold on to the device. Oxygen fought her efforts to draw it in. "It's Lei. She just texted

SOS—Davis . . . they've got her and Archie!" She clamped a hand over her mouth.

This was the nightmare that wouldn't end!

Davis was quiet. A scowl had etched itself deep into his face.

"She shared her location. We need to get to her. Now!"

He didn't speak for an agonizing minute.

"Now!" She was just about to start yelling at him when he nodded.

"Route us. And send me the location." Without slowing, he pulled his phone from his tactical pants. Tapped the screen.

Hollyn sent him the location before starting directions. Leila and Archie's location was a solid forty minutes away. It'd be dark by the time they got there. Would that help or hinder things? She clipped the phone to the dash holder, then tugged her seatbelt tighter and started praying.

A shrill ring filled the car twice before a man answered Davis's call. "Speak of the devil." His voice was deep and gruff. "I was just about to call you. Hope your death antigen is up to date, because you've got some serious stuff coming your way."

"Tell me about it," Davis answered the guy.

"Did your girl just have a run-in with someone?"

His *girl*? Hollyn's head snapped to Davis in time to see his jaw flex. And how on earth did this guy know about the accident?

"You're on speaker, Chapel."

The guy cleared his throat. "Afraid I'll spill your secrets?"

Davis looked something akin to a caged animal right now. "Someone just ran her off the road. Same way her parents' accident happened." His gaze skirted to her before he looked to the road.

In the backseat, Fury whined.

Hollyn turned to him. "It's okay," she whispered, though it dawned on her that the military working dog was probably just excited, not worried like she was. Did anything scare him? Sure didn't seem like it.

Take notes, Hollyn.

Their bodies swayed as the car veered left. She squeezed her eyes closed and whipped back around. Clung to her seatbelt.

"With Germaine's interest in your girl, we've been prowling the dark web. Found something," Chapel continued.

Hollyn's gut twisted. *Dark web* didn't sound good. Who was Germaine?

"Seems he put out a bounty. Chatter suggests someone just took a swing at the prize and missed."

Her jaw went slack. *A bounty? On me?*

Davis muttered a curse.

Chapel. "To the victor go the spoils—to the tune of three mil." He sniffed. "That's a lot of green. What in Sam Hill does your girl know?"

Davis glanced at her, eyebrows raised in question.

She leaned toward the phone, chewing her lip nervously. "I, um, don't know what they think I . . . know." She scrunched her nose. Did that sound as pathetic as it felt to say?

"Might wanna figure it out." Like Davis, his tone was all business. "You're about to have a ton of unfriendlies breathing down your neck."

Dread slithered across her shoulders as if Death itself traced its bony fingers there.

Davis gripped the wheel with one hand. "Hollyn just got word that her friends were allegedly kidnapped—"

"Alleged—" Hollyn stopped mid-word. Scowled. "Are you *serious*?" she whisper-seethed. Was there *anything* that could clear her friends' names in his mind?

Davis threw her a hard look. "Sending you the coordinates," he said to his friend. "Gonna need backup, if you can spare anyone."

"Copy. Send me your twenty. Stay frosty."

The line went dead.

Davis handed off his phone. "Send him our location. Under Chapel." He guided the car around a sharp curve in the road.

One of her hands had a white-knuckle hold on the door while the other gripped the phone. The tires of the Chevelle screeched on the pavement they'd just reached as Davis floored the accelerator.

Fresh flashbacks from her recent car crash flooded her senses.

*Keep it together. For Lei and Archie. They need you.*

With trembling fingers, Hollyn opened his texts. Found Chapel's name and sent the location Lei had shared with her. There was no reply. But *copy* meant they were going to help . . . right?

"Shouldn't we call the cops?" she managed to ask.

"I trust Chapel and his team."

Meaning he didn't trust the police?

Clinging to her seatbelt with one hand and her necklace with the other, Hollyn pressed back into her seat, eyes closed. Prayed they'd be in time.

*Hold on, you guys. We're coming.*

# 10



*ZAHDA ISLAND, ABU DHABI, UAE*

"Almost there," Davis said into the speaker phone.

"Copy," Chapel replied on the other end before hanging up.

The city was alive with lights and nightlife now that the sun was fully below the horizon. Eerie calm settled on this side of the Ba Halama Bridge that connected Reem Island to Zahda Island.

From what Davis could see, at least a dozen multistory buildings—maybe intended for offices—stood with scaffolding still around them. The ones illuminated by the streetlights looked abandoned. Unlike the main streets of Abu Dhabi, filled with people heading home from work or getting an early jump on a night of partying, the roads on Zahda Island were all but empty. A few parked cars dotted the roadsides, but he didn't see any sign of people.

The small island practically begged for trouble.

Streetlamps and city lights that refused to give way to stars overhead lit a particularly dead road Davis turned onto. At least they'd have plenty of light to work by outside. Once they stepped inside, it'd be another story.

A glance at his phone to check the directions Chapel'd sent him ten minutes ago made him bank right behind one of the unfinished structures. The location Leila had shared wasn't far from here. Maybe a couple buildings over.

Next to him, Hollyn shifted in her seat. Their kiss was still on repeat in his head. But as much as he'd slipped and let himself enjoy the moment, getting involved with Hollyn was just about the last thing he could do right now. Another time, another place.

The Chevelle's low beams splashed across two low-profile SUVs ten yards ahead. Couldn't see from this side of a huge construction dumpster, but he knew Chapel and the team were ready on the other side. Thick plastic covering over sections of the concrete buildings flapped in the breeze as Davis shifted down and parked behind the rear vehicle.

Before Davis killed the headlights, Chapel emerged and greeted them with a lifted chin. Damocles operators Cage Macklin and Nixon Hale flanked him. All guys Davis had shared ops with back in the day. Macklin and Hale were lethal on their own, but together they were an unstoppable force.

For the first time since his accident, Davis felt himself come alive with the familiar rush of pre-op adrenaline. It grounded him. He lived for this stuff. It was a rush to get another taste of the one thing he did well.

Another reason he was so irritated the Army had tossed him out like a live grenade.

A dark-haired woman he recognized stepped up to the Chevelle in full tac gear when he exited. An M4 hung loose across her small frame, and she wore a "mess around and find out" expression he could see even in the glow of the full moon.

"Ledger." Lieutenant Nora Glace greeted him with an extended hand and clasped his in a respectably firm grip. "Chapel said you've got a woman with you." She held a small tac vest and helmet out to Davis. "This should fit her better than the extras the guys have. No NVGs, but we figured that was more important for you."

He took it. "Thanks."

Hollyn came around the front of the muscle car.

The two women eyed each other in the dim light. Were like night and day in comparison—one clearly confident and full of grit, the other soft and more than a little out of place.

"Hey," Hollyn said to Glace. She looked between Davis and the LT, seemingly unsure what to do.

"Hollyn, this is Lieutenant Glace." Davis introduced them.

Glace lifted a hand in acknowledgement. "You can call me Nora."

"Hollyn."

The petite operator grinned before she walked away.

Behind them, Fury barked from the car, reminding Davis to let him out.

He opened the door. *"Fuss."*

Wild and ready for action, the RMWD jumped from the backseat. Glued himself to Davis's thigh, tail low and zipping back and forth.

They walked to the trunk, where Davis used his phone flashlight as he grabbed his knife and backup sidearm from his rucksack. Checked the Sig, then slid it into a thigh holster he strapped into place. Made sure Fury's vest was secure and discreetly tucked a roped KONG into his side pocket.

The lug was crazy for his KONG. Better to keep it out of sight, even though he knew Fury could smell it.

Chapel approached Davis. "As of today, you and Fury are officially part of the team until I decide your services are no longer required. Copy?"

"Copy." Davis nodded his understanding of the legal hoops that required his acceptance.

Chapel turned to the team. "All right, listen up."

Macklin handed off gear and an M4 to Davis, which he quickly donned while Chapel laid out the plan. Tucked the comms piece in his ear and adjusted the strap on his helmet. Slid extra mags into his vest loops.

"Eagle's in the sky," Chapel started, referencing the name of their drone.

Davis knew the one. It was operated by Sgt. Lennon Blanchard, the team's intelligence specialist and unmanned aircraft systems operator. She'd be perched somewhere offsite running surveillance for the team.

"Exterior looks clear. Multiple unfriendlies inside." Chapel continued. "Eagle has eyes on at least two hostages through an opening on the third floor."

"Germaine?" Hale questioned.

"Unknown. Our primary objective is to confirm or deny. If it's him—only way he leaves *alive* is under our control." Chapel eyed the team. "Secondary is to secure the hostages."

Davis didn't miss Hollyn's gasp.

She met his gaze, fear all over her face. "I have friends in there!" she hissed. "Aren't *they* the whole point of this?"

They weren't, but he didn't have time to explain.

"Glace, Nazari, Bennion. Gain topside infil via the building on the two side." Chapel rested one hand on the butt of his M4. "Nix, Cage, Ledger, Fury on me through blue two entry. You." He pointed to Hollyn, whose eyes went wide. "Like white on rice with Ledger—got it? No matter what. Obey that and you'll come out alive. Copy?"

Face scratched with both irritation and awareness of what she'd gotten herself into, Hollyn nodded mutely.

Chapel's brow darkened, that alone demanding a verbal acknowledgement.

Every eye swung her way.

"Play the game, win the prize," Benn muttered under his breath.

Though Davis felt for her, saw how much she felt out of her depth, it was important she was instilled with a healthy respect for what was about to go down. She was stronger than she knew, but a little fear would go a long way in keeping her alive.

"Yes, uh, sir. I copy." Hollyn sounded far from confident.

"Get her geared up," Chapel barked, then went back to the map.

Having slid his M4 behind him, Davis squatted next to her and strapped his sheathed Big Brother KA-BAR to her leg. The nine-inch blade with top edge serration was his go-to pick for hand-to-hand. Wasn't a gun, but he wasn't giving her one of those without any training under her belt.

Beneath his hands, he could feel her trembling. "Don't worry, we've got you."

Excited, Fury nuzzled his ear, trying to get him to stand and get the show on the road.

Davis shouldered the RMWD back. "Give me a sec." He stood, then helped Hollyn into her ballistic vest. Fastened it tight and prayed she wouldn't need it. Lastly, he palmed the top of her brain bowl to make sure her helmet was good to go. "Hey," he whispered.

Her eyes lifted to his, full of anxiety as she clung to her vest.

"You've got this." He winked encouragement.

For a minute, the tight creases in her forehead slackened and the trepidation in her eyes fell away. "Right," she breathed. Her gaze dropped to his lips.

Holy mother. The woman had no idea how effortlessly she could bring him to his knees.

Chapel keyed his mic. "Blank, how copy?"

"Lima Charlie," came Blanchard's reply through the comms. "Green light."

"Here we go," Davis spoke low to Hollyn.

"I'm going to be sick," she whispered.

Davis took her hand. Guided it to his belt. "Deep breaths and stay close." He nodded to Fury.

The mutt snapped his jowls closed. Tilted his head.

"Don't let go." Davis spoke low.

"No chance of that," Hollyn breathed.

Please, keep her safe.

Chapel swung a finger in the air. "Move out."

Bennion, Glace, and Nazari led the team along the rear alley that paralleled the street. They broke off at the second building and slipped through the back door while Chapel led the rest of them to the next vacant structure mere feet away. Davis's body went tense, and he strained to hear any sound out of place as they hurried through the darkness.

M4 up, Davis stayed alert at the back of the group. Bringing up the rear wasn't his usual place, but with Hollyn here, it was safest for the team to use themselves as potential shields. Fury heeled tight on his nine. Hand on his belt, Hollyn shadowed his five. Crowded his elbow a little, but at least he krew where she was.

The concrete path between the buildings was barely wide enough for two men to walk down shoulder to shoulder. That worked well, seeing as how Bennion and his team would have to jump across from one roof to the other.

They kept their steps light so they didn't draw attention should anyone be near the windows or gaping holes where glass had never been installed. A low din from nearby Reem Island filled the air along with the continuous thwapping of plastic in the breeze. Whole place looked like some kind of creepy dystopian nightmare.

Silently, they hurried to a side door. Hollyn moved with surprising stealth, hand never leaving his belt.

Chapel paused a few feet from the door. Keyed his mic. "Send the dog."

"Fury," Davis spoke low. "Seek-seek."

It was all the encouragement the RMWD needed. He clamped his jaw closed. Dropped his nose to the concrete and got to work. Sucked in round after round of deep, guttural breaths. Zigzagged as he searched the area near the door. Ears swiveling, tail high, he nosed the gaps with interest. Didn't alert, but he paused. Pawed. Paced side to side like he wanted to get in.

Davis tapped his leg twice to recall Fury. Keyed his mic. "Clear."

Chapel opened the door. Hale stalked in, swung left. Macklin followed and went right.

All good.

Then they were moving again. Into the darkened building. Unlike the upper levels, the ground floor was mostly finished with boarded windows that let in next to no light. He flipped down his NVGs, clicked them on. Made sure the door closed quietly behind him. He squeezed Hollyn's hand, hoping she read the hint to keep clinging to him. In the pitch black, she wouldn't see much.

Not affected by the darkness, Fury heeled with well-practiced ease as they maneuvered down concrete hallways. Boots gritted over sand blown in over who knew how many months. This floor was empty, so they took the stairwell to the next. Davis stayed on Macklin's six as the team silently ascended the stairs.

The landshark cleared the door on the second-story landing, and Cage slowly tugged it open. The team filed inside. Moonlight broke up the darkness, streaking through gaps left for windows.

Keeping his breathing steady, Davis stalked through the building and scanned for threats. Beside him, Hollyn's breaths were slightly labored, but she continued to keep pace with him. Why hadn't they come upon anyone yet? If Germaine were here, he wouldn't be alone. But the place seemed empty.

Sheets of wind-shredded plastic hung from the ceilings, essentially creating opaque walls. They whipped and snapped in the breeze.

Every muscle in Davis's body was on high alert. The dull ache in his shoulder was morphing into sharp pain, but he shoved away the distraction. Refused to give in to it as they searched the second floor.

No pain, no gain, right?

They followed Chapel into a secondary interior stairwell on the three side. Poured up the steps using their NVGs to see the way once more. He kept his ears trained on Fury for the slightest sign that something was off. Wasn't making that mistake again.

When Chapel held up a fist at the third-floor landing, they all paused. Didn't hear a single sound on the other side. "Where are they, Blank?" Chapel was more than miffed right now.

Fury finished sniffing the door and they filtered out. Flipped up their NVGs. Plenty of moonlight filtered in through open gaps in the outer walls. But other than some stacks of cement bags, mixers, tools, and a free-standing TV, screen blank, the space was empty.

Frustration tightened through him—another vacant floor. What was going on?

Chapel shook his head and keyed his mic. "Damocles, sitrep?"

Reports rifled off from the rest of the team—all clear.

"Blank," Chapel barked into his mic, "what the heck's going on? It's empty!"

"Negative," Blanchard's reply came over the comms. "They were there!"

"Entering from the north," Benn subvocalized a minute before a door swung open. As he and the others crossed the room, the bulky operator held up a hand in a quick *What's going on?* motion.

Chapel glowered as he scanned the room. "Blank, if you plan on having a job tomorrow—"

"I'm looking," came Blanchard's tight reply.

"Look faster."

Fury sniffed the area around them, and Davis kept track of the RMWD's body language. Still no alerts. That was good. He wasn't exactly interested in blowing up today.

Hollyn looked to him without a word.

Light suddenly splashed across her face as the TV screen

blinked to life. Weapons snapped toward the screens as Davis and the team turned to the monitor.

Onscreen, Germaine stood next to Archie in one half of the split-screen image. Twerp was gagged and bound to a chair. On the other half, Leila sat, also restrained but obviously in a different room than the other men. The walls behind her were tan, not grey, and almost appeared cushioned. Left eye swollen shut, the other lacerated, she flashed a panic-filled look at the armed guard standing next to her. Her injured face and bloodied shirt betrayed the roughing-up she'd endured.

Give Davis two minutes with Germaine. Guy wouldn't be able to harm anyone ever again.

"Ah," Germaine crooned. "Look who finally showed up. The odd squad." His posture was relaxed, as if he had all the time in the world.

"Blank," Chapel subvocalized. "Locate the feed's source."

"On it."

Davis studied the backgrounds of both video feeds. Couldn't distinguish much behind Twerp and Germaine—they were too close to the camera.

"Let's get down to business," Germaine started. "All right, Hollyn?"

Davis gritted his teeth and felt Hollyn clinging to the side of his vest.

"I know you're close with your friends. Don't make me do something permanent." Germaine lifted a hand, and the guard next to Leila jerked forward. Jammed his gun into the side of the woman's head. She yelped, chest rising and falling erratically. "Just tell me where the blueprints are, Sparrow, and everyone here walks out alive."

Davis didn't miss Hollyn's gasp. Adjusting his grip on the M4, he waited for Chapel's orders.

"I'm not a patient man. You have ten seconds before he pulls the trigger."

"Wait!" Hollyn shouted, thick tremors in her voice. "I-I don't know what blueprints you're looking for."

"Shut her up!" Chapel hissed via the comms.

Davis leaned toward her. "Don't engage."

"But he's going to kill her!" Her strangled whisper dug a figurative knife into his chest.

Germaine kept counting.

"Please!" Hollyn yelled when Germaine continued the countdown. "I don't know what—"

"Seven, six . . . "

"Blank. Give me the source of that feed. Now." Chapel demanded without drawing Germaine's attention.

Leila shook as she violently tried to break free of her bonds. She yelled something around her gag.

"Four." Germaine grinned. "Don't say I didn't warn you."

Not good.

"Blank!" Chapel barked.

"Sorry! Almost . . . "

Leila looked to the camera. Cried out.

"Two-one," Germaine finished as one word.

*Crack!*

A curse rattled through Davis. He tucked his M4 in tighter against his shoulder.

"No!" Hollyn screamed as her friend jerked and slumped forward. "No, no!" She dropped to her knees, sobbing.

Fury barked several times, feeding off the energy in the room.

"Blank, you're about to be unemployed."

"The signal's jammed! I can't get a lock on it."

"Have to be close to jam us," Davis muttered into his mic.

With a sharp nod, Chapel aimed at the screens.

*Crack! Crack!*

Glass shattered and rained down on the concrete floor.

"Move," Chapel ordered. "They're here somewhere. Two-man bounding formation." He quickly named pairs. "Find them!"

Davis spun. Grabbed Hollyn and hauled her to her feet. "Come on." He made her grab the side of his vest. Tapped his leg to recall Fury. "Seek-seek."

Fury immediately began their hunt. As they advanced, Davis could feel Hollyn shaking.

*Hang in there, Hol. We'll get you out of this in one piece.*

Germaine wasn't going to end up on the winning side tonight.

# 11



*ZAHDA ISLAND, ABU DHABI, UAE*

Darkness had never felt so heavy.

Fear and the ballistic vest strapped to Hollyn nearly suffocated her. With one hand, she clawed at the front of the Kevlar-lined straitjacket, trying to get some more space to breathe. With the other, she maintained a death grip on Davis's vest strap as they descended the stairs.

Death.

Tears burned her eyes. Not that it mattered. In the pitch-black stairwell they were racing down, she couldn't see anything anyway—terrifying, were it not for the stalwart presence of Davis. She nearly tripped a handful of times before they plowed through the side door.

Moonlight speared the dark. Breathing wasn't any easier out here. If she could just get another inch of space. But there was no time to dwell on it.

Fury led them to the back of the building. Paused for a minute in the alleyway. He sniffed back and forth as they waited, then took off like a shot.

Hollyn willed her legs to keep up with Davis and the others.

Refused to be the weak link. Leila might be gone—*Leila! You got her killed!*—but there was still a chance to save Archie.

*Please, God. We have to get to him in time!*

She couldn't lose two friends in the span of minutes! She couldn't scrub the image of Leila getting shot from her mind as they darted down the alley.

A warm breeze brushed against her wet cheeks, and the contents of her stomach began to rise.

Moving in unison, the team suddenly banked left and charged toward the side door of another building. She desperately wished she knew what was going on. Had someone said something in their earpieces? Was Archie in here?

Hollyn sank low behind Davis as the men stepped inside and broke off in different directions. When the door closed behind her, she was once again engulfed in shrouding darkness. They moved quickly, and she could just make out Fury's panting over her heartbeat thundering in her ears. The feeling of someone behind her was unnerving, and she uselessly glanced back. Almost tripped.

*It's just the team, it's just the team.*

Then barking. Furious and strong, a rhythm that jacked her heart rate with it. Gunfire erupted along with quick flashes of light.

Hollyn screamed and ducked. Pressed her free hand against her ear to try and dampen the earsplitting shots. She tightened her fist even harder around Davis's vest strap only to get yanked forward. Her shoulder slammed a doorjamb, and she wheeled past it into the open, squinting at the sudden explosion of light. Silver rays washed over the sandy asphalt. Better than nothing, but she still had to fight for focus. Blinked several times, demanding her vision obey.

Fury rocketed ahead of them at a shocking speed, heading for an Urvan microbus parked in the alleyway. Red brake lights haloed two men, one larger than the other, inching toward the vehicle in some kind of struggle.

Archie!

At least, it appeared to be him. The back of the microbus opened, and the bigger man Archie fought shoved him inside. He slammed the door closed, and the vehicle sped off a second before Fury launched himself at the guy.

The GSD all but flew through the air and latched on to the man's arm. Screams pierced the night above the gunfire still coming from inside the building behind Hollyn.

The two figures collapsed to the ground. Rolling. Fighting.

Hollyn released her hold, and Davis raced toward them, shouting at the man to be still.

*Crack! Pop-pop!*

"Take cover!"

Hollyn frantically searched for somewhere to hide in the dark. Saw a stack of crates and dove behind it as booted steps thundered near.

Davis kept his M4 trained on Germaine. "Don't move!" he shouted. Heard someone approaching on his six and spun around, gun up.

"Friendly, friendly!" Nazari yelled.

Davis turned back to Germaine as the guys surrounded them.

Fury whipped his giant head back and forth, growling around the arm. Refused to let go despite the fist crashing down on his head over and over. If anything, it amped the GSD even more.

"Get him off!" Germaine screamed.

"Freeze!" Davis demanded. "Hold still, hold still!"

Fury sucked in deep breaths around his hold as the team circled them at gunpoint. He thrashed his head a few more times. Davis didn't have to have a perfect view to know his dog was using the motion to sink his razor-sharp teeth deeper into the soft flesh.

Germaine did his own growling through clenched teeth but quit hitting Fury.

"Give me a reason!" Chapel aimed his weapon when Germaine jerked away from the RMWD.

Davis grabbed Fury's collar and tugged upward to encourage the landshark to release. His shoulder roared in protest. "Fury, out-out!" he commanded.

Finally, the shepherd disengaged.

Davis drew Fury back to let the team secure their target yet stayed close in case the guy got a second wind of stupidity. After this, the landshark deserved some solid KONG time. He stepped back as Chapel and the others rushed in to cuff the piece of trash writhing on the ground in agony.

Hollyn.

He looked around. Where'd she go? Couldn't see her. He flipped down his NVGs for a better view and willed himself to find her. Pulse ticked up. "Hollyn!" he barked.

Fury strained against his collar, trying to get a second taste of Germaine, but Davis held tight. Scanned the area. "Ho—"

Sniffs came from somewhere closer to the building. "Here." Her voice was small.

Hollyn.

Don't be hurt, don't be hurt.

He found her sitting, knees tucked up against herself, hands cradling the sides of her head as she murmured rapidly—a punch to his chest. Had she been hit in the crossfire?

Fear surged in his gut. "*Fuss*," he commanded the shepherd, relieved when his partner complied. He squatted at Hollyn's side. "Hey, you hurt? Did you get hit?" He reached for her. Felt for any warm liquid that shouldn't be on her. Didn't see any in the green oculars. When she didn't respond, he went to a knee. "Hol. I'm here. It's o—"

She launched into his arms. Their helmets smacked into each other.

Worried Fury would take a piece out of her in protecting him, he stiffened. Swung out a hand to give the "stay" command. "Hey, easy. It's okay," he comforted. Wrapped an arm around her. Tugged her close, their vests pressed together keeping him from getting her as close as he would've liked.

"Davis." Hollyn clung to him like her life depended on it, then her hands patted over his shoulders and arms. "You–you're okay?"

"Yeah, I'm fine." He was shocked she'd have the presence of mind to worry about him. "Do you feel any pain?"

She shook her head. "No. I just dropped down when everyone started shooting."

"Good move," he breathed out.

*Thank You, Lord.*

"Ledger. Let's roll," Chapel broke in.

"Yep," he acknowledged before dropping his voice lower for Hollyn. "Come on." In one fluid motion, Davis stood and took her with him.

Her fingers dug into his forearm like a vise, but he welcomed the pressure. It let him know she was with him. Alive.

"Move it." Bennion barked, coming up behind them.

Davis and Fury escorted Hollyn back to the cars. Davis kept an arm around Hollyn's waist so he could guide her past a few bodies Macklin and Hale had taken out, glad she wouldn't be able to see them in the pitch black. They hit their exfil hot. Staying eyes out, they stalked toward the waiting vehicles.

In the driver's seat of the Chevelle, Davis cast a glance at Hollyn. She looked shellshocked. Not surprising. She'd just seen her friend get taken out and been in a firefight for the first time.

They peeled away from the building behind Chapel, who drove the lead vehicle. He guided everyone back through town. Davis stayed right on their tail. E10 took them out of the city. The Al Raha Theater towered above the buildings on Davis's nine. Looked like some kind of giant blue orb and reflected the city lights in the glass sides. The UAE had some trippy architecture.

Forty minutes later they pulled onto a desolate road in the Al

Bahya area. Sand crunched under the car tires as they shot down Al Kunar Street, slowing only when they neared a home at the end of the road. The open front gate let them inside tall walls and closed swiftly behind them. Davis shut down the Chevelle as Bennion and Macklin hauled Germaine into the safe house. The way they carried the body said the guy was out cold.

"Okay, come on." Davis rushed to the other side and leaned to help Hollyn out. She felt so fragile in his grasp. Hadn't made a sound since they hit the expressway—that worried him—but he'd have to focus on that once she was safe inside the house.

Fury jumped up. Hit his thigh with meaty paws, tongue flopping out in a happy pant.

"You did good, buddy." Davis tossed the landshark's KONG into the two-story plaster structure and followed his zealous beast through the front door.

Glace, Nazari, and Hale covered their six. Locked the door behind.

"Get him to the hold. Gonna have a little *chat* with him after debrief." Chapel nodded to Bennion and Macklin.

The men roughly hauled Germaine from the living room.

Fury barked a couple times. Pawed at Hollyn's leg. Smacked his nose under her hand.

"Hey, knock it off." He pushed the mutt off her.

"Daaavisss . . . " Hollyn wheezed.

He looked down just as her eyes rolled back in her head.

*Thump. Thump. Thump.*

Heavy footsteps broke through the thick fog clouding her mind, and she felt her body bounce in movement. But it wasn't her walking. She was being carried. Her head vibrated on a strong shoulder with each step. Legs dangled over an arm that flexed beneath her knees.

Hollyn tensed. Had she been captured?

Wake up!

But her eyelids weighed a thousand pounds each. Head throbbing, she instinctively reached up to grab her necklace. Groaned with the effort.

"Easy." The deep voice was warm and familiar. Like a favorite hoodie on a crisp day.

Davis. She relaxed.

Her body shifted as he adjusted his hold. Then she was being lowered. She panicked. Hand shot out to grip his shirt but found his vest first.

*Don't leave me!*

"You're good, Hol," he soothed her.

A cozy softness enveloped her as he laid her down on a bed. She let go of him. Used all her willpower to force her eyes open. Blinked once. Twice. Davis came into focus, hovering over her, dark features handsome as ever. But deep concern was etched into his brow.

"What happened?" Then she remembered. "Leila." She choked out the whisper. "Wh-what about Archie?"

He didn't say anything.

A mental video of her friend being shot resumed its looped replay in her head, and she wanted to vomit. Fresh tears pooled. When was this going to end?

"First things first." Davis gave her hand a soft squeeze as Fury hopped onto the bed. The giant dog spun before curling into her side. He rested his jowls over her thigh, amber gaze roaming over her. Something on his vest dug into her leg, but she stayed still. "Nora's our combat medic. She'll check you over."

Nora came into the room carrying a bag of some kind. She took out a blood pressure cuff and stethoscope.

Davis released Hollyn's hand, and she instantly missed his warm touch as he stepped away, giving his teammate room to sit down.

The lieutenant slid the cuff into place on Hollyn's arm. "How are you feeling?" Nora asked as she inflated the cuff.

"I'm . . . " Hollyn licked her dry lips. Exhaustion had finally caught up to her, and it'd come out swinging. Between what had happened and the car accident, it felt like she'd been run over by a Mack truck. "Just tired." She rubbed her face. "Why is it so hard to think?"

The last thing she remembered was Davis tugging her out of the car.

"You've been through a lot," he said, hands hooked on the neck of his vest. His attention shifted to Nora. "She good?"

"One twenty-two over eighty." Nora replaced her medical tools, then looked to Hollyn. "I'll check back in a bit, but for now, you just need to rest."

If only it were that simple. She still felt like she was in flight mode. Shame at her weakness flushed her cheeks. Nora didn't seem fazed by what'd gone down at all. Probably could have taken out bad guys all night without batting an eye. Yet here Hollyn was, passing out all over the place like a sheltered lab rat.

Endurance test: FAIL.

Hollyn looked around the unfamiliar room. It was small and sparsely furnished with only the bed she was on and a single nightstand. "Where are we?"

"Safe house," Davis answered.

Fury's paw brushed at her hand, and she slowly ran her fingers over his fur.

Nora stood, bag in hand. "If you need anything or start to feel worse, let me know, okay?"

"Sure."

The petite operator stepped out of the room.

When Davis made like he was going to follow, Hollyn snatched at his hand. "Wait!"

"Just grabbing you some water." He didn't move. "Good?"

She forced a nod, heart racing again as he disappeared down the hallway. Being alone was the last thing she wanted. At least Fury didn't seem like he had any intention of getting off the bed.

He stretched his body out but kept his paw close enough for her to keep petting. His eyes drooped like she was lulling him to sleep, but the second Davis's boots thudded his approach, the dog went on alert. Lifted his head and thumped his tail against the comforter.

Davis grinned and ruffled the dog's head as he handed Hollyn a bottled water. A moment of carefree peace in the chaos.

She took a couple long swigs before capping it.

Davis sat down next to her, his presence pressing into her awareness at his very close proximity. "Feeling any better?"

"Yeah." Not wholly a lie.

His chin ticked up. "Always were a horrible liar, Holly Hobbie."

At the old nickname he'd given her, a grin tugged the corner of her lips. "Don't make me give you a wet willie like the old days." But the lighthearted feel was quickly replaced by worry over what had happened. And for Archie's wellbeing. Struggling to find the strength, she sat up. "We have to get Archie "

Davis nodded. "We will." His constant confidence proved very reassuring. Admirable. Attractive.

Wait, what?

This close to him, she couldn't think straight. All right, sitting up had been a bad decision. It put them entirely too close to each other. But she couldn't lie down again two seconds after getting up. That would be . . . weird. Her gaze dropped to Davis's mouth. His jaw twitched. She recalled how he'd kept her safe at the abandoned building. How he'd put himself between her and the madman despite the threats to their safety.

When she lifted her eyes to his again, there was something in them that hadn't been there before. An intensity. Hunger.

Stomach fluttering, Hollyn felt the hairs on her arms rising. Hands tingling, she was caught in a vortex of emotions. Leaned forward. She just wanted to be closer, to siphon more of his strength . . .

Davis didn't pull back. Instead, he slid a hand behind her

head—fingers gliding into her hair, thumb brushing her cheek—and drew closer. Maybe they'd been unsure about their first kiss. But here, now, seeing the intent look in Davis's eyes . . . yeah, this one would be for real. And the thought was electrifying.

Less than a breath separated them as Hollyn's eyes slid closed. The first brush of his lips was soft and had every nerve ending buzzing. Then he deepened the kiss, and she sank into him, lost.

Never had she felt more protected or cherished. The warning bells in her head didn't get a chance to ring this time. She wouldn't have listened anyway. After surviving a car accident and a gun fight, she was all too willing to let Davis pull her into a world where only the two of them existed, if only for a few precious minutes.

Davis's other hand wrapped around her. Tugged her nearer, and she hooked her hand around the back of his bicep. Didn't want him to ever let go of her, especially when he let out a deep moan.

Someone cleared their throat from the doorway.

Davis immediately broke off.

"Hate to break it up, but Chapel wants a word," Benn said from the doorway.

Ducking to hide the heat rising into her cheeks, Hollyn swallowed, wondering how long Benn—she was seriously questioning deciding to call him that so it was less militant—had been there.

Davis held her gaze a moment before standing and roughing a hand down the back of his neck. "Nice," he muttered to Fury around heavy breaths.

Acting like he hadn't just let someone walk up without alerting them, the German shepherd whacked his bushy tail on the comforter, then rolled over onto his back.

Hollyn braved a look and saw Benn shake his head before stepping out of the doorway. She worked hard to calm her heartbeat, but the embarrassment currently surging through her made it almost impossible.

"I'll . . . be right back," Davis said to her.

"Sure."

The sudden awkwardness between them might have been comical under different circumstances. It definitely wasn't right now, though.

"Come on," Davis said to Fury. He tapped his leg before stalking out the door, and the RMWD jumped off the bed to follow.

When the three were out of sight, Hollyn buried her face in her hands and groaned.

Seriously, what was wrong with her? Falling head over heels in love and making out with the man of her dreams while Leila had just been murdered hours earlier. And Archie. He was still being held with who knew what being done to him this very minute . . .

But as guilty as she felt, she couldn't completely snuff out the spark of hope that had been reignited in her heart. There really was something between her and Davis. She wasn't just imagining things.

She reached for her necklace, and her fingers coiled around the small sparrow char—

Sparrow!

Her pulse sped up for an entirely different reason as she recalled what the man had said before Davis's team had captured him.

*Blueprints. Sparrow.* Could it be . . .

In the chaos of the moment, she'd missed the connection. Now it was making sense . . . more or less. The project was safe, though. Wasn't it?

Hollyn stilled. "No," she whispered as dread coiled its way up her spine.

She needed her computer. Now.

# 12



*DAMOCLES SAFE HOUSE, ABU DHABI, UAE*

What a kiss.

Davis roughed a hand down his neck as he stalked to the command room. Couldn't believe he'd just done that. Couldn't believe all he really wanted was to go do it again.

Bennion tossed a stern look his way as they neared the command room. Davis worked to keep his expression neutral, but there was no denying he was in deep this time. Didn't mean he had to let the guy read him like a book, though.

Truth was, Hollyn had a way of getting under his skin like no one else. He'd have to put extra effort into keeping his mind mission-focused. It'd be more than a little difficult, but he wouldn't change what had happened for anything. Hollyn was worth the struggle.

Fury preceded them into the secondary living room the team used as command. A long table ran nearly the length of the room, and most of the team sat around it. Computers, whiteboards, and dozens of papers covered the surrounding walls. Blanchard wasn't around. Probably remaining offsite so they had less traffic coming and going.

"I want someone with Germaine round the clock," Chapel was saying when Davis dropped onto an open chair.

Fury sniffed the table near Hale's sandwich. The six-three operator was always eating. Without a word, he broke off a bite-sized piece of meat. Raised his eyebrows. Davis nodded his approval, and Hale tossed the morsel to a waiting Fury. The RMWD snatched it out of the air with lightning-fast reflexes, and Hale turned back to Chapel, taking a large bite out of his meal.

Licking his chops, the shepherd posted himself right next to Davis, eyes glued to the meal the oversized operator was inhaling, drool sliding from his jowls and plopping noisily onto Davis's boot.

He frowned.

Nice.

Davis noted the way Bennion kept assessing him. Shook his head and turned his attention to Chapel but couldn't shake the feeling that something was up.

Davis rolled his shoulder. It was still raging. He'd have to keep an eye on it. Wouldn't do him any good to push the limit and risk even more damage.

Chapel cleared his throat. "Get what we need about the arms-dealing pipeline and where they're holding that hostage."

"Assuming they haven't taken the kid out already," Bennion interjected.

"They'll keep him alive." Davis spoke up. "He's playing some kind of role in this."

A few unsure murmurs filtered through the room.

"Anything to back that up?" Bennion asked.

Davis gave a slight shake of his head. "Not yet, but I do know he can't be trusted."

"Any luck tracing the live feed?" Glace quietly tapped a pencil on a pad of paper.

"Negative." Chapel hooked his thumbs on his belt. "Blank couldn't track it."

Davis rubbed the stubble on his jaw as he listened.

"Did your girl have any new information?" The question directed at him came from Bennion. "Looked like the two of you had a lot to say back there."

Heat flared up Davis's neck when everyone looked his way. He was going to throttle the guy. Didn't care that the operator had a good twenty pounds of muscle on him. "What's your problem?" he gritted out.

Bennion's stony glower darkened. "No problem so long as your mind's on the mission and not . . . extracurriculars."

Davis clenched his fist. Next to him, Fury growled low, and he felt justified in wanting to pummel the oversized oaf. "Let *me* worry about what I'm thinking."

"Sure thing, lover boy."

He tried to ignore Bennion, but it brought up the glaring fact that Davis was slipping. Also, that he wasn't all that upset about it. Just didn't like the way it made him look to the team right now. He was all-in on this mission, despite what Bennion seemed to think.

"What do you want?"

Chapel's sharp question snagged Davis's attention. He followed the guy's line of sight to the hallway and saw Hollyn, frozen in place, eyes wide.

Fury whined in her direction but didn't break from heel to greet her. What was with the connection she had with his dog?

No. Not his dog. ABA's dog. He couldn't forget that.

Right. Just his partner for the next week or so. Then he was Crew's business.

Hollyn hugged herself. "I . . . think I know what that guy might be looking for. Though I don't know *why* he'd want it." Her gaze fanned the operators in the room.

"Which is?" Chapel prompted firmly.

Davis frowned. Wanted to tell the boss to back off, but he didn't want to get tanked twice in two weeks. So he bit down on the retort. Reminded himself he wasn't in charge here.

"A project I completed right before my parents—" Hollyn swallowed.

Davis's chest constricted.

*Come on, Hol. You can do this.*

Whatever she had to say—and he was very curious what it was—was important enough for her to step into the meeting. He didn't want her to back down now. Their eyes met and he nodded. Hoped it transferred some confidence to her. She was stronger than she knew.

Hollyn quickly licked her lips, then continued. "Before they were killed. I—um, need my laptop to get into the lab files so I can see if someone tried to access them during the break-in. Or I could go to the lab and use the computers there."

"Negative," Chapel replied. "You stay here. We'll retrieve your laptop. Tell Davis where it is and he can head over."

Davis nodded his agreement. Not that he had a choice. When Chapel gave an order, you better already be on your way.

"What's the project?" Chapel crossed his arms.

"An AI program designed to let salvaging equipment self-navigate a sunken wreck and learn as it goes."

"Salvage." Bennion mulled the word over. "You in the treasure-hunting business?"

Hollyn's chin dipped slightly. Hesitance sparked in her eyes. "Essentially . . . yes. It's one of my father's businesses. Well, was. *Is*?" She shook her head before murmuring, "Not really sure how that works now."

"All right." Chapel effectively ended the conversation. Nodded to Davis. "Retrieve the laptop and get back here."

Davis stood. Tapped his leg. Fury blew out a sharp huff in Bennion's direction before lifting his tail and walking toward Hollyn.

"Did that mutt just tell me to—"

Davis ignored the rest of the sentence as he walked with Hollyn back to her room. "So, where in the house is the laptop?"

Hollyn pinched the bridge of her nose with a soft moan.

Concern welled in his gut. "You okay?"

"Yeah," she said quietly. "I just have a killer headache and feel kind of groggy."

"You should really sleep, Hol." Much as he wanted to kiss her again, he wouldn't. Not yet. She was clearly exhausted.

"I know." Her yawn told him all he needed to know.

Fury hopped onto her bed and lay down, ears swiveling as he listened to them.

"Okay. The laptop should be in my bedroom dresser. Third drawer, under the T-shirts. The charger is plugged into the wall by my bed. There's a chance I left the laptop in the office, but I'm pretty sure I put it away."

"In your dresser, third drawer, under your shirts," he repeated.

She waved at him. "Don't with that face. I keep it there so it's not something people just see right off the bat should they go looking . . . for it." She winced. "Okay, I see how strange it sounds, but I've had my system hacked more than once and had out-of-the-blue offers of millions for my program while getting a latte." She shrugged. "It's what I do. Deal with it."

He bit down on a grin. She was cute when rattled. "Got it." He pivoted. "Fury, let's go."

The landshark hopped off the bed.

"Any chance you could grab me some clothes too?"

Davis tapped a fist against the doorjamb when he paused, feeling weird at the prospect of going through her things, but he nodded. "Sure thing." He strode outside to the Chevelle, ready to get this assignment over with. The quicker he got her things, the quicker he'd be back here to watch over her.

*It's not the responsibility you want it to be.*

Going deeper wasn't an option at the moment. He'd never said that four-letter word to anyone before—didn't plan to start now—but she'd never be his until he was man enough to say what was really on his mind.

## *DAMOCLES SAFE HOUSE, ABU DHABI, UAE*

Sunlight flared across Hollyn's face. Warmed her. Nudged her from a deep sleep. Blinking, she stretched her legs under the covers. Every muscle in her body ached. At least she felt like she was in the land of the living again.

More than could be said for Leila. Ever again.

Any lightness she'd felt seconds ago vanished. She shoved the covers back and sat up. Yawned as she squinted out the window. Sand stretched as far as the eye could see. Soft lines of red, orange, and pink hues hovered on the horizon. The sun was sinking, not rising.

How long had she slept?

She looked around but didn't see her phone. What she did find was her laptop sitting on her weekend bag in the corner of the room. Davis had already gone and come back, then. She crossed to the bag.

Voices filtered down the hall from somewhere in the house. Was the team making plans to save Archie? Or would he just be collateral damage in this twisted game? She wanted her friend back alive. Wanted them *all* back.

How many more would die before this was over?

The heavy weight of trepidation resumed its seat on her shoulders. Tugging some clothes from her bag, her hand froze over the small Bible Davis had packed along with the rest of her things. He must have found it in the dresser with her computer. She kept it there to remind herself to read a passage before any work started.

Sinking onto her knees, she brushed the well-worn leather binding and opened the book to Psalm 46, which she'd long ago memorized. "God is our refuge and strength, a very present help in trouble." She spoke the words quietly. Read down to verse five. Repeated it. "God is in the midst of her; she shall not be moved; God will help her when morning dawns."

She took comfort in the words. A strength that wasn't her own. She was far from alone, and this was far from over.

Hollyn let the verses run through her head as she changed into fresh clothes and opened her computer. Sitting on the corner of the bed, she quickly connected to the internet and punched in her work passcode to access her project files. The Sparrow Project—as Dad had insisted on naming it, despite her objections—was there. She breathed a sigh of relief and opened the file. The schematics and research were all there, but as she ran through her algorithm, the last sequence was missing.

Frowning, she ran through the code again. She must have misread. After the third time, heart beating faster, the code was still incomplete. Without the ending, the program was useless. "Where is it?" she whispered.

Hollyn scoured all of her other files to see if she'd somehow saved the end sequence to the wrong place—though she couldn't imagine how that would have happened. Still nothing.

The only thing that calmed her to some degree was that the man the team had captured didn't have it. If he did, none of this would be happening. But the question remained: *why* would he want that project?

A few more attempts only confirmed that the algorithm she'd spent years finishing had vanished. She was going to be sick. All that work . . . for nothing.

On a whim, Hollyn checked to see when her files had last been accessed.


1:23AM 9 FEBRUARY


But the attempt had been flagged.

Hollyn thought back. That was the day of the break-in. A day she *hadn't* done anything work-related. She eyed the IP address next to the attempted login. Was it possible there'd been a virtual hack that paralleled the physical break-in?

Hollyn started a backtrace on the address. The computer filtered through one IP after another. She bit her lip, tapping her fingers on her thigh. Whoever had tried to get in had used a VPN to mask their actual location. At least the system had prevented access. Still, why hadn't she been informed about the attempt?

Despite her best attempts, she came up short finding the actual location for whoever had run the hack. It just bounced around from one country to another in a never-ending loop.

She clenched her teeth and logged out before pulling up a list of the files on her hard drive. Never in a million years would she accidentally save her projects there instead of the work servers, but better safe than sorry. She dug through the programs, folders, files . . .

Another dead end.

"No." This couldn't be happening. Breathing was getting quick and shallow as her mind raced. *Where* was the rest of her work? Years of trial and error, millions of dollars spent on funding, and the key to the whole thing was just . . . gone.

"No, no." Hollyn tried to keep it together. There had to be an explanation. She slammed the laptop closed and shoved to her feet. Had to find Davis. Maybe there was someone on the team that had a greater skillset for this than she did.

The house had gone quiet. Eerily so. Where was everyone?

"Hello?" she called from the living room.

Silence was her only reply, so she turned down a hallway she hadn't been in yet. Heard muffled sounds from the end. Followed it. The hallway was wider on this side of the house, but the tile floors looked the same.

Repeating sounds played on a loop like a stuck record or something.

"Hello?" she asked again.

Still the only sounds were muffled conversation and the short soundbite. But then she heard Fury bark.

Davis!

Hollyn threw herself toward the door at the end of the hall.

Before she could turn the handle, it snapped open and Davis filled the gap. The random sounds she'd heard were louder now that the door was open. They continued to play in a maddening repeat.

Hollyn jumped. "Davis!" He didn't look injured. Good, good. But how'd he known she was out here? "W-what's going on?"

A hard look darkened Davis's face. "You shouldn't be over here." He called to Fury and they both stepped out, forcing her back.

"Turn it off!" Germaine's irritated growl clashed with the soundtrack.

Just in the two minutes she'd heard the repeated notes, Hollyn was already cringing. She covered her ear with her free hand to help dampen the sound. "What are you guys doing?" For a second, she caught a glimpse of Germaine secured to a chair in the room.

Then the door closed.

"Don't think you really need me to answer that, do you?" he challenged.

No, of course not. The only thing she wanted was to know why her family had been targeted.

"Come on." Davis ushered her down the hall and into the open kitchen.

"Is that the best way to get information out of him? How do you even stand being in there with that constantly playing?"

"This is how things are done." He spoke firmly. Zero regret tinged his eyes no matter how hard she searched. "War isn't fun, Hollyn."

"This isn't war!"

"It is! Maybe not to those with a limited, conditioned view, but—yes, this *is* a war," he continued. "And we're trying to get information from him. Trying to save people he's actively going after."

Hollyn threw a hand out. "You think that's the best course of action?"

"Yes!"

The reply was so simple. Devoid of even the smallest trace of doubt.

Hollyn searched his eyes. The only thing she saw was a sincerity that shook her to the core. She rubbed her thumb over the corner of the laptop, trying not to freak out.

Why was she even questioning this? Germaine had murdered her friend. The fight leached from her. "Is it working? Did he give you the information you want?" She hugged herself. "Who even is he?" The question had been burning in her head for a while now. All she'd heard so far was the name Germaine.

"His name's Braum Germaine. Let's leave the rest of the intel to the team, okay?" Davis roughed a hand over his stubbled jaw, and her mind flashed back to the kiss they'd shared.

Harsh reality was starting to press in on all sides, but Hollyn was determined not to let it sully what their kiss had meant. Hope and a future—God was the orchestrator of their story. That, she could trust fully. Still, the nagging what-ifs continued to whisper in her ear.

What if they were letting their past guide them? What if she wasn't good enough for Davis? What if he left?

Hollyn dropped her gaze, uncertainty growing as that last question slammed around her mind. Head lowered, she noticed the intense way Fury was staring at her. His giant tongue swept over his jowls, then he went back to staring her down, body rigid like he might strike any second.

She swallowed and took a step back.

"Find what you were looking for on the computer?" Davis asked.

"What?" The sudden change of topic drew her focus up to him again, and he tipped his head toward the laptop she held.

"Oh, right. Well, yes and no. Someone definitely tried to get into my files, and the lab system shut them out. But the ending sequence of the algorithm I created is . . . gone."

Saying it aloud made it even worse. Made it real.

His brow furrowed. "Gone how?"

"As in, I can't find it. Anywhere." Hollyn clutched the laptop against her chest. "Not in the lab system. Not on my hard drive. It's . . . like it never existed." She wracked her brain, trying to figure out what could've happened.

*Don't panic, don't panic.*

He seemed to mull that over. "What's the project about?"

"That's the thing." She sank onto one of the island stools. "It's just an AI program designed to allow underwater cameras to self-guide and self-correct themselves. It allows them to teach themselves so they avoid repeating mistakes." She huffed. "I guess *just* is the wrong word. It's important for our field, but I don't know why anyone would want to kill for it."

Davis nodded.

Fury shifted on the floor, but when she went to pet him, he jerked his head back with a growl. She recoiled, fear pricking her senses. He certainly blew hot and cold. Not unlike his handler.

"Hey," Davis reprimanded. Though he gave his dog the warning, Davis's expression clouded over as he seemed to take a full body scan of her.

What was he looking for?

Fury blew out an indignant breath through his snout and continued his stare down that matched his handler's.

Hollyn swallowed. It was unnerving to have them both eyeing her like they were trying to figure out a puzzle. "I tried to backtrace the IP address that attempted to get into the lab files but hit a wall. Do any of your teammates have backgrounds in computers?"

His jaw muscle flexed.

Something was wrong, but she didn't have the foggiest clue what. "Maybe they can do something I can't. It's not really my area of expertise. I signed out of the lab, but I can get back in anytime they need me to."

"I'll see what they can do." Stone-faced, Davis took the laptop she offered.

"You okay?" Hollyn asked.

An invisible shield slid into place, and suddenly Davis felt much farther than a couple feet away.

He gave her a tight smile that didn't fool her in the least. "Good." Davis and Fury stalked off, and she was left alone at the island.

Was he heading back in there to continue interrogating Braum?

Despite her intrinsic aversion to the whole situation she found herself in, Hollyn had no choice but to press forward. It was the only way through. She just hoped answers came sooner rather than later. For the sake of all involved.

# 13



GERMAINE'S HEAD LOLLED FORWARD, BODY STRAINED AGAINST hands tied around the backside of the chair. He squeezed his eyes closed momentarily. Laughed.

A sound that Davis was growing tired of. He clenched his fist around the lead in his hand while he stood guard with Fury in the corner of the room. The shepherd's loud barks echoed off the hard walls.

They'd paused the music to ask Germaine their list of questions over and over. Still nothing. Add to that, he was still trying to figure out what Fury had hit on earlier with Hollyn.

*Figure it out later.*

Macklin took a break. Turned away with an almost imperceptible shake of his head to Davis.

"You Americans." The Frenchman hauled in a ragged breath. Spat onto the floor. Their eyes met. Exhaustion was written all over Germaine's face. "Always think you have the upper hand. Think you know everything."

Fury traded off whining and barking.

"Yeah?" Macklin spoke firmly. "What don't we know?"

"For starters," Germaine spat again, "you don't even know who you're looking for. And to think any of this will make me tell you?" He huffed. "You'll have to do better."

Macklin held the guy's gaze evenly. "I'd say we got our man."

Germaine's lip curled. The grin that replaced it was unexpected and began to look half-crazed as the guy sized them up. His breathing was slightly strained. No matter what he said, they were getting to him. "No . . . " The word stretched out. "You're not even close. Did you really think we'd make it that easy on you?"

Davis worked to keep his expression neutral. Wasn't the first time a hostage had tried to lie their way out of things. But the twerp flashed to mind. Davis ran through the series of events back on Zahda Island. Did they have this wrong? The getaway van. Had that been Archie saving himself and Germaine taking the fall? Not a hostage extraction like they'd thought? That kid had never sat right with Davis. Maybe this was the reason why.

In the surveillance monitor attached to the wall behind Germaine, Davis could see Chapel approaching. Turned to Macklin. "Taking five."

Davis stepped into the hall with his partner. Heard the music restart before Macklin stepped into the hallway but gave Davis space. "Got a second?" Davis asked their CO.

Chapel nodded. "Sure."

They turned. Walked back the way he'd come.

"Any luck tracing the IP address?" Davis asked.

"None. It's a dead end."

"Germaine's claiming he isn't the one we're looking for." Davis unclipped Fury's lead.

Chapel grunted. "Not the first time we've heard that."

"I'm aware." Davis took a breath. This was either going to be the right call or the dumbest thing he'd ever suggested to a CO.

"Look. We've already been at this three days. Time isn't on our side." Here went nothing. "I think we should let him go."

Chapel drew up short. Pinned him with a hard look. "Not really in the business of releasing known arms dealers, Ledger."

AKA: stand down.

But Davis wasn't one to back down when he had a dog in the fight—literally. "If we let him think he's pulled one over on us by escaping, Fury can track him. Germaine will lead us exactly where we need to be."

At the mention of his name, the RMWD wagged his tail.

"Everything we've got leads to him."

"I'm not questioning he's your man. All I'm suggesting is, if there's a chance someone else is behind this, we find out."

Chapel eyed him. "And if your plan goes south? You gonna tell the families of his victims that we just let him walk?"

Davis believed in this plan. "We'll have eyes on him the whole time. Fury hasn't failed a mission yet." *Davis* might have, but the lug never had. "What if Germaine *is* a cover for him? If he's our guy, we can't leave him in the wind. Either way, we need him, and Germaine's the fastest route."

Taking a deep breath, Davis waited for a dressing-down. He wasn't even part of this team, technically. They'd been tracking Germaine far longer than he had. The stakes were high.

"I hear you. And agree." Chapel didn't look happy. Then again, he usually didn't. "But if Germaine gives us the slip, then the blame rests on *you*."

Davis knew the operator would make good on that. "Understood."

"Get ready to move."

With a nod, Davis strode to the room his things were in.

From the bed, Fury watched him prep their gear.

"You ready to work your tracking magic?" Davis asked the RMWD. "It's all on us."

Fury barked. He was ready for whatever came, no doubt.

Davis ruffed the dog's head. "Sorry. Didn't mean to insult you."

The shepherd slicked his warm tongue over Davis's hand.

*Remember, this isn't forever.*

The clock was counting down on their time together. Davis cleared his throat. He'd have to keep himself in check. Working with the lug was starting to feel too natural. Too effortless. "Come on." He stood and tapped his leg. They needed to find Hollyn.

When he came upon the kitchen, Glace was there eating an apple.

She scanned the dog and then him. "Some plan you came up with."

"I stand behind it one hundred percent."

Glace nodded. "Chapel said we're rolling out as soon as Germaine pulls off his big escape. Should be sometime tonight. From the looks of it, he's out cold right now." She nodded to a small screen on the counter.

Germaine was slouched forward in the chair, unmoving. Sleep could only be fought so long.

"We're ready." Davis peered into the empty living room. "You seen Hollyn around?"

"Out on the terrace."

Davis nodded. Stalked that way.

*Terrace* was a generous term for the cracked brick patio at the back of the safe house. But Glace was right—Hollyn had perched on a chair out here. Palm trees dotting the property provided some shade from the bright sunset. The Abu Dhabi sky had some of the most vibrant colors he'd seen.

When he and Fury approached, she quickly wiped at her face. "Hey." She spoke to him but didn't look over. Instead, she kept her gaze trained on the sand dunes beyond the house.

"Hey. Been looking for you." Davis sank onto a chair next to Hollyn. Tugged Fury's KONG from his pocket. The shepherd went crazy with anticipation. Davis chucked the toy into the air, and Fury tore off after it, sand pluming up behind him. "You okay?" he asked Hollyn.

It was a dumb question. He knew that the second it came out of his mouth—because he might not be a rocket scientist, but he could tell she'd been crying.

She sniffed. "No. My parents are dead, Leila's dead"—her voice broke—"Archie's being held who knows where. Maybe he's dead too." Hollyn wiped her face again.

Fury raced back. Dropped the now slobbery toy in Davis's lap. Davis threw it again.

"I just want this to end." Her eyes slid closed. Chin bobbed. "How much longer is this going to go on, Davis?"

Without thinking, he reached over and clasped her hand. There wasn't much that could bring him to the threshold of tears, but seeing her like this pushed him dangerously close to the limit. He hated seeing her this broken. "It's gonna be okay, Hol."

It wasn't a platitude or an empty promise. If it took everything he had to give, he *would* make things better for her.

The realization made him pause and mull over what that meant—what *she* meant—to him.

For the first time, she looked to him. His heart sank at the sight of her red eyes and splotchy face. Her fingers tightened around his, but the smile she offered wasn't convincing. "You have no idea how badly I want to believe that."

He forced a grin. "Hey. Have some faith in us, okay?" He gave her fingers a gentle squeeze.

"I do." She ran a finger under her eyes before wiping it along her jeans. "I keep trying to tell myself there's a reason for this. A purpose in the pain." Hollyn blew out a wobbly breath. "God hasn't abandoned me, even if I feel like it sometimes."

That statement hit him square in the chest.

"But now and then, grief just"—her voice hitched—"smacks me upside the head, and it's hard to see what's true. You know?"

He gave her hand a gentle squeeze. Didn't know what he

could say. He *did* know but still hadn't found the courage to actually open up a dialogue with the Big Man. How would that even go after so many years of silence?

Fury skidded to a stop, hitting Davis's knees hard, and dropped the toy. Nudged it with his nose a couple times, laser-like focus pinned to the KONG. When it came to fetch, manners went out the window. It wasn't lost on him that Fury's behavior toward Hollyn had done a one-eighty since their last interaction. He was acting like she didn't exist. Davis didn't like that he couldn't pinpoint why.

"Have you guys had any luck with finding out who tried to hack the lab files?"

Davis shook his head. "None."

"Thanks for trying. You and your team have been pretty incredible." Hollyn released a weighted sigh. "I definitely couldn't do what you do."

Guilt peppered his gut. Last team he'd been on, he'd failed miserably. Davis tossed the toy, then rapped his knuckles on the arm of the chair. "They aren't my team."

Might as well come clean.

"Oh, sorry." She considered him with concern. "I just assumed . . . Where's your unit?"

Gone. Along with the career he'd tanked.

"I'm not in the Army anymore." Davis bounced his knee. "I was medically retired."

"What happened? I know the military was all you wanted to do."

The innocent statement was salt in a wound that would never close. "A mission went south. I was at fault." So much for instilling confidence in his ability to protect her. "A good buddy of mine . . . died." No reason to get into specifics. Couldn't anyway. "I was injured. My shoulder didn't heal to a level that satisfied the medical board, so they retired me. Sent me packing."

"Davis," Hollyn whispered.

Yep. That right there was the exact reason he'd avoided talking about this in the first place. Pity. Shouldn't have gone back on his decision.

"I got the call about your parents a few hours after I formally separated from the military. Fury and I jumped on the first flight we could."

"I'm so sorry, Davis."

Fury demanded he throw the toy again. He tried to fake the shepherd out, but it didn't work. Only succeeded in nearly getting himself bit. He chucked the KONG.

"But . . . I don't understand," Hollyn went on. "If you're out, how is Fury with you? He was in the military too, right? And he doesn't seem old enough to be retired."

"We both got injured on the op, but when they tried to put Fury back to work, it didn't go over well."

Deep red and orange leached from the sky as darkness began to press in.

Fury panted happily. Tried to get Davis to throw his toy for the seventy-fifth time.

"He was on a one-way train to the Rainbow Bridge when someone suggested I take him. So I made arrangements with a buddy who procures dogs for A Breed Apart in Texas. We're heading that way after things are wrapped up here."

"Oh." The word was small. "So, as soon as this is over, you're leaving?"

Mayday! There was a bite to the words he hadn't seen coming.

"Whoa, that's not what I—"

"No, I get it." She was on her feet in the next instant. "I mean, why would you stay? There's nothing here for you, right?"

Hold up. When had this turned into an argument and he the bad guy? "Hollyn—"

"Ledger." Hale stepped outside. Nodded Davis inside. "Germaine's coming to."

"Got it." Davis stood, glanced to Hollyn, not wanting to leave her and this convo in such a bad state.

"What's going on?" Hollyn asked quietly as they all started back into the building.

He looked down at her. The argument had apparently been forgotten already. Worry replaced it. "Germaine's waking up. We're giving him an opportunity to escape and we'll follow him. Should lead us to Archie."

"Should?"

Hale turned back to them as he walked. "I'll hold back here with her. The rest of you are with Chapel."

"Copy." Davis banked left into his room. Slid Fury's vest on, then started gearing up. Hollyn followed.

She slowly sank onto the bed. "Are you sure this is a good idea?"

"It's the fastest way to find the—your friend." Probably shouldn't call the guy a twerp, considering the situation. Didn't want to start up another beef between them.

She was quiet long enough that he paused. Her bottom lip was tucked into her mouth, and he could see worry darkening her features.

"It's all good, Hol."

Make her believe it.

"This is what we've been trained to do."

She nodded. "Right. You and Fury with a team that's not yours . . . " She shrugged. "It's just—I'm concerned. I can't help it."

Davis shouldered into his ruck and tugged her from the bed. The way she willingly went into his arms pulled at his conscience and words too quickly spoken. She was putting aside whatever that'd been back on the terrace. Choosing instead to part on good terms. Her head on his vested chest and the feel of her arms around his waist was the stuff men around the world would envy him for. She deserved to be valued every day of her life. Arguments or good times, he wanted it all. Wanted her.

Didn't know what the future held, but he *did* know if he made it out of this, he wasn't leaving her alone another day in her life. If she'd have him.

"Hale will be here if you need anything." He steeled himself against the sudden intense urge to say he loved her. Wasn't putting that on her if the mission went sideways. "Stay inside, okay?"

When she pulled back, he noted her chin quiver. But she met his gaze straight on. Even grinned. "I will. You guys be safe." Her face twisted up. "I don't know, is that an oxymoron?"

Davis chuckled. "I'll take it."

So this was what it felt like to have someone that cared waiting for him when he went on a mission. Pretty sweet gig.

Fury turned in a tight circle at the bedroom door.

Davis took Hollyn's small hand in his and led her to the living room, where the rest of the team was prepping.

"I want everyone ready in five," Chapel ordered. "Get Ledger a gun."

Davis took the M4 Nazari handed him. Checked it while Hollyn stood mutely at his side.

"Aaand he just took the bait." From the command room, Hale swiveled a screen their way. Germaine had found his way out of the zip ties Macklin had loosened and was in front of the only window in the hold, hands probing the edges. He kept glancing over his shoulder.

"Let's go." Chapel circled a finger in the air.

"Stay inside," Davis warned Hollyn again.

"Don't worry." Bennion winked at her while the team filtered out of the room. "We'll keep a close eye on your man."

Davis didn't have time to form a rebuttal. Just gave Hollyn's hand one last squeeze and strode out the front door with Fury.

All right, Germaine. Let's see what ace you have up your sleeve.

Hollyn quietly walked into a larger area filled with computers and TV screens. She scanned the room. Papers and maps lined the walls, and Hayes—no, wait, Hale—was sitting near the end of a long table, focused on a video feed. It had a green cast to the images moving across it. Night vision? In the large monitor he stared at, Braum had finally pried the window open. He tried to jump through the opening. Legs flailing, he shimmied till he was halfway out, then dropped from view on the other side.

Hale tapped the keyboard, and the screen cycled through several different angles around the house. The front porch. Back patio she'd been on with Davis—wait, had they been watching her and Davis too? She tucked her chin as the rooftop came into view. They really had cameras everywhere.

Note to self: before making out with Davis next time, be sure no eyes were watching.

Hale paused on a live feed that showed Braum stumbling in the sand close to where he'd dropped. Looking around, eyes glowing, seemingly unaware of the camera focused on him, he finally found his footing. Jogged off as Hale brought up another view. This one showed Braum limp-running across the property toward a fence.

"Alpha team, be advised," Hale said, his voice low and stiff.

Hollyn looked over at him. Could see a threaded connector running up his neck to an earpiece. He must also have a mic somewhere.

"Germaine is moving along the north wall. Heading toward the back of the property." He looked like he was listening to someone, then nodded. "Copy." With a heavy sigh, he leaned back and crossed his arms over his thick chest. He was huge. He was—looking at her.

Hollyn caught a gasp in her throat. She ducked, cheeks heating. "Sorry."

Hale—she wished she knew his first name. It was weird calling someone by only their last—shrugged. "No skin off my nose."

She pushed her gaze to the screen. It was just a green-cast view of a chain-link fence, sand, and some desert plants. Nothing in frame moved. "They're going to be okay, right?"

His steady expression didn't waiver. "They know what they're doing."

No false promises. She appreciated that . . . at least, she thought she did. The way her palms were sweating told her maybe she would've liked to hear a white lie just this once. She needed to know Davis was going to be okay. They couldn't have been brought back into each other's lives just for her to have him ripped away again.

Along with everything else, she didn't know if she could handle that.

Hale studied her. "How long have you known Ledger?" His knee bounced just like Davis's did when he was thinking. Must be a guy thing.

"Uh, we met when we were ten." She grabbed one of the pencils on the table. Rolled it back and forth under her hand.

He shot her a look of appreciation. Nodded. "Ten. Long time."

"Sometimes it feels like a lifetime."

"Feels like a lifetime for most of us," he joked. "Nice to meet the famous Hollyn, though."

Wait, what? She fidgeted in her chair. "Famous?"

"Oh yeah. Ledger talked about you all the time when we were deployed."

"He did?" Why was her heart racing all of a sudden?

"For a while there, I thought the two of you were married."

The laugh that shot from her mouth sounded equal parts crazed lunatic and dying cat. Could this get any more embarrassing?

Hollyn turned, shaking her head. "No, no. Definitely not married. No, he . . . we . . . never."

"Yeah." Hale chuckled. "Picked up on that."

So many questions were going through her mind. At the

forefront: If he had talked about her to the point his friends had thought there was something between them, why had Davis shut her out of his life so completely the day he left for Basic? And what was going to happen when this mission was over and he left her again?

# 14



Crack! Pop-pop-pop!

"He's in the building!" Davis barked into his mic as he and Fury bolted across the sand toward a door Germaine had just disappeared behind.

So much for covert.

Fury had tracked the guy for over two hours before the team had all but walked into an ambush outside an industrial building near the Ba Al Ghaiylam area. It nagged at Davis that the tangos had been prepared for this. How had Germaine communicated his approach? They'd searched him thoroughly for any kind of communication device before his interrogation.

*Zip. Ping!* Davis ducked, the firefight raging around him, unyielding. Damocles continued to lay down suppressive fire. Gripping his M4, he steadied his breathing. Dug his boots into the loose ground. Locked his gaze on his partner. The air was thick with salt this close to the shore. Made everything sticky, including the door handle he yanked back on. Nazari right behind them, they slid inside. Fury shot forward and they followed, clearing the area as they ran.

Don't lose him.

Footsteps peppered the floor somewhere ahead. Retreating, not advancing. Germaine? Fury was getting dangerously close to slipping out of sight. Davis growled. Freaking—the RMWD was fast.

Movement above caught his eye a second before bullets sparked off the floor. He snapped his weapon upward and responded. Neutralized the threat and doubled down on his pursuit of Fury.

"Augh!" The masculine scream down a hall echoed in the air.

Davis slid to a stop at the corner. Did a quick check. Saw Fury with the arm of an assailant in his mouth. He pulled and tugged with deep growls.

Weapon up, Davis advanced.

The tango reached for a gun he must have dropped when Fury took him down.

*Not today.* Davis eased back the trigger.

*Crack!*

The tango's body went slack. Fury whipped his head side to side a couple more times.

"Out," he directed the shepherd.

Fury kept his grip for another few seconds before he decided to release.

"Seek-seek!" Davis gave the command.

The RMWD took off down the hall. Davis and Nazari checked the doors—all locked—as they hustled. When Fury skidded to a stop in front of a door on the right, Davis slowed to a stop, reading the shepherd's body language. "D'you find something, buddy?" he asked, more in hope than with proof.

After dragging in some deep draughts of air at the threshold, Fury clawed at the door.

Davis stalked forward, waiting for Fury to settle back. He flicked the handle with his nondominant hand and eased the door open. Angling for a better view, he traced the interior with his reticle. A small office. Empty. A desk sat in the middle, papers and file folders piled high all over it. A whiteboard on one wall had a hand-drawn schematic of . . . a missile? Half of it had been wiped off.

Fury dropped his nose to the ground, tail up. Beelined to a bookshelf at the back of the room. Pawed at one of the shelves before looking back at him.

"Give me a hand," Davis said. Slid his M4 behind his back.

"Yep." Nazari joined him and they each took an end.

At first, the bookshelf didn't budge, then something clicked, and it easily slid aside.

Nazari took point and entered. "He's here."

There, in the middle, Archie sat tied to a chair—unconscious. A dozen discordant elements pinged in Davis's head as he put Fury in a "down" and moved in to assist with the twerp. Not exactly how he'd expected to find this leader of a terrorist group.

This guy had supposedly been tortured, yet there was no blood on his clothes. Just dirt. Not how you'd expect to find a hostage. Was it a setup?

He assessed the twerp for a minute. Always had bugged him. But this . . . it wasn't right. Something was off. It hadn't been difficult to find him or breach the room. No one was standing guard, and if the twerp really were a liability—and not in on things—why not waste him before they engaged Damocles? It was sloppy work to leave him alone where anyone could capture him.

He eyed Nazari, whose furrowed brow suggested he was having the same thoughts. "Doesn't add up," Davis muttered. Sliding a pocketknife from his tactical pants, he looked around the room. Didn't see any cameras, but that didn't mean they weren't there. They'd need to be quick about this.

"Hey, man." Nazari nudged the twerp.

The kid moaned but didn't come to. The knot on his forehead said he'd probably been knocked out cold.

Davis slid the knife blade through the zip ties like butter.

The twerp pitched forward. Davis and Nazari grabbed him before he fell off the chair.

Another groan and this time Twerp's head lifted. "What do you want?" His reply was weak as he slowly lifted a hand in defense, and Davis noted one of his fingers was jutting out at an unnatural angle.

Okay, so maybe Archie being the mastermind behind all of this was off base. A curse rattled through Davis. Which meant they were back at ground zero. They'd better get hands on Germaine again, or it was his backside up a pole.

"Get off me," Twerp growled.

"Take it easy," Davis said to him. He keyed his mic. "Alpha Actual, package secure."

"Good copy," Chapel comm'd. Gunfire crowded his words. "Suggest you clear out. More unfriendlies inbound."

"We need to get Germaine back."

"We will. But not now. Head back."

Davis balled a fist. Cursed and turned to Nazari. "Let's go." While Fury paced the opening of the room, he knelt beside the chair supporting Archie and hooked the twerp's arm around his neck. His buddy did the same. Together, they hoisted him up.

"Hold up." He slid out his phone in the front room. Quickly took video of everything in the office. If there was any useful intel, he'd have a record of it. "Okay." He glanced down at Fury. "*Fuss.*"

The RMWD snapped into position, and they hurried back the way they'd entered the building. Side-shuffled through the door into the deafening cacophony of war blanketing the night. Outside, the firefight was near deafening.

Shots flared against the night as they ran toward the rest of the team.

"Come on!" Chapel yelled. "Blank's about to bring the place down!"

Davis bit back a curse. Nodded to Nazari, and they hustled it toward the rest of the team. "Move move move!" Chapel took point while the rest of the team queued up at the rear so Davis and Nazari wouldn't get shot in the back hauling Archie away from the building. Legs aching, back pinching, Davis ran as fast as possible, each punishing step feeling too slow against a raging fireball.

One klick out, Chapel keyed his mic. "Blank! Drop it."

The familiar sound of the incoming suicide UAV neared. Blanchard guided the remote aircraft loaded with C4 overhead and into the side of the building at their distant six. The eruption shook the ground.

*Booooom!*

The concussion punched Davis in the back. He stumbled. Caught himself and shoved forward alongside Nazari. Gripping Archie's wrist, he hiked the guy's weight higher for a better hold and did his best not to faceplant and kill them all. Pain tightened his shoulder.

Archie sagged against them, weak. His feet dragged as they hauled him to safety. At his side, Fury gave a low whine—not liking the tension in the air, apparently.

*Me either, buddy.*

An intense wave of heat and debris lunged toward him and the team. A massive plume of wind obliterated the structure. Light from the fire lit their path. Screams of those unfortunate to be caught in the blast mixed with the creaks and groans of bending metal. Several chunks of shrapnel pierced the ground nearby.

Gritting his teeth, sweat sliding free of his helmet and down his temple, Davis pushed his body to the limit. Didn't slow. Didn't stop. Didn't look back.

The slow creep of dawn forced itself into the black night as the team reached the relative security of the safe house. Each step made his calves and back scream. His legs trembled as he climbed the steps. He and Nazari delivered Archie to the couch, and the guy slumped against the cushions, breathing hard. As if *he'd* just hoofed it five klicks in full tac gear carrying a hundred-

and-thirty-pound sack of potatoes. Sweat beaded his forehead, pain written all over his face.

Good.

"Archie!" Hollyn rushed in from the command room, and trailing her—Hale.

Davis caught her before she could reach her friend. "Wait," he cautioned. "Let Glace look him over first."

"And you?" Her eyes searched his, voice quiet. "Are you okay?"

He nodded. Man, her concern for him felt good. "I'm fine."

She nodded while Glace strode over with her kit and got to work. The rest of the team subconsciously formed a half circle around the combat medic. If Archie so much as sneezed in her direction, he'd regret it.

Davis turned to his four-legged partner and ran his hands over the furry spine, hind legs, and forelegs. Verified there weren't injuries he'd missed. "Did good, buddy." He hiked back and tossed a KONG in the air. The landshark snatched it. Trotted to a corner of the room and plopped down with a huff to chew on the toy.

"I'm going to reset your finger," Glace said to Archie.

Grimacing, Archie nodded.

Hollyn pressed a hand over her mouth, flinching when her friend grunted in pain.

At her side, Davis removed his brain bowl, then laced his fingers with Hollyn's. Ran his thumb back and forth over hers while Glace splinted Archie.

The twerp smirked at Hollyn—something that irritated Davis to no end. "Hey, Hol."

"What happened?" she asked.

"That's what we're going to get to the bottom of," Chapel stepped in. "Benn, Macklin, take him to the hold."

"The *hold*?" Hollyn stepped forward. "Clearly he's not who you're looking for!"

"Hollyn," Davis warned. Now wasn't the time.

Benn and Macklin were already hauling Archie toward the hallway. And for the first time, the guy did something smart—he didn't fight them.

Fury neared, gaze intent on Hollyn.

She took a step away from the shepherd. "You guys can't be serious!" she yelled at Chapel. "What do you think you're doing?"

The burly guy nailed Davis with a hard look.

She got the message, stepping back as Chapel disappeared after the others.

"You too?" Hollyn turned on Davis. "I know you guys never saw eye to eye, but come on! Archie is my friend—he *isn't* behind all of this. You saw him!"

Fury planted himself in front of her in guarding position, body rigid with focus, clearly sensing the rising tension.

"Yeah." Davis angled in. Kept his voice even. He could understand why she'd feel that way, and truth was, he didn't think Archie was behind it either. "Protocols are in place for a reason. When we circumvent them, people die."

Preaching to the choir.

"Germaine in the wind?"

Davis hadn't realized Hale was still around. He nodded curtly. "Chapel said he got away on a boat before they could reach the dock."

The way this had turned out was less than ideal. He owned that. But with the info they'd had at the time . . .

Hindsight and all that. One thing he could guarantee—Germaine hadn't seen the last of them.

The video he'd taken needed to be combed through—quickly and thoroughly—before the next A-bomb blew up in his face.

When Hollyn took a step toward the hallway, Fury launched his ninety-pound frame at her. His paws punched into her chest as she screamed.

"Whoa, whoa!" Hale bellowed.

"Fury, no!" Davis reached out too late.

Fury and Hollyn tumbled to the ground. He grabbed the RMWD's collar and hauled the dog off, afraid he'd clamp on to the arm Hollyn lifted to protect herself. But as he tugged the landshark backward, it registered that while the shepherd had brought her down, he wasn't *aggressing*.

Drawing in deep breaths, tail swishing back and forth in the air—he wasn't trying to hurt her, he was scenting. Davis drew Fury around and held the lead tight to keep him under control as Hale helped Hollyn, who scrambled backward.

"You good?" Davis's heartbeat punched his chest. How many times was he going to ask her that?

Hollyn clutched her throat. Red scratches streaked across her neck. So much less than Fury could've done. "I'm . . . " She swallowed. "I think so."

That'd been way too close.

She patted her neck, then her motions became more frantic. "My necklace!" She scanned the floor, turning in agitated circles as she searched.

Fury kept straining against Davis, pulling in the opposite direction of Hollyn. He released the RMWD, who shot forward. Within seconds, Fury sat, attention laser focused on the floor.

Davis neared. Saw the missing necklace. "Good boy." He ruffled the shepherd's head and stooped to grab the item.

Hollyn took the proffered necklace. Gasped. "No!" she cried out, looking at the pendant. Then him, her eyes watery pools. "It's broken."

Flip.

Davis glared down at Fury. Of all the things he could have ruined.

"Hollyn, I'm—"

"Wait, what's this?" She sniffed. Messed with the globe. Dug her fingernails in and pulled out a tiny rectangular object she identified immediately.

A microchip.

## *DAMOCLES SAFE HOUSE*

"Why would a microchip be in the necklace?" Hollyn turned to Davis like he'd have an answer. Her gaze dropped to Fury, who was still looking at her like she was a slab of bacon. And as if he could read her mind, the hairy beast licked his jowls.

Fear still fresh from being attacked, she distanced herself farther from him.

"What's going on?" Chapel stalked into the room.

The permanently stony expression he wore chilled Hollyn to her bone. Rendered her mute when she should speak up. Clearly, today wasn't the day she'd find her nerve.

"Not sure yet," Davis answered. "Fury got a hit on Hollyn."

Well, that was one way of putting it.

"Broke her necklace—found a microchip hidden in it." He extended his hand to Hollyn.

"Where'd you get the necklace?" Chapel demanded.

Which sounded a lot like he was blaming her. "M-my dad."

"The dad," Davis said pointedly, "who was killed had developed military-grade technology."

"No," Hollyn objected. "He developed technology. Someone else wanted to weaponize it."

Chapel studied her hard. "Let's check it out."

She set the piece in Davis's hand, deliberately avoiding the grumpy team leader and the four-legged force of nature.

Davis nodded to Chapel, who didn't look happy as he trailed Hale into the command room.

Hollyn's hands were shaking by the time she sat in front of the computer.

Dark-haired Hale dug through some things on the desk and tugged a chip reader out.

Hollyn held her breath as he opened the file that popped up, then swiveled the screen to her and slid the mouse her way. "What?"

"It was in your necklace from your dad . . . " Hale shrugged. "Figured you might want to open it."

"Oh." Right. Sure. But that awakened a whole new level of dread. What had Daddy hidden? Was it a message? Did she really want to even know if it'd gotten him killed?

Chapel and Davis stepped up behind her chair. To her relief, Fury kept his distance this time, his teeth squeegeeing over his KONG. She rubbed her neck. Nightmares about him jumping on her were going to plague her sleep for a while.

She opened a folder and found several files, all with numbers instead of names. "Here goes nothing . . . " She clicked open one of the files.

"What are we looking at?" Davis asked, apparently leaning in, because his words whispered along her earlobe.

With a shiver, Holly struggled to focus. Blinked and looked again at what was on the screen. Heart in her throat, she gasped. "That's my algorithm!" Bending toward the screen, she squinted, processing the information there. "Not my whole algorithm, but the part that was missing from the lab files."

"And what does that do?" Chapel gruffed.

"The algorithm?" She peered over her shoulder at him. "It just . . . makes the program run. Without it, the drones are just drones."

"With it?"

"The drones become . . . intelligent. Responsive. Intuit and resolve situations. I was looking for a way to eliminate underwater accidents from divers having to do dangerous grunt work around wreckages. Drones are expendable, people aren't."

Davis pointed to another file icon. "What about the others?"

Still rattled that the missing piece of code was here, hidden in her necklace, she had to haul her thoughts back in line. Clicked open the next icon.

A dozen documents populated the screen. She strained to

identify them. "Emails . . . shared between two people calling themselves *Old Lace* and *Crossfire*." Finger to her lips, she read the emails. "Okay, the first one is dated a year ago and contains source code to my algorithm." Which made no sense. Who had gotten hold of this? She hadn't shared it with anyone except Daddy.

"Do you or your dad always share source code so easily?" Hale asked.

"No." She balked. "In fact, that's *encrypted* source code that could have only been accessed by someone *inside* the lab. No one else had access."

Which made Hollyn sick to her stomach. Its implications were too terrible to fathom. No . . . it couldn't be . . . a traitor . . . spy?

She shook off the daunting thoughts and checked the other emails. The one called Crossfire said they were getting close to figuring out the missing piece in the AI program and the deal could close soon.

"Unbelievable . . . " She drew the word out as she kept reading. "These are negotiations to sell my program."

How dare whoever this was try to steal her work!

Hale whistled low. "Nice chunk of change, there." He indicated a number with enough zeros to give coding a run for its money.

Hollyn clicked through the rest of the emails. "'We'll be ready for the demonstration soon . . . There are a few chess pieces to eliminate from the board.'" She sucked in a breath and glanced at Davis, whose expression went grim. So that did mean what she thought it meant. She swallowed and returned to the message. "'Stick to the plan. Any attempt to double-cross me will end poorly for them.'" Her stomach twisted. "I can't believe this . . . my parents! My parents were the *chess pieces*. This—*this* is who killed them!" Tears pricked her eyes, and she gulped down the lump in her throat. Glanced over her shoulder to Davis. "What demonstration?"

"Don't know," he replied. "But we need to find out."

In another folder, a note from Dad waited.

*Sparrow,*

*For some time I've suspected that our lab had a mole, but until these emails were intercepted, I didn't have proof. Unfortunately, I'm still unable to determine who's behind this. As a precaution, I held off uploading the last section of your algorithm so the lab files were rendered unusable. As you've probably figured out, they're on this chip. You know how meticulous we were about protecting your launch. These prove that someone from the lab has betrayed us. I pray I find out who and what they planned to do with the program before you ever see this. However, if I don't, as I said in my letter, trust no one but Davis.*

Hollyn rested her elbows on the desk and braced her mouth against her fisted hands for a moment, struggling to process this revelation, to understand that her dad had known someone was betraying them. "Someone from the lab is behind this." She said it more to solidify the truth than as a repetition of the email's contents. Her heart was so heavy. Someone she'd worked with—maybe even *daily*—was to blame, and she hadn't suspected a thing.

"Archie," Davis said dryly.

Hollyn turned. As much as she wanted to argue, she couldn't empirically say he was wrong. And that hurt. A lot. "We should talk to him."

Surprise flashed over his face.

"No, *we* will talk to him," Chapel countered.

She gathered every ounce of courage she could muster. "All due respect—"

He scoffed. "Which just means up y—"

"This is my code and my lab." For once in her life, she was taking a stand. "Like it or not, I'm part of this, and I know Archie better than any of you." She resented that everyone had already decided to blame Archie.

"Which is part of the problem—he means something to you. Can you do what's necessary if he's guilty?"

His challenge rattled her. But she realized something. "If he's guilty, then that means he killed my parents." The thought of that struck a powerful chord. "I'm done being a peacemaker. We need truth, not just a head to hang." *She* wanted truth. Whatever it may be. If he was the one behind this, she'd find a way to accept it. But if he wasn't, they were wasting valuable time going after the wrong person.

Chapel stared her down.

Was it her imagination, or had Davis and Hale just collectively leaned away? As the seconds ticked by, Hollyn understood this man had more experience in this arena. A more attuned sense to liars and terrorists. Maybe she should let him handle it. Admittedly, that'd be so much easier than—

"Good." Chapel gave a sharp nod. "Let's go."

She didn't give him time to second-guess his decision. Just stood to follow him. Sidestepping Fury, she took in a steadying breath.

"We'll hold back and comb through the video Ledger took," Hale said. "See what else we can figure out about where Germaine went."

Without a word, Chapel took off toward the hold.

Following the grizzly operator down the hall bolstered her resolve to stay strong. She could do this. After all, she'd held her ground and stated her position and he'd agreed. So she was doing something right.

His broad frame blocked the light as he ducked into the hold. Inside, she spotted Archie on a medical gurney, Glace and Macklin hovering over him. Where was the rest of Damocles?

"Hollyn." Relief filled Archie's tone.

She forced herself not to rush forward.

*You have to find out what's going on.*

"Are you the mole, Archie?" she asked him point blank. Wanted to see his reaction.

His face scrunched in confusion. "What're you talking about?"

Hollyn pressed on. "We found the emails."

"Emails?" Archie didn't look at anyone in the room but her. "I don't know what you're referring to."

"Crossfire and Old Lace."

He frowned again. "What does that even mean?"

The tether on her temper burned, and she stomped forward. "My parents are dead, Archie! Leila is dead!" She spoke with more ferocity than she'd known she possessed. "Stop messing around! Was it you? Did you kill my parents?"

"No!" Archie balked, anger replacing confusion. "It wasn't me. On a stack of Bibles, it's not me. I swear." He blanched. "I'm not the one you're after."

Chapel's muscular form wedged in. "Then who is?"

Archie looked between them. Looked like he might not say anything else. Then his shoulders slumped and his head dipped. She thought she heard him whisper *forgive me* before he straightened. "I don't know who's behind it . . . but I know what they're going to do with the program."

# 15



HE'D KNOWN? THIS WHOLE TIME—POSSIBLY LONGER THAN THE emails revealed—and he'd never said a word?

"All right." Chapel lowered his hands out to his sides, a move that reminded her of cats when they turned sideways to make themselves look bigger, fiercer. And this guy definitely seemed more intimidating than usual. "When, where, and what? Now."

Archie shook his head again. "I don't know. All I found out was that they're going to militarize the program to guide missiles. They're planning a demonstration. Soon."

Hollyn swallowed. Same message from the emails. Was he telling the truth or blowing smoke about not knowing more?

"What kind of demonstration and where?" Chapel pressed.

"Again," Archie bit out, "I. Don't. Know. I heard them talking about missiles and the Sparrow project. Wasn't hard to put two and two together from there." He bobbed his head toward her. "I know what her program does."

Hollyn wracked her brain. This wasn't right. Archie's behavior. His apparent regret. None of this was adding up. And did anyone else find it unbelievable that his captors hadn't cared that he could overhear them? "They can't make the program work without the whole algorithm." Better not tell him she had the missing part, just in case he was lying. "You saw the test runs fail."

He lifted a shoulder in a half shrug. "Sounded to me like they had someone working on that."

Who? Her stomach squirmed. Yet . . . "Even if they had everything they needed, the program is currently only able to support a short-range launch," Hollyn went on. "No one is dumb enough to try to guide a missile into an area they're standing in themselves."

"How short?" Chapel gruffed.

Hollyn lifted a shoulder and shook her head. "Fifty yards max. I hadn't developed the long-range sequence yet."

"I don't know," Archie said. "But they're definitely getting ready for something."

Expression granitelike, Chapel leveled a hard look at Archie. "And you expect us to believe you just managed to overhear all this?"

Chapel voicing what she'd just been thinking boosted her confidence. Yet she couldn't quite squelch the nagging thoughts in the back of her head that had her doubting Archie could be at the heart of all this.

*But you can't deny the facts.*

Her friend's lip twitched with ire. "Not like the door was all that thick, GI Joe."

Chapel didn't acknowledge the quip. Instead, he turned and spoke quietly to Macklin and Glace before looking at Hollyn. "That's good for now." He jutted his chin toward the door, and she took the hint.

She didn't want to press her luck by insisting that she stay, so she stepped out of the hold. Stopping by the command room to grab the microchip—she didn't want it far from her for long—she saw Davis and Hale were still wading through whatever footage they'd been talking about earlier. She had been going to slip into a chair near them, but Fury lifted his head off the floor and let out a low growl, effectively ending that idea. Why he wasn't a fan of her now, she didn't know. That was an animal for you, though. Especially one like the RMWD.

The guys glanced over their shoulders.

Davis straightened. "What'd he say?"

Hollyn leaned her hip against the door jamb. "Says he doesn't know who's behind this, but he overheard that they're planning to modify the program to work with *missiles*." She rubbed her temples. "I had a completely nonviolent intention with that program. That someone wants to militarize it . . . and they've got a demonstration planned . . . It doesn't sound good. Missiles! Can you believe it?" When his face went somber, her pulse sped up. "What?"

Davis stood. "Chapel still with him?"

"Wh—yes." She frowned. "What's wrong?"

"I'll bring you up to speed later." He gave her arm a squeeze when he and Hale brushed past her, Fury hot on their tail.

"Well, okay then," she murmured to herself in the empty silence of their departure. A nearby clock read almost noon. No wonder she didn't feel on top of her game. She'd been awake for over twenty-four hours without food or rest.

Hollyn stepped over to the chip reader on the desk and took out the microchip, then shuffled to her room. Sinking down onto the bed, she looked at the tiny piece of tech in her hand. It'd been with her the whole time, and she'd had no clue. If she'd found it sooner—

No. It wouldn't do any good to go down that road now.

Eyelids heavy with exhaustion, she set the microchip on her nightstand. The fluffy pillow lured her to lay down. She yawned.

Maybe just a quick nap.

"Hollyn?" a voice tugged her from the clutches of sleep.

With a yelp, she bolted upright, wide awake. Archie stood in the doorway, looking sheepish. Why was he here? The team was just letting him walk around the house now?

An uneasy feeling bobbed in her stomach.

"Archie . . . hey." She rubbed her face. Yawned, feeling like she'd run a marathon. So much for a nap helping. She felt more confused and tired than ever. What time was it?

The Abu Dhabi sky was a pool of pink and purple hues. Drat. She'd been asleep longer than she'd planned.

"What are you doing?" She shoved her blanket back and folded her legs. "Isn't the team questioning you?"

Cradling his injured hand, he stepped into the room. Lowered onto the bed beside her. "They decided I was in the clear."

They had? That didn't sound right. Call her crazy, but she didn't think Chapel would decide *anyone* was in the clear.

"What?" He eyed her.

She tried to stop staring as the uneasy feeling grew stronger. "Sorry." What was it about him that seemed different? He looked basically the same as always—minus the dirtied clothing and tired eyes. When was the last time *he'd* slept?

He flashed a grin that didn't reach his eyes.

*Something's not right.*

Hollyn bit her lip. "Maybe you should go back and rest, Archie. You've been through—"

"Did you know I have a couple sisters?"

"What?" Hollyn twitched. Talk about a jarring subject jump. "Uh, no. I don't think I've ever heard you mention them."

Hollyn stood and tried to nonchalantly maneuver so Archie would come away from the door. If she could just get a clear shot, she could bolt out of here and find Davis.

"They're younger than me. Haven't seen them in a while."

Where was this going? The dregs of sleep clogged her thoughts. "You should visit them when this is all over. Family is important."

"Sorry, Hol. Didn't mean to go there." He smiled.

The nickname coming from him didn't feel the way it did when Davis used it. Instead, it felt forced and highly awkward.

Archie tapped the edge of the bed with his good fist then stood. "Remember that game we used to play in the lab?" He looked at her. "Hypothesis: people will go to lengths they never imagined to protect those they love. Agree or disagree?"

Her heart was thundering in her chest now. She felt like a caged mouse a snake was about to devour. She could yell for help . . . but he was still too close. He could easily attack her, or worse, before any of the team reached them. Speaking of which—*where* was the team?

"Agree," he prompted, "or disagree?"

"Agree," Hollyn replied quietly. "It's human nature."

Archie nodded, seemingly in thought. "I loved you, you know."

Hollyn widened her eyes. What was she supposed to say to *that*? "Archie . . . "

"Yeah, I was always too chicken to tell you. Then it was too late."

Yes. It absolutely was too late. He'd *always* felt like a brother to her. And even if he hadn't, she'd been in love with Davis since high school.

The realization surprised her, but it was true. She *was* in love with Davis.

*Trust no one but Davis.* Dad's warning replayed in her mind.

"Look," she started softly. She just had to placate him. Keep him calm. If he'd just take a couple more steps, she'd have a shot of escape. But he wasn't moving now. "A lot has happened in the last couple of days. I really think you should get some sleep. I'm sure Glace could give you something to help." She swallowed and tried to force a laugh, which just came out flat. "We both know we're not at our best when we're sleep deprived."

"Right." Archie nodded. "That would probably be good. I can't really think straight."

Hollyn seized her chance. Stepped toward the hallway. "I'll just go get—"

But Archie blocked her path in one fluid movement. Before she knew what was happening, he was kissing her. Hollyn tensed, her entire body revolting. She jerked her head back. Pushed him away as hard as she could. "Stop!"

"Hollyn—" he tried.

"No!" Hollyn forced distance between them, continuing to hold up her hand. "Never, Archie. No, that's—it's not going to happen."

He dug his hands into his hair, a frenzied look twisting his expression. "I'm . . . sorry, Hollyn."

Without another word, he slipped out of the room.

Heart racing, Hollyn tried to think straight. *What* had just happened?

Davis. She needed Davis.

She reached for the microchip on the nightstand. Froze.

"No," she breathed. Rushed over. "No, no." She ran her hand along the entire top of the stand. It'd been right there! Where could it have gone? Maybe she'd knocked it off in her sleep?

Hollyn dropped to her hands and knees, dragging her hands over the floor, feeling dirt and rocks and food crumbs—gross!— but no chip. What'd happened to—

She gasped, her gaze whipping to the door.

Archie.

Hollyn shoved to her feet and raced into the hallway. Nearly collided with Glace.

"You good?" the petite medic asked.

"Where have you guys *been*?"

Glace's look hardened. "In a meeting. Why—"

"He took it!" Hollyn jogged toward the command room and Davis. She couldn't believe she'd just gotten played. Stupid, *stupid* girl. "Archie's got the microchip!"

## DAMOCLES SAFE HOUSE

"I can't believe I let him take it," Hollyn murmured for the dozenth time since she'd rushed in to tell them Archie had stolen the microchip. Over and over she wrung the baseball hat she'd been given to wear.

"It's done, Hol," Davis said. "Don't worry—"

"Don't worry?" she cried. "They're planning a demonstration, and now that he has the missing code, they can do it!"

"We'll stop them in time."

Davis didn't like telling her things he couldn't actually guarantee, but she needed to hear that she hadn't irrevocably screwed things up.

Not like he had, anyway.

He was livid—along with the rest of them—that Twerp had given them the slip. None of them could figure out how Archie had escaped undetected, but Davis especially felt the weight of their mistake. Should have chained the guy to the wall. Held him at gunpoint. Anything but let their guard down a fraction of an inch, even if they'd thought he was secure.

While Chapel had chewed them up one side and down the other, they'd checked through surveillance footage without unearthing any clarity on what'd happened, so they turned their focus to the footage from their raid. Time wasn't on their side.

Davis and Hale had discovered a pamphlet for the Emirates Palace Hotel lying on the desk. On the whiteboard adhered to the north wall was written today's date, along with a missile schematic that had been partially erased. A little online digging had revealed a high-profile gala with ranking dignitaries and their families being held tonight.

However, they'd also found out from dark web searches that a general in the UAE Armed Forces was recovering in a nearby hospital across town. The guy was waist-deep in some shady dealings. That paired with the volatile relations between the armed forces and local anti-military organizations made him another possible target—though not as likely since they hadn't found anything pointing to him in the footage.

Davis secured more mags in the ankle holsters under his suit pants. While some of the team would provide cover around the Emirates Palace, he and Fury would go undercover as party security, so Fury would have full access for his EOD search. Davis tucked the forged security clearance Blank had created for them into his pocket.

Hollyn looked especially out of her depth, back in her ballistic vest with his KA-BAR strapped to her thigh. She, Bennion, and Glace would head to the hospital and away from the most likely target.

"Hey." He tried to calm her. "It's going to be okay."

She nodded but continued to chew her lip. Kept shifting her weight from one foot to the other. She clearly wasn't made for this, but he was proud of the way she was still holding it together after all she'd been through.

A realization he'd never thought he would come to slipped into his mind: This would be his last rodeo.

Soon as they were on the other side of this, he was making sure Hollyn had as much peace and quiet as she could handle. He'd gladly spend the rest of his life protecting her from having to deal with anything like this ever again. The internal calm that followed the decision was confirmation enough. Couldn't have imagined living to see the day he'd willingly step away from this life.

She was worth it, though.

Hooah.

Chapel had decided that they'd cover their bases and have teams set up at both the hotel and hospital. But with one a more likely target than the other, Hollyn would go with Bennion and Glace to the hospital—the safer of the two. The rest of them would set up around the hotel and try to intercept Archie and whoever was with him.

Foregoing his M4, Davis checked his Sig and slid it into place on his waist holster. Grabbed the tuxedo jacket. The team had done a decent job finding a passable outfit for the black-tie gathering on such a tight turn around. He ran a finger along the neck of the dress shirt that squeezed tighter than he would've preferred. Tugged it from his skin. The ensemble was made even more uncomfortable by the low-profile Kevlar vest underneath.

Flipping monkey suit.

"OTG in ten." Chapel was the first ready. "Sixty mikes to head this off."

The rest of the team double-timed their efforts.

"Are you sure about this?" Hollyn stepped up to Davis.

Amped up, Fury spun and knocked into her legs. She practically jumped away.

"Sure about what?" He double-checked her vest.

"About splitting up."

He wanted her as far from danger as possible. "I'm sure. Don't need you getting hurt."

She nodded without another word, and he almost missed her arguing with him.

"Move out." Chapel spun a finger in the air.

They hurried toward the waiting vehicles. Fury leapt inside after the rest of the team.

"Be careful." Hollyn suddenly wrapped her arms around Davis's neck.

He tugged her close for a quick second. Kissed the side of her head. "Always." Then they were heading in different directions.

The farther they drove, the stronger Davis's gut feeling grew—something was wrong.

Hale knocked his knee with his own. Nodded and held out a fist that Davis bumped with a gloved hand. It surprised him that, even though missions and team were the only things he'd ever lived for, now that he had someone important in his life, the only thing he really wanted to do was protect *her*. Life goals that had once been held in concrete were breaking loose. Morphing into something he couldn't have predicted.

*Just one more mission. Then I'm done. For good.*

On his terms this time.

When they arrived at the hotel, it was nearing 2200 hours. Which was ideal because the darkness allowed the team to disperse undetected while Davis and Fury walked into the party.

The six-story structure was more extravagant than any place he'd been invited to before—or rather, *not* invited to. Near the center of the expansive setup, a wide stone path cut across a large but shallow pool. Hundreds of guests in black-tie attire congregated around dozens of café-height tables set up around the rest of the open area. Rows of highly manicured bushes lined the space between courtyard and sandy beach. Not exactly Fort Knox.

They were given a few hard looks from actual security patrolling the outskirts of the Emirates Palace courtyard, and for a moment, Davis wondered if their cover was blown. But he threw them a chin-up greeting and acted like he was supposed to be there. The guards returned the gesture and moved on.

The din of the gathering was barely edged out by the crash of ocean waves to the building's twelve. There were more people here than he'd anticipated, dressed in everything from evening gowns to traditional saris to military suits.

He and Fury maneuvered around the stamped concrete pathways. The dark sable shepherd sniffed the air, and Davis watched for the slightest hint that his partner had a hit

A woman in a white-and-gold sari detoured in their direction, champagne glass in hand. She grinned at Fury. "Awww, what an adorable puppy!"

The shepherd seemed about as thrilled with the term as Davis and surged toward her with enough ferocity to bring the woman up short.

"He's working," Davis warned. "Keep your distance."

"Well!" She glared at the two. Hurried away.

Davis thumped a hand on the landshark's side. "Nice," he murmured.

"Blank. Update." Chapel came over comms.

Davis listened as he scanned the guests. Neither Archie nor Germaine had shown yet.

"Nothing on facial rec," Blank updated in her usual calm and quiet tone. She was manning their eyes in the sky once more.

"Stay frosty, people," Chapel comm'd the team.

Didn't have to tell Davis twice. The uneasy feeling he hadn't been able to shake in the Jeep was still going strong out here. Loose grip on the leash, he finished their loop around the courtyard. "Let's run it again," he muttered to his four-legged partner.

"Possible confirmation on Archie," Blank comm'd. "Stand by."

Here we go.

# 16



*DOWNTOWN, ABU DHABI, UAE*

Driving down Corniche Street late at night was like being hit upside the head by déjà vu.

Hollyn closed her eyes, fighting back memories of that night. Would this one forever change her life too? She clutched the straps of her Kevlar vest and prayed for everyone's safety—especially Davis's. City lights of downtown Abu Dhabi splashed over her face through the rear passenger window. How different her life was compared to a week ago.

Then? Mum and Dad had still been alive. She'd been happy, celebrating a victory . . . Tears pooled in her eyes as she remembered taking Dad's arm at the gala. The way he and Mum had laughed at each other. Neither of them had let slip even an ounce of worry over what had been going on. For a moment, Hollyn wondered if her mum had known about any of it or if Dad had chosen to keep her as blissfully unaware as Hollyn.

Maybe if they'd all known, they could have—

*Don't do it. It's impossible to know and will only drive you crazy.*

Benn whipped around a slower car. Accelerated slightly to

avoid a red light. He kept glancing at the rearview mirror, and for a moment, Hollyn wondered if someone was following them.

No, no. He'd be acting differently . . . right?

"Right up here." Glace directed him from the front passenger seat.

They were just a block away from the hospital now. Rows of palms lined the street with cityscape on one side and the dark expanse of ocean on the other. Lamp posts in the center divider held illuminated butterfly sculptures she'd always loved. A touch of whimsy in the heart of the hustle and bustle.

Hollyn watched the people walking down the sidewalks. Some laughing together, others on their phones. Still others were out for an evening jog, their lives going on as if nothing had happened. As if her parents—the only people who'd believed in her, loved her, chosen her, *adopted* her—weren't gone. She'd told herself before . . . everyone leaves. Eighteen years with a permanent family had almost convinced her it was forever. Her parents were amazing, and while this loneliness wasn't the same as what she'd experienced as a little girl . . . it was still loneliness. Emptiness.

She spotted the skyscrapers and felt a hollow sense of desperation, knowing once this . . . adventure was over, she'd be back in Minlan, TN. With Mum and Dad gone, she would leave this incredible city. Alone. There might be gorgeous mountains in Tennessee, but there certainly weren't any skyscrapers that looked akin to futuristic space towers like the Etihad Towers or grand leaning buildings like the Capital Gate. But like this ever-changing city, which had a lot in common with the States, she was once again smacked with change. Heartrending change.

They turned onto Al Ladeem Street heading toward their destination. She'd never been inside LLH Hospital, but Bongani had driven them past it several times, and she was familiar with the area. As Benn maneuvered their vehicle through the more populated part of the city, Hollyn was struck by the seriousness of why they were here in the first place.

Benn stopped at a red light, and she stared out her window.

Davis and the team seemed sure that the palace was the location for the demonstration . . . but if they were wrong? Countless lives could be lost if they didn't stop Archie in time. And whoever he was working for or with. Her stomach twisted just thinking about his betrayal. He—

Wait.

Hollyn sat up straighter. Squinted at the darkness competing against the city lights. She peered through the window toward the hospital. Was that—him!

"It's Archie!"

"What?" Glace jerked to her. "Where?"

"Right—" She lost sight of him as a thick mob pressed in front of him, blocking her line of sight.

"Where?" Glace demanded.

"There—he was right there! Green shirt, crossing the . . . " Even as she tapped the glass, he was again lost amid the sea of people on the street. She grunted. "Well, he was."

"I . . . don't see him," Glace said.

Hollyn strained to see around the intrusive group.

Benn let off the brake just as Archie came back into view. Definitely him. As he hurried along, he kept casting glances over his shoulder. Seeing if he was being followed, maybe?

"There!" Her hand was on her seatbelt buckle before she knew it.

Benn braked again. Cursed. "Can't just park in the street. I'll—" He gunned the engine just as Archie turned and jogged down an alley between the hospital and an apartment high-rise.

"No!" He was *not* getting away! Without another thought, Hollyn threw the door open and launched out. A car in the next lane slammed on its brakes, tires screeching on the pavement. A loud horn blared around the driver's angry slew of Arabic curses as Hollyn palmed the hood, heart lodged in her throat. "Sorry!" Momentum from jumping away spun her but she quickly rebounded and took off in the direction Archie had disappeared. She heard more car horns and yelling behind her—she was sure the team was mad at her for bailing without warning—but didn't hesitate.

*This is dumb. They're going to be ticked when they catch up. Forget that—what if you get lost? Or in trouble.*

She had her phone. No, wait—trying not to slow down, she patted her pants pockets. Drat! She'd left it on the Jeep seat next to her hat. So much for triangulating her if they lost sight.

Hollyn pumped her arms as she raced. Not much she could do now. But she could handle their anger as long as they caught Archie and stopped whatever was about to happen tonight.

She desperately wished Davis weren't across town right now.

*"Intabehe!"* yelled a man she nearly plowed into.

"Sorry!" Hollyn vaulted forward, shoes slapping the concrete. She struggled to keep Archie in view. Saw him duck around a corner. She really wished she'd been a long-distance runner. But no. She'd spent most of her time at a desk in the lab, and trying to haul in a decent breath burned. Her lungs and calves ached, but she wasn't quitting, because he was not going to get away.

Even this late at night, the air was still very warm. It coiled around her and tightened her chest. Made it even harder to breathe. Beads of perspiration formed on her brow. She gasped a breath as Archie vanished around a four-way junction. "No!" she rasped. Shoved herself onward. Tripped over a curb but caught herself and vaulted forward. Banked hard right around the corner of the high-rise.

And slowed. Where . . . where had he gone? No no no. He couldn't—

There! He disappeared through a back door of the apartment building, and Hollyn didn't have time to wonder why he hadn't gone into the hospital. She pitched herself after him. Dove through the opening seconds before the door closed. Stumbling to a stop, her eyes roved the interior. The scuffed cream-and-speckled laminate had seen better days. Two old-school fluorescent lights struggled to fight off the shadows. But the hallway was empty. No Archie in sight.

Fear cuffed her throat as the lights tinkled and blinked out. Back on. *Yeah, not helping . . .* She was alone, armed only with a knife she had no idea how to use except sharp-side-out . . . Right. And here she was charging after someone she should have never trusted. Doubling down, she threw herself around the corner of the empty hallway.

Right into a blur of black. Thudded hard against a chest. Hands grabbed her.

Hollyn screamed as she was thrown to the hard ground. Though her tactical vest buffered her fall, it also impeded flexibility. Pain flared up her arm as she rolled.

"What are you doing?" Archie gritted out.

"Get off!" Fear alive and chugging through her veins, she clawed away from him and shoved off the ground. "Me? How about *you?*" she demanded. Gulped oxygen amid the heavy doses of adrenaline.

"You shouldn't be here!" His good hand fisted. "Run," he hissed at her.

"What?" She must've misheard him. Hollyn peered over his shoulder, praying Glace or Benn would catch up any second.

Aaany second . . .

*Of course they aren't coming. When will you get it that you're alone?*

Davis. She needed Davis.

Archie's eyes widened and he went rigid.

The sudden change in his demeanor concerned her. She frowned. "Wh—"

"Didn't expect to see *you* here." A voice intruded from behind.

Hollyn pulled in a sharp breath as chills skidded down her spine. She knew that voice well, but nothing could have prepared her to hear it. Not now. Not here. When she gathered the courage to slowly turn, she felt the world tilt on its axis.

"No," she whispered.

There, in the middle of the dim hallway . . . was Leila.

## *EMIRATES MANDARIN ORIENTAL PALACE HOTEL, ABU DHABI, UAE*

"Negative confirmation," Blank comm'd, bringing the team up to date on the situation. Davis shook his head as he and Fury continued their search of the hotel exterior.

Where was the twerp? He veered from the group. Decided to search a wider perimeter. In alcoves. Around trees. Under tables. Fury drew in deep breath after deep breath but never alerted.

They were missing something.

One of the perimeter guards walking the other direction nodded to him. "Nothing like babysitting billionaires," the man said in Arabic. The sneer on his face deepened.

Davis huffed like he thought the same, surprised the guy had even acknowledged him, unlike the rest of the security staff. "Least it pays the bills, right?" he replied back in the language he'd been forced to master in Special Forces.

The burly guy hesitated.

Flip . . . had he said it wrong?

The guard barked a laugh. "Barely."

Expelling a breath he'd held, Davis noted Fury sniffing the air around the newcomer. Davis scanned the guy and didn't like the way he tensed. Was he trouble? He prayed not. But then Fury moved on, giving Davis a glance that said *Negative, let's keep searching.*

With a nod, Davis excused himself. After a glance back, he let Fury lead them inside the hotel through a back door. The interior matched the exterior. Everything from the luxury marble floors to the gold accents and fifteen-foot stone walls screamed extravagance.

Fury sniffed around to a point.

Davis reached for his mic, but the shepherd lifted his head and moved on, panting happily.

No alert.

Frustration streaked over Davis's shoulders. "Seek-seek." He refocused his working dog.

Fury trotted down the hallway.

"Alpha Seven." Chapel's voice in his ear rattled.

"This is Seven, go ahead," Davis replied, watching Fury move past every door without so much as a tail wag. *C'mon, dude . . .*

"Einstein is MIA," Chapel stated. "Two and Three are unable to locate the objective but are Charlie Mike."

Davis paused. So Bennion and Glace hadn't found Hollyn. Anger rattled through him. How the blazes had she gone missing?

"Einstein sighted our target but Two and Three could not confirm."

He knew Chapel paused for him to give the expected "good copy," but that was not anything good, and he didn't trust himself to speak.

"Take Fury and haul it over there and put that force multiplier to work."

Now that . . . "Good copy." Davis stalked farther from the party. "*Fuss.*" Fury threw him an annoyed look but snapped into place. They hustled for the Jeep. It would take at least fifteen to twenty minutes to get across town. Minutes they didn't have.

Never should have left her side.

## NEAR LLH HOSPITAL, ABU DHABI, UAE

"*Leila?*" Hollyn couldn't believe her eyes. "I saw you die!" Yet here she was. Standing in the hallway. Very much alive.

But this woman before her wasn't the same one Hollyn had come to call best friend over the last year. Gone was the kindness that had always been one of her most admirable traits and made her approachable. Instead, this version of Leila was a roiling ball of anger and distance. Something dark—sinister, even—hung in the air and made Hollyn take a step back. Right into Archie.

"Surprise." Leila grinned like the Cheshire cat. The nefarious vibe radiating off the woman was almost palpable.

*Get out of here. Run. Now!*

Even as she took a step back, Hollyn registered two giant men standing behind Leila like club bouncers on steroids. Dressed in solid black, they matched Leila. Death squad.

Not good. When the flight part of her instincts finally seized her, Hollyn spun and tried to dart around Archie.

In a flash, he had her. Restrained her.

She kicked. Tried to yank free. "Let me go!"

Powerful hands wrapped around her flailing arms in a vise grip. Halted her efforts to get away. One of the bouncers crushed her back against his granitelike chest.

Leila sauntered forward, eying the tablet in her hands. "Seems your entourage lost track of you." Brown eyes lifting, she clicked her tongue, then cocked her head to the side. "I have to hand it to you guys, though—didn't think the team would split up. It would have been my preference that you all remain at the hotel. Fewer loose ends to tie up separately."

Hollyn swallowed. "So sorry to disappoint you."

"Your boyfriend sure thinks he's on the right track." Leila turned the device around, revealing a live feed of Davis and Fury moving down an Emirates Palace hallway.

*Davis, get out of there!*

This couldn't be happening.

"What's this all about?" Hollyn demanded. She wished more than anything that she'd never gotten out of the vehicle to chase Archie. That she'd listened to Benn. Until the team found her, she'd have to bluff her way through this. Delay them . . . talk. They *would* find her . . . right?

"Oh, come," Leila said, wrinkling her nose. "You're a smart cookie. You tell me."

Anger pulsed through Hollyn's veins. The last thing she wanted to do was entertain or comply with anything this woman said. But each word bought her time. "The lab, the missiles . . . my *parents*." She choked out the last word.

Leila didn't even have the decency to look regretful. Instead, she shrugged. "Collateral damage. I gave your dad the chance to hand over what I wanted before anyone got hurt." She ambled forward. "I know you aren't biologically related to Ansel, but you sure have his thick head." She sniffed. "Do you know what he did with my offer? He refused. Refused!" Another shrug, this time with pursed lips. "What happened next was on him. Not me."

"You can't be serious!" How had she *ever* been fooled about who Leila really was? "Does that logic really work in your twisted brain? You're psychotic, killing innocent people."

The woman rolled her eyes. "Oh please. I did what I had to do." She tapped the screen in her hands. "And I'll *keep* doing what I have to do. You should keep that in mind."

The threat was far from empty. After a few more taps on the device, Leila nodded to Bouncers One and Two, and they forced Hollyn down the hallway.

Digging her heels in, she fought their manhandling, afraid she wouldn't come back from wherever they were taking her. "Where are we going?" If she was going to die, she didn't want to do it being a doormat. "Tell me!"

"I hardly think I answer to you."

It was strange that she didn't seem to have an issue with divulging anything. Eerily so. And if she kept Leila talking and distracted, it might delay . . . whatever was coming. At least long enough for Benn and Glace to find her. *Please, find me. Please, be that good.*

Bouncer Two punched open a door to a flight of stairs, and Bouncer One wrangled her toward the concrete fire well.

Hollyn stuck her boot against the jamb and shoved backward.

Bouncer One stumbled, but it was more like the leaning tower of Pisa—he wasn't going down. Not easily, anyway.

Bouncer Two was there and grabbed her legs. Secured them. Together, the bouncers moved into the fire well.

Hollyn let out a screech that echoed up and down the concrete jungle of wrought iron and mildew. Desperately hoped someone heard it. Anyone. She hauled in a breath to scream again.

A hand clamped over her mouth. It was smelly and clammy. The thought of where his hand had been made her squirm. Struggling to breathe, she bit his palm. He nearly dropped her, and Hollyn realized that hadn't been nearly as smart of a move as she'd thought. If she'd fallen . . . she could've cracked her skull.

Something cold and hard pressed against her temple. Still captive in Bouncer Ones's arms, she stilled. Peered to the side, sickened when she saw the fire in Leila's eyes . . . just past the gun.

"Be a good girl now?"

Bouncers One and Two set her down almost like they were waiting for her to make a move and get herself killed.

Hollyn wanted to rail, argue. But . . . this was a delay. She gave a faint nod. Hoped this gave Benn and Glace time to get closer. And Fury . . . if they got him here, he could track her, right? She needed to leave a scent. How could she make it really clear for him?

An idea struck and she pretended to trip. Quietly spat on the ground.

"Get moving!" Bouncer Two gruffed, yanking her up the stairs.

Gathering every gram of strength she could muster, Hollyn

walked compliantly. Decided to use the time to her benefit. "Why did you fake your death?"

Leila didn't answer. Just kept taking step after step

"The night of the gala"—Hollyn wanted answers—"why did you get me out of the car? Why not kill me too?"

"On the off chance my people could not figure out how to modify the program, I had to keep *someone* alive who could."

She didn't know what she'd been expecting, but it wasn't that.

Leila didn't look back as she climbed the stairs. "After I brought Archie into line, he was only successful in obtaining the first half of your code. So I had to keep you around as insurance." She went silent for a moment before continuing. "Did you tell her about how *you* contacted *me* to sell the program, Arch?"

Shocked, Hollyn faltered. Her stomach churned. "What?" She looked to Archie, who did have the decency to look remorseful. "Is that true?"

The look in his eyes was answer enough.

"He bragged"—Leila really dragged out that word, the resonance echoing in the stairwell—"about having access to a groundbreaking program and offered it up to the highest bidder. Lucky for me, I convinced him to give me a great deal."

"Great for *you*," Archie muttered from behind. "More like blackmail."

More like, but not completely? That meant . . . "I can't believe I ever trusted you," she bit out. Tried to jerk free of Bouncer One, but it only resulted in him clamping her arm even tighter. "I defended you at every turn. How could you do this?"

Forehead creased, he swung a hand out. "I—"

"Do you know how many more people will die now?" Was she the only one of her so-called friends with a moral compass? Compassion? "The fallout could be catastrophic. You of all people knew how adamantly I rejected the military's bid to buy the program because of what they could've turned it into. Why my dad and I insisted we not go public. Then you . . . you . . . do *this*?"

With that, his mouth drew into a firm line. He looked away. "I have my reasons."

Hollyn couldn't stop her jaw from falling open. "What reason could convince you that killing my parents was okay? We welcomed you into our lives, and you destroyed everything!"

Head lowered as he climbed the stairs, Archie was decidedly silent.

Anger shot through her veins, burning hotter and hotter. He was responsible for her parents' murders and . . . he wouldn't say anything other than he had *reasons*?

Then again . . . there wasn't a defense in the world she'd accept! Her parents would still be alive today if not for him.

On the landing, with that thought lingering, Hollyn reconsidered the whole "good girl" thing. A distinctive poke in the back—not a finger, but likely another weapon—nudged her through the door and down a hallway to the right.

Leila stopped at a door, and Bouncer Two opened it.

They stepped into a large apartment. Four marble columns added a touch of over-the-top luxury to the main space, though with a long table and about a dozen chairs, it reminded her more of the command room back at the safe house than the living room it was meant to be. The far side of the room was just a wall of windows.

On another wall, five screens were mounted in a row. Each featured a video feed, different angles around the high rise—no sign of Benn or Glace on the streets below. There was one camera that showed the hospital across from their location and one of the Emirates Palace across town, but both views were highly zoomed out to the point that the whole building could be seen. That likely wasn't a good sign.

Bouncer One shoved her away from the screens toward a pillar near the windows that looked out over the busy street below.

As he bound her hands around the pillar with zip ties, she could feel defeat rising. She didn't bother trying to fight him off. Between the bouncers and the gun holstered at Leila's hip, Hollyn wouldn't get far anyway.

But before the brute blocked her view, Hollyn saw a familiar Jeep parked halfway onto the curb.

Hope welled anew. Maybe the team would find her before it was too late. She needed to stall.

Hollyn's mind raced. "It wasn't you who attacked me, and it wasn't Archie that the team captured before, so who was that back at my home?"

Leila didn't take her eyes off the screen. "Someone who'll be dining with Nemo from now on."

Unsettled at the ominous answer, Hollyn faltered. "What's your end goal here, Leila? If that's even your name."

"My name makes no difference," the woman who was now a stranger answered. In one of the screens on the wall Benn and Glace slid into view. They were searching the perimeter of the apartment high-rise.

Hollyn desperately wished there was a way to warn them what was happening.

Leila typed something into the system, then spoke into a radio. "They're around the east corner."

Near the wall of windows, Archie stared out into the darkness.

Hollyn dropped her gaze to the table, unable to stomach the sight of him. "You're not going to get away with this."

"I already have."

"Davis and Fury will find me." Hollyn's heart raced in her chest. "And when they do—"

"You'll be dead." Leila shook her head. "I just wish I'd be around to see his face." She indicated to the screen where a couple other men similar to Bouncers One and Two stalked along the side of the building. "I'd start saying your prayers now. Once I finish this, I won't need you."

The sickening realization that Leila never intended for Hollyn to make it out alive hit her like a brick wall. No wonder she hadn't held back details.

*What did you do? No matter where you go, people die around you.*

Tears welling, Hollyn trembled. Her bound hands strained against the zip ties, and bile rose in her throat.

"If we're done with the dramatics, I'd like to get on with business. The buyers are waiting, and there's a lot of money poised to fall into my account." Leila glared at Archie. "Watch her. She escapes, you die." With an unaffected sigh, she turned to Hollyn. "I'd say it's been nice knowing you, but who has time for lies? But really, I do owe you thanks. Without that brain of yours, none of this would be possible."

"Don't do this."

Leila grinned as she and the bouncers trudged out of the room. "I'll leave the live feeds up so you have a front-row seat to the deaths of your friends."

"Leila!" Hollyn yelled. "Stop!"

The only response to her demand was the sound of the door lock clicking into place.

# 17



DAVIS NAILED THE ACCELERATOR, BEGGING THE JEEP TC BEAT THE GPS-predicted arrival time. In the backseat, Fury panted heavily. Paced back and forth, his whine piercing the road noise. On Corniche Street, traffic started to slow. "C'mon, c'mon," he muttered, yanking the wheel around one car. Darting behind another. Gunning it. Dang, he needed another route. He took an opening between cars and swerved onto Al Bateen. The dash screen rerouted.

"Find her yet?" He spoke to Benn and Glace through comms, eyes on the road.

"Negative," Benn growled, clearly ticked off.

Davis didn't blame the guy. They didn't have time for this. What had Hollyn been thinking? He tugged his tie free. Undid the top button of his shirt. Stretched his neck. Better.

Looking in the opposite direction, a lady stepped off the curb to cross the road. Her head jerked his way, and the headlights lit her wide-eyed expression.

"Come on " he yelled. Punched the horn and swerved around her.

It'd been years since this level of panic had amped him up. But this was Hollyn he was talking about. The one person he wanted to protect more than anything in this life and was failing at right now. Squeezing the wheel, he knew what he had to do.

"Okay!" he prayed aloud. "You've got my attention now, all right?" He felt dumb verbalizing this but continued. "I can't do this without Your help. I get it now."

He swung around a BMW.

"Please," he continued. "I need You to get me there before anything happens to her. I'm sorry I've been MIA for so long thinking I could do everything on my own. Just . . . don't let her pay the price for my silence."

Immediately, something he couldn't quite put a name to flared to life in his chest. He'd take that as God letting him know he'd been heard. His resolve not to let this end badly doubled. Hollyn put her trust in the Big Guy. It was time he did too.

Streetlights splayed over the windshield like a blinking bulb as the Jeep barreled down the street. Davis swung in and out of traffic.

Fury whined his feelings near Davis's ear.

"Same, bud."

They took another couple turns before pulling alongside the curb. Davis threw the vehicle in Park and shot out of the driver's seat to release Fury. His eighty-pound beast surged from the vehicle, whipping Davis around and racing down the street to where Benn and Glace were waiting in the shadows across the alley from the hospital.

"Still nothing?" Davis ran after Fury toward the team.

"She left her phone in the car when she bolted," Glace updated him. Then handed him the baseball hat Hollyn had taken with her when they left the safe house. "Also left this, but there was no way to track her without the dog. We lost eyes around the corner there." She pointed toward LLH Hospital. "We've searched but found no trace of her."

"Thinking she's close by," Bennion said. "Could be in the apartment building, but it'll take time to search."

Davis frowned. Nodded curtly at the implied *time we don't have* tag. "Fury will find her." He keyed his mic. "Alpha Actual, update?"

"Negative visual."

This wasn't adding up. Maybe he and Hale had gotten it wrong.

Locals eyed them with keen interest, likely due to the M4s Bennion and Glace were carrying. They murmured to each other in Arabic. No doubt the authorities would show up soon. The team needed to move.

As if on cue, Blank's steady voice came over comms. "Two, Three, and Seven, be advised: multiple emergency calls to ADP about suspicious gunmen. We count three ADP response vehicles en route and closing fast."

What he wouldn't give to have her drone in the area instead of at the hotel.

"Let's go," he said to the team members. Leaned down so Fury could sniff the baseball cap.

The shepherd sniffed it intently. Nosed it around, tail still as he took in a few deep whiffs of scent.

"Seek-seek."

Fury's head dropped and tail went up. He tracked in a circle before taking off in the direction Glace had indicated earlier. Pacing his landshark, Davis watched him plow scents along the street. Could feel the team hustling behind them.

Between the hospital and another tall building, the sidewalk widened and the crowd thinned. Gasps and yelps seemed to push the pedestrians from Fury's pace. They were smart to give him a wide berth at this point, but it definitely wasn't the way he'd hoped this would go down. Probably get their butts chewed out by Chapel once this was over.

"Someone call the police!" one person shouted in Arabic.

"Already did!" another replied.

Great.

Fury tracked, unfazed by the chaos and the complaints about his presence. Zigzagging down the path—once trotting toward a woman who dropped her purse as she scrambled away, afraid he was coming for her—he worked the scent cone. Paused now and then only to press on a second later. Around the corner, an alley opened up behind the Golden Tower. Aptly named seeing as every piece of the structure of glass reflected like sun in a brilliant gold.

"K9, update?"

"Fury is tracking a scent, but nothing yet." No signs of Hollyn, no proof she'd come this way. But Fury's nose never lied. The shepherd's scent cone narrowed rapidly, leading him straight up to a back door. He shoved his snout against the threshold and hauled in several long draughts. He eased back and pawed it. Jumped up on his hind legs and pressed before dropping and spinning in a tight circle. He looked to Davis and barked.

"Here!" Davis spoke to the others. Lowered his weapon and inspected the handle. Looked clear. And Fury hadn't planted his backside to indicate explosives. He gripped Fury's lead and nodded to Bennion, who took point and breached with Glace behind him to clear ahead. Davis trailed the duo with Fury.

Two dim lights lit the hallway. At the first corner, an earsplitting alarm rang out.

Benn swore. "Move, move!"

They jogged forward. Cleared the corner just before screaming sounded from the upper floors. Doors slammed and the rumble of dozens of people running could be felt. It mingled with the piercing screech coming from the alarm. Fury seemed to sense the urgency and sped up his track.

Davis followed his partner, watching for any alerts. Prayed Hollyn was here and he wasn't too late.

Benn nodded toward the staircase and paused.

Everyone in the building was about to be headed their way.

## *GOLDEN TOWERS, ABU DHABI, UAE*

Street noise from several stories below the apartment room filtered in despite the thick glass. From her place in one of the corners, Hollyn glared at Archie as he paced back and forth.

"Hollyn, please hear me out." He took a step toward her.

"Hear you out?" She balked, adjusting her stance to reduce the strain on her shoulders from having her arms hooked around a marble column, hands zip-tied on the other side. "Look at me! You have me tied to a column. You killed my parents. And you want me to *hear you*?"

He huffed. "You were always too smart for your own good. That column is insurance. I don't want you to get hurt trying to escape."

"Is that a threat?"

Archie faltered. "No—that's not . . . I didn't mean—"

"What kind of monster are you, doing this to someone who called you friend, took you on trips, spent countless hours debugging your code?" she growled, her throat raw. But who cared? "What did my parents ever do to you to deserve being murdered? What did *any* of us do that you'd betray us?"

He took another step. "Nothing—"

"Exactly!" she spat. "Yet you couldn't help but seize your chance to steal from us to make a buck." Hollyn strained against the zip ties but felt her shoulders scream in protest. "I can't believe I ever trusted you! You *snake*!"

His face went ashen and he slumped back. "I don't expect you to understand."

"Well, good! Nothing you'd say could make this okay or bring my parents back!" Hot tears pricked her eyes, and she blinked them back. She was so far beyond shedding another tear for him. Time for another tactic. "Be thankful I'm tied to this column."

A smirk said he wasn't concerned about what she could do to him were she freed. Anger bubbling, she focused on the ties. She'd prove to him he had something to worry about. The zip ties caught on a notch in the marble. Hope leapt. If she could just use that nock in the marble . . . maybe she could wear down the integrity of the ties, break them. Just like she'd do to him. The coward!

"It's not going to work," Archie said quietly.

Hollyn gritted her teeth. Kept going. A burn started in her wrists where the sharp edges of her binding bit into her skin. What was a burn if it kept her alive? Determination dug deeper.

"Stop!" he yelled, launching forward.

She started, meeting his gaze briefly, but then resumed. If he wanted her to quit, she'd try harder! She refused to quit.

"Hollyn, it's never going to break. Give up."

Glowering at him, she didn't.

"Fine." He lifted his chin, anger darkening his eyes. "But we both know you're never going to break them like that."

In fact, she *did* know. That's what ticked her off more. Here she was, trapped with the man responsible for murdering her parents and destroying her life, and she had no way to get free. No way to tell Davis or the others where she was. No digging herself out of the hole . . . the one she'd jumped into.

*Looks like you're shouldering your fair share of the blame, Hollyn.*

Arms aching and burning, she slowed to a stop. Slumped against the column and shook her head. Studied the guy she'd considered a friend. Worked with. Laughed with. What had possessed him to do such a horrible thing to her and her family? She knew things like that were as unanswerable as existential questions, but . . . she had to know. "Why did you do it?"

Brown eyes slowly dragged to hers, and there, for the first time, she saw . . . apology. Regret. It permeated his posture. He dropped into a chair. Tapped the armrest in that irritating way of his that always drove her mad.

"Why!" she demanded.

"My sister" He pushed his glasses up. Stared at her as if that explained everything.

"Your sister *what*?"

He huffed and bent forward, shoving his thick black hair from his forehead. The curls hooked together and stayed in place but made him look slightly crazed. "She was diagnosed with a condition I can never pronounce, and it'll take hundreds of thousands of dollars to treat. No insurance will touch it. Too risky."

She wasn't exactly unfeeling, but how did his sister's life take precedence over her parents'? Over her own? She guarded her expression when he looked her way, not wanting him to think she was caving.

"Yes, I stole from you," he croaked out. "But it was to help *her*." His eyes turned to muddy pools beneath unshed tears. "I didn't realize who or what I was getting involved with until it was too late."

This . . . this was the side of Archie that had made her befriend him in the first place. But still . . . "People buying black-market data don't typically live by the golden rule, Archie." He had to see that, right? "It's not rocket science."

"In a way, it is . . . okay, *missile* science." He looked miserable as he paced to the windows. "You aren't telling me anything I haven't already told myself a dozen times over. But . . . Leila threatened both of my sisters if I didn't help her get the rest of the code."

"Why didn't you just tell us?"

"Tell you what? That I was a thief?"

"Yes! Something. Anything! You had every chance in the world." Hollyn tried to keep calm, be understanding, but it was difficult. The if-onlys bouncing around her brain were shrieking at her. She could think of a dozen different paths he could have chosen. Hugging the column, wrists and shoulders aching, she slid to the floor. Rested her head against the cold surface, feeling defeated. Frustrated. Secretly hopeful that Davis and Fury would come barreling through the door . . .

"I'm sorry," Archie said quietly as he slumped against the wall. "I'll never be able to tell you that enough."

"Save it. I'm not interested." Who knew if she could even trust his words? Maybe he was just playing her again, manipulating her to get what these other people wanted. "How does Braum fit into all of this? What she said before—did . . . did she kill him?"

Archie nodded. "She makes good on her promises."

Which meant she only had till Leila came back to get free. "Help me escape."

"Are you crazy? I can't do that!" Eyes wide, he pushed his glasses up the bridge of his nose again.

"Seriously? So what you said about being sorry—that was just a load of garbage?"

He started pacing again. Looked at the screens on the wall.

Hollyn couldn't see Leila in any of them—or anyone else she recognized, for that matter. "So, letting her kill my parents wasn't enough—now you'll let her kill me too?" She sniffed. "Guilt is going to be your only friend when this is all said and done. And if you think she'll really do anything to help your sisters, you're out of your skull." Her heart was pounding. She *had* to get him to help her, or she was as good as dead.

"Stop talking!"

A sharp siren pierced the rest of his sentence, and Hollyn ducked, forehead brushing against the cold pillar. Wished she could press her hands over her ears. "What is that?" She tried to think. "Is it the fire alarm?" Pushing to her feet, she tried to shift around to see him. "Archie! Please—help me!"

But he just darted to the screens, frantically searched each. For what, she wasn't sure. Could hardly think straight with the screaming alarm. Hollyn started rubbing the zip ties up and down again. "Archie!"

He turned. "I can make this right. I'll show you."

Never. He could *never* make this right.

"Wh—"

He ran across the room to the door. Before she could yell his name again, he was gone.

"No, no!" She panicked, gaze skidding around the room, trying to find something, some tool to free herself. "Please," she cried out to God, "I don't want to be burned alive."

So this was it? Whether by Leila or a fire, she was going to die?

Hollyn jerked her hands, trying one last time to get free, but the ties wouldn't budge. It was no use. A ball of emotion lodged in her throat as she stopped fighting. She couldn't free herself, and no one was going to find her in time. Bouncing her legs, whimpering, she yanked again on the ties. Dagger-like pain sliced into her wrists. Warmth slid across her inner forearm.

Defeated, she broke down crying. Why? Why had all this happened? It wasn't fair! She'd tried to create a technology to *help* people! Now Mum and Dad had died for it. *She* would die! Tears choking her, she could only think about her parents. They'd been so senselessly robbed of their lives. The only people who'd ever cared about her, who'd adopted her, made her their own. And they were gone. And now she'd never know a life with Davis.

*I didn't even have the guts to tell him I loved him.*

That ache bloomed across her chest, tightening. Squeezing. If she could just have one more chance . . . but no. It wasn't coming. No one was coming. Because nobody was promised tomorrow. How many times had that been proven throughout her life? Enough to believe it.

Through teary eyes, she scanned the room. Saw through the far window that night had stolen into the day. Oh, she wished to see the stars one more time.

Her gaze hit the door. Was there smoke? She sniffed. Didn't smell anything . . . "Help me!" she screamed, and gave a hard yank on the ties. Cried out as the ties became like scalpels, slicing into her wrists. She rested her cheek on her arm and cried, tugged again. The pain was too much. But if she stayed, she'd die. Alone.

It always ended up that way, didn't it?

Could she . . . reach something? Maybe from the desk. Blinking around her tears, she eyed the table . . . papers there. The desk below the wall of TV screens. Shoot! Nothing to use. The grating claxon hammered her head, made it ache. From the hall came the thuds and screams of people running. It was going to be the last thing she ever heard. How depressing was that?

No. She wasn't a quitter. Never had been. But what on earth could she do? She rotated herself around the column, again searching for something to help her break the zip ties. She bobbed in frustration, desperate to be free.

She was not dying like this!

"God, please!!"

Wait wait wait . . .

Her knife.

Leila's guards had taken it off her once they got inside the room. With more focus this time, she shimmied around the column, searching the table and desk. Recalled hearing it clatter against a surface. She prayed it was still here.

Not on the desk. Or the table. Defeat punched her in the gut.

Of course it wouldn't be. They wouldn't have left—

A glint snagged her attention. She sucked in a breath and strained to see by the chair in front of the screens. There! It'd fallen. And thank God, because they'd have probably pocketed it.

"Thank You!" she cried.

Without wasting a second, Hollyn lowered herself to the ground. Stretched out on her stomach. Reached with her toe toward the chair. Inched closer to the beacon of hope. Screams and thuds pounded the hall. Thankfully, no smoke filtered under the door yet, but that might not mean much.

Her shoe connected with the blade. She sucked in a breath. Applied pressure and tried to drag it backward. The sole of her shoe slid over the blade. With a grunt, she tried again. Lengthened her body out as long as she could be and felt the sting of the zip ties digging into her flesh. Failed again.

Thumping her head against the column, she cried. It was useless. She was useless. She'd been right—she would die alone. Those she loved always . . . left. One way or another.

*"It'll be okay, Hol."* Davis's words played in her head. Gave her an iota of strength to build on. She had to believe that. It wasn't over till it was over.

Growling into the pain, Hollyn stretched . . . stretched. Pinned the hilt this time. Slowly, firmly drew the toe of her shoe toward herself. The knife surrendered. Exultant, she had to force herself to stay calm, keep the blade coming closer. Once she got it close enough, she hiked onto her knees. Angled awkwardly to get the knife even closer. Then she stood and nudged it to the column. Again, shimmied around and went back to her knees, grasping the blade. Relief rushed through her, and she took a moment to let herself shudder a few tears.

Okay. "Now for step two." She winced as she slowly, carefully manipulated her hold on the knife so she could saw through the ties. One wrong twitch and she could lose control of her only chance at escape.

Carefully—so carefully—she tried to work it into a solid grip but couldn't get the right angle. Man, her head was throbbing from that stupid alarm. With the lack of smoke, she was starting to wonder if someone had pulled it on purpose.

*Worry about that later. Refocus.*

"Come on," she muttered.

Finally! Had the knife firmly in hand. She positioned the blade under the zip ties—fingers trembling—and started to saw.

When she glanced up, she froze. Squinted for a better look at one of the video feeds. Was that . . .

Davis! And Fury!

A relieved whimper scampered up her throat. But where were they? She realized then she didn't even know where the feeds were coming from. But by the look of the laminate stairs and the sea of people fleeing in the opposite direction, Davis was here. In this building!

"Davis!" she screamed. Oh my gosh. They were here! Looking for her. She wasn't alone. Hollyn watched them jog up a flight and then another, Benn and Glace close behind. Just the sight of them gave her confidence that she'd be rescued.

So happy, she nearly lost her hold on the knife. Barely recovered. "Focus!" she told herself as she started rubbing the blade along the plastic as best she could. Which wasn't great considering the only angle she could get made it difficult to apply much pressure. But it was a start. She'd take it.

Hollyn kept an eye on Davis. He and Fury would disappear from one security camera just to appear in another. Then the miracle came—she saw him stalking down a hall . . . and heard heavy footfalls. A keening. In the hall.

"Help!" She screamed at the top of her lungs, even though the fire alarm masked most of her voice. "Davis! *Help*! I'm here!"

# 18



"Move! Out of the way!" Davis barked in Arabic at the people running the opposite direction down the stairs.

Fury threaded the legs of the hundreds moving en masse down the stairs in a panic. He dodged more than one person unwilling to move and bounded up the stairs like the master tracker he was.

Davis struggled to stay with him, people not as willing to yield their path to him. Clearly, the landshark had a scent he was tracking, so Davis wouldn't call him off. They needed to find Hollyn before the twerp got her killed.

Gun in position, he negotiated the fastest path through the flood of bodies. The deafening claxon of the alarm drilled into his nerves. His gut tightened when he realized he'd lost line of sight on Fury. "Moving to third floor," Davis huffed into the comms. "Fury has a scent."

"Copy," Glace replied. "Two and Three twenty meters behind you."

Good. Davis strained to find Fury.

A blur of fur ahead keyed him into Fury shooting left at the landing.

Davis plowed through the oncoming throng and hauled it up the last few steps. Weapon tucked close in position sul once more, he cleared the corner and moved into the passage. Past seven stragglers making their way toward him, he spotted Fury hauling scents up and down the hall.

Two faltered halfway down the hall and pinned themselves to the wall, terrified of the dog working the scent cone.

"Clear out, clear out. Move," he ordered the three, motioning them past him as he closed the distance. They bolted for the stairs as soon as Davis stalked by. He shifted and gave his four-legged partner room to work. Listened for anything out of the ordinary. Which was difficult with the alarm still trying to split their ears open.

When the shepherd went from a brisk walk to a full-on run, Davis took off after him. Near the midway point of the hall, Fury suddenly slid to a stop. Head swung back and forth, tail up. "Whatcha got, bud?" he asked, closing the distance, keeping his weapon held close and down as he visually searched the door and threshold. He strained to listen around that stupid fire alarm—which was clearly a false one. Who'd triggered it? He advanced to his dog and heard a noise. Paused. Cocked his head to hear better.

Was that a muffled yell?

Fury bolted two doors down and, snout pressed to the threshold, dragged in thick draughts of air. He did a head tilt, then planted his butt in front of the door. Stayed there, statue still, gaze boring holes in the door.

"Good boy," Davis breathed, moving to the door. He palmed it to verify it wasn't hot from a fire, even though he saw no smoke. Ear to the barrier, he listened again. Rapped on the door. "Security! Anyone in there?"

He heard something that blended with the alarm. "Hollyn?" he shouted.

"Yes! I'm here!"

Davis saw Benn and Glace hustling up on his left, so he stepped back, lifted his right leg, and nailed the door with his boot. It bucked, but a crack splintered down the jamb. He did it again amid an excited whimper from Fury, who barked.

The door surrendered. Cracked open.

Fury sailed into the room like the landshark he was

When nobody fired at Fury, Davis moved into the room, weapon up. First thing he spotted was Hollyn anchored to a marble column like a horse at a hitching post. It ticked him off, but he kept himself in check. Knew that was a classic lure—get him to rush into the room to save the hostage, then kill him. So he focused on clearing. Heard Bennion do the same and Glace rush to Hollyn. The room held a table littered with papers and a wall of monitors. Checked a door—closet. Another accessed a bathroom.

"Clear." Davis holstered his weapon and pivoted toward Hollyn. Dropped to a knee and produced his KA-BAR. "You okay?"

"Light bruises. Nothing significant." Glace provided the medic's rundown of her condition.

"Yeah . . . "

The tremor in her voice punched his gut. He sliced through the zip ties, his gaze scanning her for injuries. In a blink, she leapt at him. Thudded into his chest, arms coiled tight around his neck.

"You're okay. I've got you."

"You came. I can't believe you came."

Davis swallowed at how deeply those words dug past his tac vest and years-hardened heart.

"I'm sorry," she murmured, her lips moving against his neck as she shuddered. "I'm so sorry! I should've listened. Stayed put."

Surprised at her words and the way she'd thrown herself at him, Davis held her tight. Heard as much as felt Fury sniffing

Hollyn's face and swiping his tongue along her cheek. He ruffed the shepherd's head, knowing Fury wasn't too thrilled when others "attacked" him. "You're okay now. It's okay. I wanted to kill you when I heard you'd left."

He tried to laugh but couldn't. Felt a primal need to know she was okay, wasn't injured. "You're safe now. That's what matters." He wasn't sure if he was saying that for her or for himself. That's when the desperate, frantic realization rushed through him—he loved her and would do anything for her. "I'll always come for you." When she eased back, he framed her face with a hand. Swept his thumb over the bruise forming on her cheek. He bent in to be sure she was listening, she truly heard that. "Always."

Her blue and green eyes took him in.

Somehow, his mouth was on hers. He sealed the promise, letting the kiss linger. Letting himself become entrenched in that commitment.

"Hey, lovers, we need to wrap this up," Bennion groused.

Davis cupped her face. Wanted to say so much more, but he knew, in her life, words had been cheap. So many had left. Even her adoptive parents. He helped her upright but didn't let go of her hand.

"Give us a rundown on what happened."

Grief played havoc on her features. "I've been so stupid."

"Not possible. You're the smartest person I know."

Something faltered in her expression as she stared at him. Swallowed. Then wiped her eyes. "It's Leila—it's been her the whole time."

"The dead girl?" Glace balked, giving Benn a confused look.

"She's not dead—she was here. She's the mastermind behind the whole thing, and holy wow, that girl has a cold, wicked streak the size of Alaska!"

Behind them, Benn's curse wasn't completely drowned out by the fire alarm.

"You're sure?" Glace asked.

"I told you—she was right here. Held a gun to my head. Trust me, I know my fr—" Hollyn stopped mid-word, sickened that she'd ever called that woman "friend." She nodded. "It was her. And she's not alone. Archie's working with her—blackmailed, but he chose money over my parents' lives."

Davis grunted. "Knew he was a piece of—"

"Any idea where they went?" Bennion asked as he slung his M4 to his back, folded his arms, and studied the screens. "Not seeing him on the surveillance feeds."

The words drew Davis over. He saw the hall, apartment foyer. The back alley. Exact one they'd use to infil . . . "Saw us coming."

Benn nodded to a lower-right screen. "A klick out."

Davis eyed another more active screen. "That's the dignitary event." He rubbed his jaw. "She had a contingency plan."

"What does that mean?" Hollyn asked.

Davis shifted to face her. "D'you know where they went? Did they say?" He noted Fury searching the room. Kept track as he listened.

"No . . . I don't know." She shrugged. "Leila and the bouncers with her left . . . maybe ten or fifteen minutes ago. Then Archie took off saying he was going to stop her."

"Stop her?" Glace challenged. "Thought you said they were working together."

"They are—*were*—I don't know." She kneaded her temples. "Archie tried to sell my program to her, but that's where the blackmail came into play. We have to find her." Her eyes widened, and she caught Davis's sleeve. "She said the buyers were waiting, that she'd have a lot of money soon."

"Not good," Bennion muttered.

"Missile launch," Davis suggested with a nod.

"Has to be," Hollyn said gravely. "She's trying to prove that it can do what she promised—that has to be it because she said she wouldn't have a need for me. If I can get my hands on the tablet she's using to run the AI, there's a chance I can hack in and stop the launch even after it's been started."

"How much of a chance?" Glace asked.

"Doesn't matter. *Chance* is better than *no chance*," Benn said. But a scowl was etched onto his face. "So, clear the hotel and palace?"

Thinking through what they'd learned, Davis considered the guy. "If not an entire square mile." His gaze shifted to the screens again. "Anyone got eyes on them?"

A round of "negative" answered.

"Can't move against them until we know where they went." He returned his attention to Hollyn. "You have any ideas?"

She gave a halfhearted shrug.

He touched her shoulder. "I know it's been a lot, but . . . we need actionable intel."

"Leila didn't say."

There was something in her voice and expression that made Davis still. He frowned at her. Couldn't believe what he saw in her eyes. "I . . . don't believe you."

Those eyes widened almost imperceptibly. Her lips parted and color flushed her cheeks. "Are you calling me a liar?"

Her tone, the flush that now seemed infused with anger, warned him to tread carefully. "Hollyn, I'm not—"

Fury's incessant barking drew them around just in time to see his sable coat vanish out the door that hung crookedly on its hinge.

Davis hissed an oath and darted to the hall. "Fury, heel." His boy bolted down to the stairs, barked loudly, hackles raised.

"Stay with her," Benn muttered as he hurried that way, M4 at the ready and Glace trailing him toward the stairwell.

Ear trained on the room—all quiet—Davis watched the two. Whistled to his boy, who suddenly whipped around and came trotting back. "What was it?"

"Didn't see anything." Benn shrugged.

Davis turned as the alarm suddenly fell silent, the emptiness of that noise suddenly deafening and gaping.

Davis's ears rang in the wake of quiet emptiness. "'Bout freakin' time." He shifted just as a loud creak popped from his left. He pivoted that way, weapon out and trained on the shadows. Saw a smear of green duck through a door. No. Couldn't be . . . Heart in his throat, confusion rank, he jerked his gaze to the room—to Hollyn. And pitched himself down the hall. "Hollyn!"

He whipped open the door marked Roof in Arabic and shoved himself up the stairs. Saw her boot round another flight. He sucked in a breath. Toed the next step. Threw himself up, reaching out . . .

Caught her boot even as the steps thumped his chest.

She yelped and tripped.

Davis lunged and caught her calf.

"Let go," she cried out. Turned and tried to kick him off.

Hardcore determination dug into him. He fisted her shirt and held her in place. "What're you doing?"

Watery eyes held his. "Please—just let me do this."

He dragged himself up until they were even. Found his knees, huffing out the effort it took to interdict. "No."

"I can't put anyone else in dan-"—a sob choked her word—"-ger. Please . . . "

Heart rending, Davis pulled her to her feet. Braced her against the wall even as he heard the others shift into place around them. "What'd I tell you? Down there in the room—what'd I tell you?"

She considered him, locked in a visual duel it seemed, then realization fell over her fair features. The dam broke and she dropped her head to his chest. "That you'd come for me."

Holding her close, hand cupping the back of her head, he breathed against her ear, "Always. Even if it means protecting you from yourself."

"I can stop her," she moaned. "If I just—"

"Her brand of evil only uses people."

She swallowed her tears and her grief. "If I help her, then—"

"Then your hands are bloodied too. For what? At what cost? How many lives?"

She gripped his shirt. "I don't want anyone else to get hurt because of me. Everyone I love always does . . ."

He smirked. "I'm not hurt . . ."

Bennion groaned loudly. "I can change that."

"Shut up." Davis grinned as he guided her into the narrow corridor. A tall, thin window gave them light. "We'll talk more later—what do you know? What sent you up this maintenance passage?"

Gnawing her lip for a moment, Hollyn hesitated. Her brows knotted, her eyes again watering.

"Trust me, Holly Hobbie."

"Not fair, using that nickname."

"Wasn't meant to be."

She shuddered a sigh. "The roof. I think that's where she is."

The rest of the team needed to get out of the hotel vicinity. "Why the roof? Only exfil would be a chopper, and if they struck the hotel with the dignitaries, the smoke would inhibit visibility."

"She's hosting a demonstration of the drone-guided missile. She said the buyers were waiting. That means showing proof. Best place for that is—"

"The roof." He struggled to breathe. "You really think she'd do it right here?"

"She's cocky," Hollyn said. "She was shocked we figured out where she was operating. And she thinks I'm tied up and with Archie, so I'm guessing she wouldn't think she needs a backup or exit strategy. She left me in the room with the intention of returning to kill me."

Davis tensed. "How do you know that?"

Hollyn shrugged, her lower lip trembling. "No loose ends, she said."

"I'll be very happy to send Fury after her." As he keyed his mic, he glanced at Benn and Glace, who looked both relieved to have intel and frustrated that Hollyn hadn't shared the intel when they'd asked. "Base, this is Actual."

"Go ahead, Actual," Chapel replied.

"Evacuate the hotel."

"Say again—"

"New threat targeting the hotel with a drone-guided missile. Known terrorist is Leila Pierce."

"Thought we were hunting Archi—"

"Complicit minion. Recommend immediate evac of the building."

A curse sailed through the comms as Davis made a signal for Two and Three to get moving. "We will hunt down and interdict. We could use some eyes in the sky."

"Actual, this is Blank. Eagle heading your way."

Benn peered out the wall of dark windows. "Looks like we've got company. Paw Patrol on-site. Heading into the building."

He nodded to Davis and Glace, and they were on the move. "Stairs only," he said.

"Looks like I'm about to get my steps in," Glace said with a winsome smirk.

Benn frowned.

"Twenty-six flights . . . minus three," she explained.

"Lady," he said to Hollyn. "Next time, can't you try to escape using an elevator?" The big guy huffed and cocked his head. "Twenty-three floors of fish-in-a-barrel." He stretched his neck. "Fun times, here we come."

Blank's soft, Southern voice twanged through the comms. "Actual, drones show four unfriendlies on the roof—three males, one female. Confirmation on Archie Durand. Negative facial rec on the others."

"Good copy. Base, we're heading topside." Davis whispered a prayer of thanks for thermal imaging that the drone could use.

It wasn't lost on him how easily that response of turning to God had just come. Maybe there was hope for him yet.

"The female has to be Leila," Hollyn said. "If they confirmed Archie, then he's with her."

Legs aching, lungs burning, they continued their climb. Finally hit the twenty-sixth floor. Davis deferred lead to Glace and Benn, who shouldered the wall next to the door, peering through the small window.

Davis stayed with Hollyn, and she'd vowed a couple of times that she wouldn't run again. Fury, on the other hand, though he panted heavily, was still a ball of energy. The elevators Benn had moaned about were still inoperable after the fire alarm, which locked them down automatically. Not that they'd all climb in and make their deaths easy for the enemy.

"What'd you see?"

"Four, just like Blank said," Benn confirmed with a nod. "I can take out two of them but wouldn't have a clear line of sight because of that transformer."

"Okay, neutralize them, and I'll come up around to our nine." He eyed Glace and Hollyn. "Take cover behind the transformers." Anticipating Glace's rejection of hiding instead of fighting, he nodded to her. "Keep her safe for me. Please."

Lips thinned, she gave a curt nod.

"On my count. Three . . . "

Benn adjusted his stance to erupt out the door, weapon tucked into his shoulder.

"Two . . . *one!*"

# 19



HEAD DOWN, BENT OVER, HOLLYN RUSHED OUT BEHIND NORA before the door could close. The scent of saffron and cistus wafted up from the street below as they shimmied up behind a transformer even as shots peppered the air. Heart in her throat, she could only pray that Davis wasn't hurt or killed.

She knelt next to Nora, who inched closer to the end and peered around the large gray steel box.

"What's happening?" she whispered. The gusty wind and droning machines swallowed her words.

And then Glace was gone, striding forward, shooting.

What?

Hollyn scooted forward. Saw a dozen more men coming from a secondary fire well on the other side of the roof Oh no . . .

Leila stood near the edge of the roof, holding Archie hostage. More like a shield, because they all knew the woman would kill him if—no, when it suited her. A snarl yanked her attention to Fury, who fought with Davis against two men. Guns clattered to the roof.

The chaos of the conflict was mind-numbing. Hollyn prided herself on her ability to multitask, but this situation nearly shut her down. Who was she supposed to help? Nora Glace was clearly a skilled operator, moving with determination and precision, taking down one target, then going hand-to-hand with another.

And Hollyn was sitting here cowering.

Archie somehow broke free from Leila. Lunged toward one of the weapons that had clattered across the rooftop.

Oh no you don't.

Hollyn raced toward it and kicked the weapon, her boot connecting first with Archie's hand, then—inadvertently—his head. She should feel bad, but after all he'd done to her . . . all the grief he'd caused . . .

He whipped back and his head struck something. He collapsed with a strange wheeze that somehow carried over the din. His body went still.

Hollyn's heart did a double beat. Had she just—

*Ping! Ding-ding!*

With a yelp, she realized she was standing in the middle of a gunfight. She ducked—and even as she did, she saw Leila crouched along the safety wall at the edge of the building, tapping furiously on her device.

Oh no. No no no.

Hollyn peered out. Could Davis or Bennion intervene? "Stop her," she called out.

Bullets pinged the metal transformer, forcing her back.

Blinking around the dust and debris kicked up, she looked over at Leila. Still crouched. Still tapping. Absolutely unfazed by how many men had fallen in her defense in the past few minutes. They were only numbers to her. "C'mon . . . c'mon . . . " She willed Davis or Benn—someone—to see her. But they were all engaged in fights. The last time she'd leapt without looking—to pursue Archie—hadn't ended up well. In fact, she'd been a hostage. Nearly killed.

She had to do something. Couldn't let more people get killed. With one more check to Davis and Fury, fighting a vicious battle with two different guys now, Hollyn thrust herself up. Sprinted across the distance. Dived into a distracted Leila, who looked up too late to stop her. Knocked her back. Took her to ground.

Momentum carried Hollyn into the concrete wall. *Crack!* Pain skidded down her neck and shoulders. Her vision blurred.

She groaned but struggled back up. Knew Leila—

"You stupid—"

A missile made of fur and teeth careened into Leila Clamped onto her arm. Her scream ricocheted as the two tumbled. Leila bent backward—and the two went over the wall.

"No!" Hollyn screamed, shoving herself forward.

Davis manifested out of nowhere, his face a mural of rage and panic. He careened toward the edge, and Hollyn's stomach climbed into her throat.

He collided with the edge of the roof.

"Fury!" Davis barked.

She half expected him to go over the side as well, but he wedged himself in. Straining. That's when she realized he had hold of the shepherd.

A strange, foreboding silence dropped over the roof sans any other attackers. Light seared their vision as a chopper whirled overhead with a spotlight.

Bennion darted forward and grabbed hold of Davis's belt as the two struggled to pull the dog back up.

A sickening compulsion pushed Hollyn to peer over the edge. That's how she saw a panicked Leila holding on to the dog, who was yelping and whining as Davis struggled to keep the two from dropping. Without warning, Fury shook his spine and snapped at the clinging Leila. A chunk of fur came loose . . . and freed Fury of the weight of the woman, who fell away . . .

Hollyn gasped. Couldn't watch. She jerked back and dropped with her back to the wall, squeezing her eyes tight, willing that last image of shock and terror on Leila's visage to go away. She didn't need that image seared into her brain. The sound of fading screams was enough. Please, God . . .

"Hollyn!" Hands gripped her.

She looked up at Davis, who shoved something into her hands. When she glanced down at what landed in her lap, she felt sick. The program . . . "She launched it."

"Stop it!" Davis barked.

"I . . . " Her fingers obeyed his command, even if her mouth and brain weren't there yet. "I don't know if I can . . . "

"Base, this is Actual. Missiles launched," Davis spat. He leaned in to examine the tablet. "Two mikes to impact."

"Can you stop it?" Glace crouched next to her.

It took a hot second for her to simply bypass the security protocols without an error. Her shaking hands had been defying her efforts. "Now to redirect the navigation . . . " She worked through it and breathed in relief.

Correcting navigation.

She gaped at the message on the screen. "No." She redirected again.

Correcting navigation.

"No no . . . " What was going on?

"You can stop it, right?" Bennion's voice was gruff, urgent. "Hurry up, Hollyn. We aren't made to withstand a detonation."

"Hollyn?" Davis leaned in slightly.

"If everyone would shut up!" Regret tugged at her, but gratefully, silence ensued. "Sorry." She typed as fast as she could, brain straining to figure out why . . . "The AI is fighting me . . . " Her heart leapt. "No, it's thinking . . . protecting its purpose." Which was good in a lot of situations . . . but really bad right now.

"Not that I'm rushing you, but we're negative one minute." Bennion's voice was low. Tight with irritation.

"And you'll be negative a body part if you don't stop talking," Glace hissed at him.

It was terrifying enough with the clock countdown that

hovered in the upper right-hand corner. To have him telling her to . . . *Just focus. Get it stopped.* But . . . why wasn't it working? She'd entered the right . . . "The code . . . it's not working."

"What code?"

"The AI's kill code. I have to kill the AI because it's correcting the misdirection I sent it so it'd detonate in the ocean." She growled as she tried again. "Why isn't it working?" It was the right code. Why? What was she doing wrong? "The AI . . . "

45 seconds.

Dad had changed it . . . preventative measure . . .

"Thirty . . . "

Which meant . . . "I've got it. Hang on." She found the program where her algorithm was nestled. Accessed it.

The system prompted: Password

Hollyn stared blankly at it. Password? What password?

Wait . . . my algorithm . . . Mine!!

"Hollyn," Davis said with more than a little warning, the sound of the incoming missile terrifyingly distinct.

She typed in the only password she could figure Dad would use for her: Sparrow.

Incorrect password. Two chances left.

"Hollyn!"

Panic thrummed. What was—

Leetspeak. She and Daddy had made more than one joke of her affinity for that internet hacking language. Hurriedly, she typed in 5P4rr0w.

The screen blipped. Characters on the page seemed to fall to the bottom as a bird fluttered from one side to the other, its wake spelling *I knew you'd do it, Sparrow.*

She clapped her hands over her mouth and fought the tears. Daddy . . . But how . . . how had he known?

A shriek overhead drew their gazes skyward. The moon caressed the hull of a missile that rocketed past the buildings.

Davis lowered his gaze to her. "What . . . just happened?"

"I redirected the missile into the ocean. My dad anticipated someone would try to use the program for something military and created a counter-code to neutralize the code." She fought the tears again. "It was me. My dad knew I'd find a way to intervene."

"And save thousands of lives."

# 20



## *REINHARDT HOME, ABU DHABI, UAE*

Leaving Abu Dhabi was going to be hard. Strike that. Leaving *Hollyn* would be hard.

Davis cinched the strap on his duffel while Fury supervised from his sprawled out position on the bed.

One week had passed since the mission had come to a head. One week, and he still hadn't been able to bring himself to say those three words to Hollyn. But with damage control after everything, and the funeral, it hadn't felt like the right time. Now he was *out* of time. Crew'd called him mere hours ago saying the ranch was ready to take Fury.

Davis's hand stalled over the last strap. Guilt plagued him for what he was about to do. But this wasn't forever. It was just for now. They'd talked it over and agreed that Hollyn had a lot of things to take care of as far as the company she was now in charge of and wasn't in a place where she could move. Still, she'd been very quiet since he'd broken the news about Crew's call.

With a heavy sigh, Fury tracked him. The RMWD's gaze was

relaxed but heavy. He didn't know it yet, but they'd be on a 747 back to the States in about two hours.

Clearing his throat, Davis secured the last strap. "Look. Things are going to change soon."

Fury lifted his head, all ears. Tail thumped on the bed as he listened.

Flip.

If it was this hard to try and distance himself from the shepherd, doing the same with Hollyn was going to be amplified a hundred times over.

Regret pressed on his shoulders. Drained him. Reminded him how much he was putting on the line by leaving Hollyn now.

Still. He couldn't say what he needed to say and then jet off for who knew how long. But this time he wouldn't make the same mistake as when he enlisted. He *was* coming back for Hollyn, but it would take time to train a new handler for Fury. Time to make sure the transition was smooth. Weeks. Maybe a few months. Then he was free to do what he wanted.

First things first. Get Fury settled.

He owed the RMWD that much after all they'd been through.

"All finished packing?" Hollyn's soft voice brought him around.

Davis swallowed down the *wow* that almost slipped out of his mouth. Even in jeans and a simple tee, she was a knockout.

"Yeah." Davis slung the bag over his shoulder, and Fury popped up, ready to go.

Hollyn nodded, and he couldn't deny the sadness written on her face before she turned to walk with them down the hall. His resolve faltered, but he steeled himself to what needed to happen.

Feeling like a class-A jerk, Davis followed her outside and down the front path of the house to where Bongani was waiting to drive them to the airport.

"If I find anything you left, where should I send it?" Hollyn asked as he and Fury stalked to the other side of the car.

She wouldn't find anything, but he wasn't going to say that. "The A Breed Apart ranch. I'll be staying there while I train a new handler for Fury." He paused. "Hol."

She looked to him over the top of the black Mercedes without saying a word.

"This isn't forever. Just . . . for now. I'll be back."

A halfhearted grin tugged at the corners of her mouth. "Right." She ducked into the car, and they settled in their seats.

Fury sat between Davis's legs in the backseat, happy to be out for a drive. Trying—and failing—to find *something* to say, Davis noted Bongani eyeing them through the rearview mirror a handful of times during the half-hour drive from Saadiyat Island toward the airport. But the guy didn't say so much as one word. Only the sound of Fury's panting from the backseat broke up the silence.

Cautiously, Davis reached for Hollyn's hand. Wanted to give her some kind of physical reassurance that he wasn't leaving her willingly. She clung to his hand but didn't look over at him.

Palm trees and sandy beaches whizzed by the car as they drove down Sheikh Khalifa Bin Zayed Street.

They pulled up to the curb with Davis still wrestling for something to say. Coming up short. There was nothing that would make this easier.

Bongani opened Hollyn's door, and Davis grabbed his duffel from the trunk. He could hear several people murmuring awe at Fury's size as they walked past.

"Thank you, Davis. For everything." Hollyn moved in for a hug.

Davis held her close. Didn't want to let her go, but it was time.

*Don't do anything that will make this harder on her.*

"Try to stay out of danger for the next few months, okay?" he joked.

Her laugh was less than wholehearted, and it cut him deeply. "I'll do my best." She pulled back and gave him a small grin, chin quivering slightly.

It almost tugged those three words out of him then and there, but that would be selfish on his part, wouldn't it? He'd seen too many people start off relationships long distance that crashed and burned a few weeks later. He cared about Hollyn too much to risk that.

Once he was back here, he'd never let her go. Just had to make it through the next few months.

Fury sat at Davis's side, observing everyone around them. Always on sentry duty. He was going to do great things for ABA.

Regretfully, Davis turned to Bongani. Shook his hand. "Thanks for the ride, man."

"Of course." Bongani nodded.

"Let me know when you two land?" Hollyn asked.

"Sure thing. I'll see you later, Hol."

With one last look, Davis clicked his tongue to Fury and turned toward the airport.

The next few months were going to suck. No two ways about that.

"Are you all right?" Bongani's voice held genuine concern.

Hollyn was grateful that he was driving. She didn't think she'd have been able to see the road clearly through the hot tears pooling in her eyes. She nodded her head. It was all she could do without completely breaking down.

Bongani pulled out of the terminal. "Come now," he gently pried from the driver's seat next to her. When she didn't answer, he continued. "Why didn't you go with them?"

She drew in a shaky breath. "He didn't ask me to."

And that was the simple truth of it. Though they'd talked

things over and come to an agreement, she couldn't deny that if Davis had asked her to go with him, she would have found a way to make her obligations to Reinhardt Tech work. Would have built a new life by Davis's side now instead of possibly later. But clearly, he didn't feel the same way.

A moment of silence passed between them. "I'm sorry to hear that."

"Me too."

Hollyn thought back to the kisses they'd shared. The conversations. The looks. She knew she hadn't made it all into something it wasn't, but maybe what was between them had simply been born out of chaotic circumstances. After all, he'd never actually *said* he loved her.

Now that things had calmed and returned to a normal pace, it was possible Davis was thinking clearly again—or *not*, if you asked her—and regretted how far things had progressed between them. He was human, after all. Allowed to feel the way he felt. She only wished they'd had time to talk about things in more depth. He'd said he was coming back, so why did she feel like she was on her own once again?

After the funeral for her parents, Davis had gotten a call from Crew that the team was ready to take Fury. A whirlwind twenty-four hours later, he was ready to leave. It had all happened so fast. So soon. Her mind was still reeling from the events of the last couple of weeks. She needed some clarity. Wished that her parents had been buried here so she could talk "to" them, but Randall had seen to it that they were laid to rest in the family plot back in Tennessee.

Hollyn was grateful for that . . . but nevertheless it amplified the feelings of being left behind. On her own. Again. Still, there was comfort in the knowledge that even though everyone in her life might leave her, God never would. The question was: could she let that be enough?

She could head to the lab . . . but for the first time in her life, it didn't feel like she'd find what she was looking for there. She wouldn't see Dad sitting in his office or hovering over his next project with that familiar gleam of joy in his eye. No. The lab was the last place she wanted to be.

The ocean, then. She always felt close to her parents there.

"Would you please take me to Saadiyat Beach?"

Bongani nodded. "Of course."

He guided the Mercedes through town, and Hollyn let herself stare mindlessly out the window. Watched families walking down sidewalks, mothers dressed in elegant kaftans that rippled in the breeze blowing in from the gulf. Children laughing while they talked with their fathers. The skyline of the city behind them was filled with a mix of gorgeous curved architecture seemingly a throwback to times past as well as modern skyscrapers ushering in the future.

Why didn't it feel like *her* future was here anymore?

Abu Dhabi had never felt so distant to her as it did now. It no longer felt like home.

When she felt the car come to a stop, Hollyn blinked. She sat up straighter in her seat, staring at the gulf that stretched on for miles ahead.

"Would you like me to walk with you?"

Hollyn looked over at the older man.

Bongani was a blessing that maybe she hadn't always appreciated the way she should, but she did now.

"That would be nice." She knew he wouldn't pressure her with conversation. In his quiet way, he'd let her set the tone. It would just be nice to have him beside her.

He grinned and came around to open her door.

As she'd predicted, Bongani was silent as they slowly trekked through the white sand for a good half mile. Wave after wave crashed on shore. Hollyn let her shoes dangle at her side, her fingers hooked through the laces.

It was unusually empty on the beach today, but she was grateful for that. Pausing, Hollyn turned and stared out at the water.

"I don't know what to do." The words slipped out. It felt both defeating and liberating to say that out loud.

"Don't you?"

The question surprised her. When she looked up at Bongani, kindness shone through his dark brown eyes.

"What is Holy Spirit saying to you?" He shot her a knowing grin. "Listen."

Hollyn chewed her bottom lip and squinted back out at the water. One name—one face—came to mind no matter how hard she tried to push it away.

Davis.

"I'm not positive he wants me." She lifted her shoulder in a one-armed shrug.

"Did he *say* he didn't want you?"

"Well . . . not in so many words. But if what was between us was real, why would he leave without me? Maybe all of it was just in my head. If he loved me, he would have told me. His actions could have been spurred on by the life-and-death situations we found ourselves in. Science has proven the effect that stress has on the brain. People don't think clearly."

A weighted sigh pulled from the tall man beside her. "You are a smart woman, Hollyn. But it is times like these that I believe leaving your head out of it would serve you better. Instead, let the Father guide you. As Jeremiah twenty-nine declares: 'For I know the plans I have for you.'" Bongani looked down at her. "There is One who will never abandon you. One who has far greater plans than you have even for yourself. Trust that."

Her pulse ticked up as hope flared back to life. Another set of waves crashed into the sand in front of them. The salty scent of the water tinged the air.

She tried to be still. To listen. But she couldn't stop thinking about Davis. She was in love with him. It was that simple. If she never told him, she'd always wonder what could have been. Even the pain of hearing him say he didn't return the sentiment would be better than the not knowing. At least she'd have closure.

Hollyn nodded more to herself than anyone. Knew what she was going to do. "How do you always know what to say?"

Bongani scoffed softly. "Just take it from an old man. When the Spirit prompts, don't ignore it."

She nodded before grinning. Tapped her shoulder against his arm. "You're hardly an old man, friend."

Bongani laughed. "From your lips to God's ears. And may I live to see another seventy-five years."

"If you're seventy-five, I'll eat my shoe," Hollyn joked, holding up her sneaker.

He chuckled again, shaking his head. "Back to the airport, then?"

"Not yet." Hollyn took in a steadying breath. "I have some things I'm going to wrap up here first."

As much as she wanted to leave right this second, now that she wasn't fighting for her life, she would make sure the businesses that Dad had spent his life building were taken care of. Appoint people for the everyday running of Reinhardt Tech and hire movers for her things. But the moment that was done, yes, the airport was exactly where she'd be headed.

Bongani turned and started back the way they'd come, but Hollyn waited for a moment, eyes on the horizon.

"I'm going to be all right," she whispered to her parents, though she knew they couldn't hear her. Tears pricked her eyes. "No matter what else comes, I'm not alone in this world. I love you . . . always."

# 21



THIS WAS CRAZY, RIGHT?

Hollyn fidgeted with the strap of her purse in the backseat of the town car that had picked her up from the airport just under an hour ago. It was cooler here in Texas than she'd anticipated, and she kind of wished she'd packed warmer clothing. Too late now, though. The jeans and T-shirt she was wearing would have to suffice. Even though she'd lived most of her life in the States, she'd never been to Texas before, and her brain had been telling her it never got under ninety degrees. Well, it did. But that realization was soon eclipsed by the sight of the A Breed Apart front gates.

Hollyn swallowed as the driver turned down the long driveway. It had only been a week since Davis had left for the States, but every day had felt like an eternity. She'd worked as quickly as she could to arrange coverage for the running of the lab and the rest of the business side of things that she was now in charge of. The second she'd been free to hop on a plane to Texas, she had.

*What are you doing? Maybe this was a bad idea.*

She swallowed down the doubts creeping up. She'd been in communication with Davis since he'd left, but his days were long and their conversations short. One truth remained unchanging, though: her feelings for Davis had only grown since he'd come back into her life, and—beyond the shadow of a doubt—she was in love. If he didn't feel the same way, then at least she was about to find out for sure.

Hollyn tucked her loose hair behind her ears. Smoothed a hand down the front of her maroon shirt. Maybe she should have grabbed one of the barf bags from first class on the flight over. Her stomach was in knots, and the queasy feeling rumbling around in there was escalating by the second.

As the town car driver came to a stop in the parking lot near a large building, a woman with white-blonde hair was heading down the front steps. Beside her, a reddish colored dog with a lean, muscular build eyed the car with ferocity. A slight motion of the woman's hand brought down the dog's intensity a few degrees, but it was still unnerving.

Hollyn thanked the driver and asked him to wait for a moment before she stepped outside. This place was much bigger than she'd pictured. From here she could see several large structures and at least two very large fenced fields. Some people were working with dogs in one, but Davis didn't seem to be one of them. Barking came from one of the buildings.

"Can I help you?" The woman and her dog stopped a few feet away.

"Uh, I hope so?" Hollyn stood a couple inches taller than the blonde but definitely didn't come close to the tough presence the woman naturally exuded. Oh yeah, she was out of her comfort zone here in Davis's world. "I'm . . . looking for Davis Ledger?"

The woman chuckled. "Is that a question or a statement?"

Hollyn laughed nervously and told herself to relax. "A statement. Definitely. I just—I need to speak with him. If he's available," she tagged on quickly.

The blonde scrutinized her for a moment, something that was

heavily mirrored by her dog. They must have decided she wasn't a threat, because the woman nodded over her shoulder. "We were actually on our way near where he's working. We'll take you to him."

Relief washed over Hollyn. She turned and grabbed her backpack from the car. As it drove away, Hollyn chewed her lip, hands squeezing the straps of her bag.

"You coming?" the woman asked behind her.

Hollyn spun and hurried to catch up as she hooked her arms through the straps of her bag. "Yes, sorry."

"I'm Rio, by the way." The blonde gave Hollyn a smile. "And this"—she reached down and patted her dog's side as they walked—"is Chaos."

The dog panted happily, and Hollyn could almost swear she saw it smile.

"It's nice to meet you both. I'm Hollyn."

Rio's step faltered. "Hollyn?"

Uh-oh. Not the reaction she'd been expecting.

"Is that bad?"

"No, no," Rio said before a grin spread across her lips. "Just so . . . interesting. We've heard a lot about you."

In the span of a week? Curious. Davis wasn't exactly the chatty type. Maybe he was different with these people, though?

Hollyn swallowed, unsure what to say as she followed Rio behind one of the larger metal buildings. Barking from inside grew louder along with the voices of a couple men. Rio slid open a door and motioned Hollyn inside.

When she saw Davis, her heart skipped a beat, and she couldn't wipe the grin off her face. There he was. Dressed in black tactical pants and a long sleeve T-shirt that hugged his biceps and broad shoulders in a mind-scrambling way His back was to her, and he was speaking to another guy who held a lead attached to Fury.

"All right, that was decent, but don't let him get away with giving you attitude. Run through it again."

"Ledger!" Rio called out.

Davis turned. Surprise flashed across his face when he spotted Hollyn. Surprise and . . . something else she couldn't put her finger on.

Oh man, she was so in love with him. She prayed desperately that this hadn't been a bad idea. That he'd say he felt the same way about her. Could she handle it if he didn't? Maybe she should have waited back in Abu Dhabi for him to make the first move. Or come at a different time. Or—

"Hollyn." The way he spoke her name didn't give her any clues to if he was happy or disappointed to see her, and she tried not to let that get to her. More, he seemed like he was in shock that she was standing here.

Well, that made two of them. This was by far the riskiest thing she'd ever done.

He blinked like his brain had just short circuited and then turned to the guy working with Fury. "Keep going. I'll be right back."

"Sure thing," the guy replied.

Fury gave a few jerks of protest before complying with what he was being asked to do, and Davis jogged over to where Hollyn stood with Rio and Chaos.

"What are you doing here?" he asked, still clearly in disbelief. "I didn't know you were coming."

"Yeah, I, uh . . . surprise?" Hollyn opened her arms wide in an attempt at humor.

Oy. Could she be anymore awkward? So much for planning out exactly what she was going to say and how things were going to play out on the flight over. She'd chalk it up to exhaustion. Probably should have at least gone to the hotel to take a nap first. But no, she'd jumped right into the town car and asked to come straight here.

"I'll just get back to work." The grin on Rio's face was as unnerving as the surprise on Davis's. "It was nice to meet you, Hollyn."

"You too."

Standing here, alone, Hollyn suddenly didn't know what to do. Gaze locked with Davis's, her heart told her to say what she'd come to say, but her head told her this had been a stupid idea. Not a shocker—her head was winning. "I . . . um . . . hi."

Davis grinned. "Hey."

None of this was going the way she'd thought. She'd just go with the flow, though. "Can—" She glanced over his shoulder to where Fury and the handler were working somewhat haphazardly. Yeah, she probably should have waited till the end of the day to do this. "Actually, this can wait till later." She took a step backward. "I wasn't thinking, and now I'm interrupting your day and—"

"Hol, breathe." Davis reached out and took her hand. Gave it an encouraging squeeze, which bolstered her confidence. "What's going on? Is everything okay?"

She could do this. She *needed* to do this.

*For once in your life, be bold.*

Hollyn swallowed, gaze still locked with his. "Can we talk?" she forced herself to ask.

Put the ball in his proverbial court. Then she'd know how to continue.

"Of course." He didn't even hesitate to pause work for her.

The gesture warmed her from the inside out. Maybe there was a chance he still felt the same way he had when he'd kissed her. Or at least, what she'd been thinking he felt. She should probably think a little *less*, but then again, that wasn't who she was.

Davis turned and called out to the guy across the arena. The man unclipped Fury, who ran over to them. Hollyn's heart flew into her throat seeing the RMWD charge their way. But at the last second, he slid to a stop in the loose dirt. Glued to Davis's side, he stared up expectantly. Davis ruffled the shepherd's head.

"Good boy," Davis said before looking up. "Want to take a walk?" he asked her.

"That would be great."

But she'd need to get to the point of her trip soon, or she was going to lose her nerve.

Davis led her out of the building. A slight breeze had picked up, bringing with it a scent she could only describe as *country*. Fresh air mixed with recently cut grass and hard work . . . if hard work could be a scent.

Fury nudged her hand.

"Looks like someone else missed you."

*Else*? Meaning he had too?

Hope had her heart racing.

*Tell him! Tell him now.*

Goosebumps formed on her arms. It was chilly out here.

"So." He cleared his throat. "What brings you all the way here?" There was something in his tone that conveyed reservation. When he cast a look over at her, Hollyn noted a seriousness in his eyes that hadn't been there earlier.

They stopped at the fence line of the outdoor training field, and Davis pulled a toy for Fury from his pocket. Chucked it hard. The German shepherd cleared the fence and tore off after the KONG.

Hollyn swallowed. It was now or never. "There's something I have to tell you."

"Okay, sure." He nodded and faced her while Fury ran back their way. He skidded to a stop but didn't relinquish the toy. "*Af*," Davis commanded, glancing away for a second.

Fury lay down, panting around the slobbery toy in his mouth.

Having Davis's full attention was more than a little unnerving. Hollyn worked a loose sliver of the fence between her fingers. "So." She licked her lips. "There's something I've been wanting to say for a while now, but it never felt like the right time with . . . just everything. I mean, you know. You were there."

Rambling.

Davis just nodded, steady gaze pinning her.

Her heart was beating so fast, and her whole body felt flushed. "I don't really know the best way to say this"—a concerned look drew his eyebrows together—"so I'll just blurt it out. And don't feel like you need to say anything right now. Just hear me out and think it over."

Arms crossed, his broad shoulders rose in acknowledgment as he waited for her to continue.

"I love you." The words hung between them for a moment before she forced herself to press on. "I've known for a while now. I mean, I thought I knew back in high school, but these last few weeks .. well, what I feel for you now is so much deeper. You feel like home to me, and I love who you are." She couldn't read his expression. That worried her. "And I get it. You might not feel the same way, and that's okay. You did leave, and maybe I'm projecting Maybe you feel like we just got caught up in the chaos of the last couple of weeks and you need space. But I had to tell you how I feel, otherwise I'd always wonder what-if. I understand if this is just a one-sided thing but—"

A small smirk spread across Davis's lips as he lifted his hands to the sides of her face. She went still under his touch. "Do I get a chance to reply?"

His thumb brushed back and forth against her cheek, and all she could manage was a nod.

*Yes. Please, put me out of my misery.*

Hollyn drew in a breath, afraid to move. She searched his brown eyes. His nearness and the way he was so carefully cradling her face infused her soul with hope that he might feel the same way about her that she did for him. But was that too much to wish for?

"I love you too."

The air whooshed from her lungs as she stood there, dumbfounded, afraid she might have misheard him. She tried to get her bearings. "You do?"

Was she dreaming this? She'd waited what felt like her whole life to hear him say exactly that, but it seemed too good to be true.

"I do."

"But . . . you left."

"Just to get Fury situated here," Davis defended gently. "We talked about that."

At the sound of his name, Hollyn saw Fury's head pop up in her peripheral vision.

"I didn't want to tell you I was in love with you and then get on a plane and leave you for weeks or maybe months." He lowered his hands to her arms and down to thread his fingers with hers. "No matter how many ways I played it out in my head, it seemed like I was abandoning you." Davis searched her eyes. "I'm sorry, Hol."

Hollyn's brain stalled around a few words of what he'd just said. "Say it again."

"I'm sorry."

"No." She grinned and wrapped her arms around his trim waist. "That you're in love with me."

Nothing else mattered to her in this moment except hearing him repeat that.

Chuckling, Davis gently slid a hand behind her head and tugged her closer. He leaned down to press his lips to hers. The kiss was warm and completely mind-scrambling. When he pulled back, he slid his arms around her as well. *Happy* hardly began to describe how she felt right now. "I'm in love with you, Hollyn."

Her eyes slid closed as she relished the words.

*Thank You, Lord! Thank You for this incredible man!*

Davis drew her closer, and Hollyn happily pressed her cheek against his chest. His heartbeat thundered almost as quickly as her own.

He loved her. He. Loved. Her.

A sound from the fence preceded Fury bumping her arm with his giant head. Hollyn dropped one hand from around

Davis and held it out to the RMWD, who pressed his weight into her leg. He happily accepted the careful scratch of his head that Hollyn offered.

This, right here, was all she'd ever wanted. To be loved. To be part of a family. To be right where God wanted her to be. And she'd do her best to make the most of every moment they had together from here on out.

# EPILOGUE



"I think that's it." Hollyn locked the door to her massive childhood home.

Davis watched her from the bottom of the front porch steps. Wanted to make sure she didn't feel pressured to wrap this up faster than necessary. A bug landed on his neck, and he swatted it away before wiping the back of his hand over his forehead. The forest of red oak and sugar maple trees surrounding the house rustled with a slight breeze. Wasn't enough to do much, though. July was definitely one of the worst months in Tennessee, if you asked him. Too humid and hot if you couldn't take a dip in the lake. Today was no exception. He preferred the drier heat.

As if in response to his thoughts about the heat, Fury whine-panted at his side.

Davis reached down to run a hand over the goon's head, and the dog went silent.

Hollyn stepped back and stared at the log cabin for a little while.

He knew saying goodbye to the place had weighed heavily

on her for the last couple months, but ultimately, she'd decided to sell. As soon as she was done here, they'd head to the title company so she could sign papers. Then she'd head back to Austin, where she was renting a small home, and he and Fury would head to Texas Hill Country.

Somehow, Crew had managed to reel Davis in as a handler for A Breed Apart. And truth be told, he loved the gig. Having Hollyn an hour away was great too—though not as close as he'd prefer. Or as close as he hoped she'd be soon.

Turning, she wiped her eyes. Descended the front stairs. Fury nudged her hand with his nose. Their hot-and-cold relationship had evened out, and lately the shepherd almost seemed to prefer her over him. Traitor.

"Hey, buddy," she crooned in an even tone. Scratched the place behind his ear he loved best.

Davis appreciated that Hollyn didn't use baby talk with him.

"Doing okay?" he asked.

Hollyn slipped her arms around his waist. Nodded against his chest as he held her close. "Yeah. This is for the best. That family is going to be very happy here. Besides." She tilted her head up to meet his eyes. "My life is in Texas now. And you still have the cabin here, so it's not goodbye forever."

Just knock him down with a feather, why don't ya? He kissed her temple. Didn't deserve her or her resilience. She was one of the strongest women he knew.

After she'd left Abu Dhabi and he'd gotten hired on at ABA, Hollyn hadn't wasted any time hiring an architect and crew to build an extension lab for Reinhardt Tech. It split the distance between ABA and Austin. If things went to plan, it'd be ready in about ten months. She was happy overseeing every aspect of her future lab, and that made him happy.

While she wasn't part of the daily running of her father's company, she still had monthly board meetings via telecommute and had plenty of say in the direction they were heading. It suited her. She'd told Davis more than once, *"I'm a scientist. Not a CEO. I'm happiest in the lab."*

"Well." She sighed. "You guys ready to go? If we leave now, we'll make it over there on time."

They'd be early. But that was good—gave him time for what was next. As far as Hollyn knew, selling the house was the only reason they were here, but he had other plans. Ones that right now were making him more nervous than he'd ever felt in his life.

He looked down at her. "Let's take a quick walk."

"A walk? Do we have time?"

"Always time for a walk. We have something to show you. Right, Fury?"

Fury barked and ran toward the tree line. Paused and looked back at them to bark, tail wagging. His tongue lolled out the side of his mouth.

Hollyn grinned and laced her fingers with his. Something he'd never get tired of. "Lead the way, boys."

Davis took a covert breath as he led them down a path they'd walked hundreds of times before. But instead of following it all the way down to his cabin, he veered them off the path to a spot he'd never shown her before.

Fury was loving life. He sniffed the dirt path. Darted back and forth through the wild grass.

Hollyn trapsed through the foliage. For a second, he wished he'd thought to cut it down. But she didn't complain.

When he stopped them in front of a wide oak, she looked around. Squinted against the sun. "You know, as long as I lived here, I don't think I ever came out this way."

"Too many bugs?" he teased.

Fury caught the scent of something and started to take off.

Davis whistled. *"Fuss!"*

The RMWD spun on a dime and zipped back to his side.

"Hey." Hollyn laughed. "I just prefer the clean environment of a lab. Nothing wrong with that."

"Such a girly-girl." He grinned. Shook his head.

"And you love me exactly the way I am."

"You got me there."

"And I love you and kind of like hanging out with you, so don't let me die out here." Humor lit her blue and green eyes.

"Promise," Davis replied. "I wanted to show you this before you sold the place."

She eyed him. "So mysterious."

Davis cleared his throat. Man. He used to tease buddies about their proposal jitters, but this was honestly harder than he'd thought. "I used to walk out here every time I came over," he started. "The summer of our junior year, after things got really bad with my mom, I'd sit here thinking about what I wanted my life to be like. How I could have what you guys seemed to."

Hollyn nodded knowingly. The breeze blew a strand of her strawberry-blonde hair across her face. He reached out to tuck it behind her ear.

Not to be outdone, Fury pressed his ninety-pound frame into Davis's leg.

"Anyway." Davis mentally steeled himself. It was now or never. "I carved something in the tree that I never told you about." He tipped his head.

She turned. Gasped when she saw what he'd carved. "Are you serious!?" Hollyn rushed up to the trunk.

Touched the roughly carved D + H.

Davis reached into his pocket and slid out the ring he'd been holding on to for the right time: a delicate gold band—she'd been adamant about not wanting a diamond or jewel in the setting so it wouldn't get hooked on any of her projects at work—he'd purchased a few weeks prior.

He took a knee behind her. "*Sitz*," he whispered to Fury.

"I never knew you felt that way back then!" She turned. "I thought—"

When she saw him kneeling there, he heard her gasp again. She looked at the ring. At him. The ring again.

"I should have told you a long time ago, but it took me a while to get my head on straight. I love you so much. Think you could be happy with a couple hammer-head soldiers like us?"

"Yes!" she squealed, bouncing with excitement. Calmed herself a little when Fury got antsy. "Yes, of course I could!"

Davis stood just as she threw her arms around his neck. Kissed him. He gladly returned the gesture, arms around her waist. Held out a hand to stay Fury but rubbed his ears. "Mind if I put the ring on?" He pulled back.

"Please!" she wiped tears from her eyes. Held out her left hand so he could slide the band into place. "I love it!" She smirked at Fury. "You helped him pick it, didn't you? 'Cause we had more than one conversation about this."

Fury tilted his head to one side, then the other. Listening.

"Are you sure you don't want a diamond? Because—"

"It's perfect," she said emphatically. "Now I don't have to worry about taking it on and off at work." She was practically beaming as she stared at her hand. "It'll stay on from now till forever."

Now till forever.

Davis liked the sound of that. He sent up a prayer of thanks for the woman standing in front of him—something he'd been doing a lot more of these days. Thanks to Hollyn's encouragement, he was rebuilding a solid foundation with God.

"I didn't think I could be happier than when you first told me you loved me. I was wrong," Hollyn said. "We're a family. You, Fury, and me. *My* family."

Davis grinned wide.

Yeah. Forever with her was just the beginning.

# ACKNOWLEDGMENTS

Thank you to EVERYONE who's encouraged me along the unexpected journey of writing this book! There were times I didn't think I'd be able to finish it but your prayers got me through. I absolutely couldn't have done it without you and thank the Lord for you!

A special thank you to Ronie for everything you've taught me and for the incredible mentorship. Working with you has been the BEST!

Thank you for reading *Fury*! Gear up for the next A Breed Apart: Legacy thriller, *Surge* by Ronie Kendig and Voni Harris, releasing this fall.

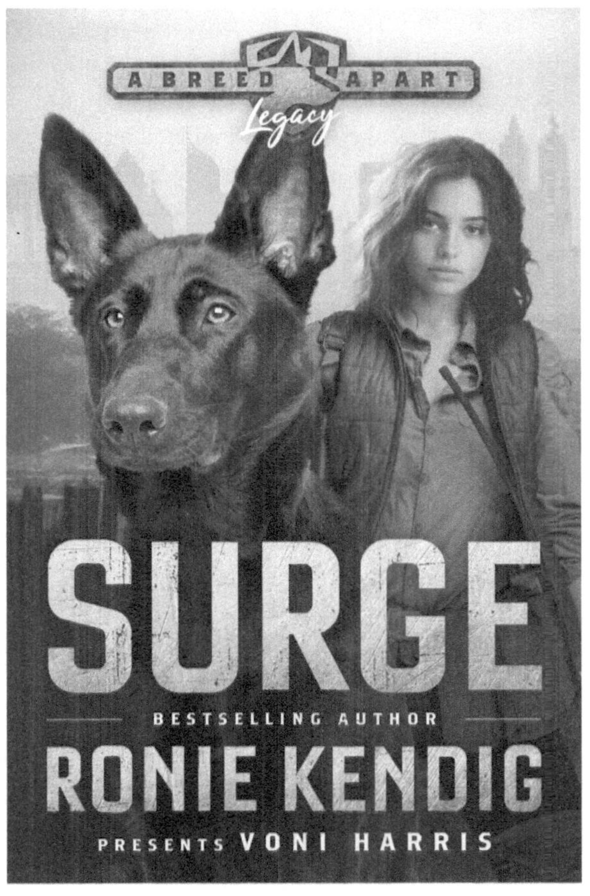


**In a race against time to stop terrorists, will the truth destroy their lives—or save thousands?**

Delaney Thompson is not a warrior, and doesn't want to be. She's happy as a dog trainer at A Breed Apart ranch in Texas. More, she has a particular connection to Surge, a former military working dog. Still, the last thing she wants to do is go out in the field with the animal, who struggles with his own brand of

PTSD. But when a terrorist with a chemical weapon is spotted in Singapore, they need Surge . . . and her . . . to help—whether they're ready or not.

Bossy, wounded former Navy SEAL Garrett Walker doesn't want a civilian on the trip, but he needs Delaney's help if he hopes to track down the weapon. What he doesn't expect is a grudging respect for her. Or, for her to get under his hard exterior to mend the broken places inside. Delaney can't deny her feelings for a man who is so much more than he seems. But will she only get in the way?

As they track the weapons dealer through Singapore, and then discover his lethal plans, they must find the weapon and stop it before it kills thousands. With time against them, can they work together to stop tragedy?

A pulse-pounding addition to the A Breed Apart: Legacy series, Surge is full of romance amidst deception, danger, and daring rescues that will keep you on the edge of your seat until the final breathless moment.

READ ON FOR A SNEAK PEEK AT SURGE.

# SURGE | A BREED APART: LEGACY, BOOK 5

## PROLOGUE

*SOMEWHERE OVER DJIBOUTI*

"The chance we've been waiting for is finally here," Navy SEAL Master Chief Garrett "Bear" Walker said as Charlie team huddled in the hangar. "According to COMINT, Sachaai terrorists have been training in their homeland for a purported large-scale attack on America, but they were spotted boarding a C-17 to return to their Tadjoura workhouse early tomorrow morning and will effect that attack."

Communications Intelligence hung slightly below Human Intelligence on the intel ladder, but that was harder to come by in Djibouti City and especially with these terrorists—cowards, who poisoned the air and people rather than facing their enemy head-on like real men.

Petty Officer Third Class Blake "Zim" Zimmerman—the newb on the team with a couple degrees in chemistry—let out a low whistle. "They deal in some nasty stuff."

"To put it mildly," CIA operative Bryan Caldwell said as he strode across the hangar. Leathered skin spoke of many hours in the sun. Gray hair at the temples spoke of stress. Probably because the guy didn't have friends. He slid images—satellite

261

photos, pictures of men, structures, an aerial shot of a village, and a picture of a container—onto the table. "Sachaai is Urdu for *truth*," Caldwell said, " and their goal is to make Pakistan the world hub of Islamic truth. They will stop at nothing to remove all obstacles in their way."

The *thwump* of rotors and engine whine of the Black Hawk powering up on the tarmac fought to dominate the air.

"Hold up," George "King" Kingery said with a scowl, his thick red beard twitching as he frowned and took in the spook. "This op is vetted by *him*? The guy who burned us in Burma?"

"I didn't—"

"And we're going to believe he's giving us everything and *not* risking mission success?"

Grunts of agreement skidded around the hangar from the rest of Charlie team.

Caldwell huffed. "I'm giving you everything you need—"

"*Need*? That's a load of—"

"Bury it." Garrett didn't bother to hide the growl in his voice. Nobody was happy about operating on intel from the operative. "We've been champing for a chance to get these pukes, and now we have it. The chemicals they're using are lethal. I'm going to hand it over to Zim for a quick brief, but the second thing is that we need to get in and out before first light. We aren't exactly American Idols here. So, we have a few hours to get in and get back here." He nodded to Zim. "Brief them on the chems—but fast. Helo's waiting and the clock is ticking."

"When we head in there, we'll be looking for metal lockboxes with an indicator like this," Zim said, holding up his phone with an image of a red-and-black panel. "We've all heard about sulfamic acid and potassium cyanide—not a big headache, but the Sachaai love to make hydrogen cyanide gas with those chems."

"Symptoms?" Garrett asked.

"Nausea. Vomiting. Temporary blindness. Heart palpitations...or heart attack. Shortness of breath...or no more breath—but if this stuff disperses into the air, we have seconds. If that." His dark eyes were wide.

"Their chemist has found a way to stop it from doing that," Caldwell said, "so if we can get hold of him, we could possibly shut down the Sachaai for good. Or at least long enough to decimate their infrastructure."

"We know who that is?"

Zim sagged. "No, but this guy is a genius. Being able to do this and keep these chemicals—"

"See your nerd coming out," King teased in his deep Southern drawl.

"Which is why we're all going in with chem gear," Garrett said, not willing to be turned into a blistered corpse. "HAZMAT will be on standby to come in behind us to secure the site, if we find anything."

"Okay," King said, stroking his beard as he stabbed a thick finger at the image with the white buildings. "Djibouti City?"

"SATINT tracked Sachaai to a neighborhood a kick inside the southern border of Tadjoura before signals got scrambled, impeding analysts from narrowing the target location any further." Garrett grunted. "That's a quarter mike of potentially unfriendly territory to sort through. HUMINT has an informant describing their headquarters as a small white building."

Laughter filtered through the space.

"Reckon it'll be a challenge to find the Sachaai's 'small white' HQ in that sea of white structures," King said, eyeing the device with the SAT imaging of their target location.

"Doesn't matter," Zim said, pointing to the MWD team. "We've got the Mal to sniff 'em out."

All eyes turned to Petty Officer Third Class Sam "Samwise" Reicher and his military working dog, Tsunami M501—also a petty officer, but Second Class, one rank above his handler. MWDs were force multipliers and morale boosters all wrapped up in one aggressive package.

Samwise patted Tsunami's tac vest. "Tsunami has all the

training of a military working dog with the added special forces training. On top of that, she is the only MWD with specialized training to rout the signature lipid that's unique to the Sachaai."

"So make sure the dog lives," Garrett said. "We'll chopper in, hit the beachhead a klick outside Tadjoura. Hoof it to the sector defined by intel. Let the MWD do her thing and sniff out the workhouse. Then sensitive site exploitation: Secure the site. Document the site. Search the site to learn what the terrorists planned against the US. All to rout that lipid. Any questions?"

"Negative," came a chorus of replies.

"Lives are depending on us. We fail, thousands die. This time, it's our own—Americans." He skated Caldwell a glare. "This mission can't fail or we fail them. Let's move out."

The team checked their gear. Garrett clipped his M4A1 to his sling harness, double-checked his Sig and the comms piece in his ear. He started toward the hangar doors.

"What's this?" King taunted as he snatched something from Samwise.

"Hey!"

Garrett looked over his shoulder and saw the big guy angling away from the handler, which amped Tsunami.

King whooped. "What?" The big guy whipped out a huge smile. "How did you get a beauty like this to marry your ugly mug?" He looked closer. "I need one of Zim's microscopes to see the diamond. Cheap, man. Too cheap."

Samwise snatched it back and, over the rotor, shouted, "Because unlike you, I have style."

King barked a laugh and headed out to the tarmac.

Eyeing the picture his friend held, Garrett saw him start to tuck it away. "You asked her."

Grinning, Samwise nodded.

They fist-bumped over Tsunami's head. "Finally. Good job." But why did this feel like a bad omen? Every mission they went on was one they might not come back from. And Sam wanted to put a wife through that? Too much risk…

In the helo, the MWD team sat across from him, the fur missile stuffed between both Garrett's and Samwise's boots.

Jutting his jaw at his buddy, Garrett dropped on the net seat and felt his back pop. A dozen years as a SEAL had battered his body. Broken fingers, twisted ankles, a few bullet wounds, whiplash…This was it. His last mission. Time to get out before he came back in a pine box or sans a limb. He wasn't signing the reenlistment papers. Not that he had Samwise's attractive reason waiting back home.

Home…They had to do this mission right, or thousands of Americans would die.

That's why he'd become a SEAL—for the people, the innocents. No re-upping meant he couldn't help people in the only way he knew how and was skilled at. How could he not sign the papers? This was his life's purpose, even when a pre-mission briefing meant listening to CIA operative Bryan Caldwell. When Zim crowded in around him, Garrett felt the gas mask providing tension. He shifted it…and his thoughts went to the mission in Burma. Caldwell had been a jerk then too, but the HUMINT he'd brought to the table had been flawless.

Garrett narrowed his eyes. Okay, mostly flawless He could admit that…Either way, a threat against the good ol' US of A wasn't one he'd take standing down. No way he'd sit on the bench while terrorists attacked his country. It was the only reason he'd listened to the man's lecture about the Sachaai and the political landscape fueling them: America was friends with the "westernized" Pakistani president, whose politics stood in direct opposition to the Islamic terrorist cadre's goal.

Garrett refused the headache trying to take over his brain. *God, help us.*

Hand still on the mask, he scanned Charlie team. Felt the buzz of adrenaline as the chopper zipped them closer to target. These were the best of the best. Warriors. Hunters. SEALs. His men.

Warmth pressed against Garrett's calf, and he eyeballed

Tsunami. In the dark, the pure-black Malinois looked more like a phantom than a dog. Soulful brown eyes squinted at the terrain, blurring a hundred feet below. Her pink tongue dangled, and she shifted her position, those keen eyes sweeping up to him. When she noticed him looking at her, she jammed her snout up under his hand and thrust upward with that powerful Malinois neck, insisting he pet her. This hard-hitting Malinois and her snout were the key.

"You help us do this, and I'll buy you a steak," he muttered, knowing the Malinois could hear him over the thunder of the chopper and elements. When Garrett didn't immediately pet her, she nudged his hand again.

With a quirk of his lips, Garrett gave in. Always did like a girl with attitude. "One day," he said in a quiet tone, "that attitude will get you in trouble." A double pat to his shoulder drew his gaze to the flight chief, who held up both palms.

Garrett nodded and keyed his mic to Charlie team. "Ten mikes out."

Tsunami stood and her tongue disappeared, ears up and trained on the beachhead. The four-legged warrior was ready for action.

Garrett looked out at Tadjoura. Home to around 45,000, it was the third-largest city in Djibouti and had a smattering of white houses that all looked alike.

The flight chief held up three fingers.

"Three mikes out," Garrett announced to Charlie as he shifted to the edge of the nylon seat. Brought his M4 around in front of him and lowered his NODs.

The helo descended, dust and dirt swirling in a cloud as it held station over the tiny sheltered beach they'd mapped out one klick north of Tadjoura.

Garrett hit the beach and rushed forward, dropping to a knee to provide cover as the rest of Charlie deployed behind him. He scuttled up to a six-foot wall and pressed his shoulder against the concrete. He scanned up and down the beach as the rest of the team dropped in. Zim patted Garrett's shoulder, giving the ready signal, and he pushed up, his boots digging into the sand. Eyes out, ears alert, and heart steady, he trekked down the deathly quiet street that paralleled the gulf.

As they reached the outskirts of the neighborhood intel had targeted, lit by the moonlight, Garrett pulled aside and motioned the MWD team ahead. The neighborhood was empty and quiet. He looked over at Samwise. "Go."

The handler caught Tsunami's collar. "Tsunami, seek-seek-seek."

Garrett trailed the duo, who were checking shadows, windows, doors, rooftops, the hard-working nose taking in scents.

With all her spunk on full display again, Tsunami charged forward to do her job, towing Samwise as they took point. Just like Charlie, the dog ran toward the trouble, anxious to seek it out. Ears swiveling, the Malinois rushed onward, sleek snout drawing in long, puffing breaths as she zigzagged up the street. She hugged the first row of structures, sniffing out each door and moving on to the next.

Keeping pace, Garrett patrolled the street, monitoring the dog's progress and the comms chatter, anticipating trouble. Which would come. He could feel it in the air.

Tsunami hurried to a house, passed it. Lifting her head, she took in long draughts and circled around. Took more time sniffing a corner of the building. Paced the scent trail back and forth. She angled toward Garrett and brushed against his leg. He'd swear she did that on purpose, almost as if telling him to give her room to work the scent cone.

He backed up. Samwise had once explained that the scent trail started wide and narrowed—like a cone—as it got closer to the scent source.

Tsunami planted herself in front of a door.

*Attagirl.*

Samwise glanced at him and gave a nod, then drew his Malinois aside.

Shoulders taut, Garrett stepped up to examine the barrier and spotted a digital lock. *Well, that's different…*He visually traced the jamb for tripwires or plastique. If the dog said the lipid was here, then the lipid was here. He just didn't want to get blown to kingdom come proving that. "Zim, you're up," he subvocalized to their communications specialist as he shifted aside and saw Charlie holding watch.

The five-nine SEAL hustled up, phone in hand as he eyed the digital lock. In what felt like seconds, Zim overrode the electronic lock, then snapped up his weapon and stepped back.

"Send the dog," Garrett said.

Samwise caught Tsunami's lead and unclipped it. After a nod from Garrett, he sent the black Malinois into the white house.

M4 up and tucked into his shoulder, Garrett glided and banked left, checking the corner, then swung right along the wall. A series of *clear*s told him the immediate area was clear. The winey smell of cookstove ethanol, with a hint of mold, permeated the tightly packed space. The four-legged operator trotted down a long hall, ducking into a room and out of another.

Garrett moved through the plaster home. Around a wobbly table, a threadbare cushion lazily tossed in a corner. Soda bottles and cans littered the dirt floor.

"Clear," Zim called via comms just before he reemerged, moving methodically to the next room, weapon tucked firmly against his shoulder.

Ahead, Tsunami emerged from a back room and headed for the stairs.

Stairwells were notorious for creating an incredibly risky fish-in-a-barrel scenario. Garrett nodded to the handler, who sent the dog up.

Tsunami vaulted from every third step till she reached the top and rushed to the left and an open door barely visible from the lower level. Spine to the wall, Garrett swept his weapon up as he climbed the stairs, expecting contact any second.

On the second level, he peered around the corner.

Tsunami was hauling in scents as she headed down a narrow hall straight to the farthest door on the left. The Malinois sniffed at it. And she again planted herself with a double thrust of her snout at the door. Ears pricked, she stared at the barrier, then shot a glance to Samwise as if to say, "Right here, Boss."

After Zim swung to his right on the top stair and readied himself, Garrett took up position. King and Brooks lined up behind them on the stairs. He'd learned long ago to trust MWDs. The team had to breach this location. But what was on the other side? Explosives? Was the door rigged? Wouldn't put it past Sachaai.

Unexpectedly, the door jerked inward.

Garrett snapped his weapon up as a tall, lean man jolted at the sight of the dog.

"Hands, hands!" Garrett shouted in English and Urdu.

Samwise lunged at him as the man's hand went up—revealing a small round device.

Without warning, Samwise and Tsunami dropped like wet blankets, bodies convulsing…then…unmoving.

No! Instinct pushed Garrett forward even as he smelled… nuts? What was—

*Thud!* In a blink, the local was laid out on the floor too. The device tumbled from his hand and slid across the hall.

Was the guy dead? Garrett moved in to check—

A hand slapped his chest—Zim's. "Masks!"

The shout was enough to jack Garrett's heart into his throat. He snatched his chemical mask and stuffed it on, quickly securing the straps. He gave Zim a nod of thanks, then glanced back to the team.

King backed down the hall to the stairs, grabbing his mask off his belt, Brooks doing the same.

Backstepping, Garrett aimed for the stairs and eyed Tsunami

and Samwise. "Eagle One, this is Bear. Possible chemical agent. Samwise and Tsunami down. Local male down."

"Copy that, Bear. Advise immediate exfil and head to rendezvous site."

"Good copy, Eagle One." Garrett darted into the invisible chemical fog and caught Samwise's drag strap. Hauled him back, even as Zim shifted a now-limp Tsunami around his shoulders and snagged the man's odd device. Hiking Samwise onto his shoulders, Garrett hoofed it with Zim back down the suddenly cold hall. The floor shifted—and Garrett collided with the wall. Oh no. Dizziness. He'd been infected! A fog edge into Garrett's mind, but he forced himself on, away from the bitter almond smell. "Charlie team, clear out," he comm'd as he headed to the stairs.

Ahead, Zim began stumbling.

Garrett hooked his arm up around the nerd and shoved them both down the hall.

At the stairs, Zim whispered, "I'm okay now, Boss."

Taking in the area, Garrett wondered about that scent. Where'd that come from? Didn't matter. Men were down, the dog was down. Samwise's weight made him take care as he hustled to the first level and rushed out the front door, where the team waited. He rolled his shoulder, releasing Samwise into the capable hands of the corpsman. "Chemical. Passed out." They laid him out and Garrett shifted aside.

Brooks went to a knee, bent over Samwise. "Unconscious. Breaths are light and fast. Pulse is normal." He huffed. "We need to get him to Lemonnier and their medical team. And a decon team for all five of you, considering that chemical effect."

"How's Tsunami?" Garrett asked.

"Same."

He turned and spied Zim still up and moving. Then he took a long draught from his CamelBak and caught one corner of the tactical litter Brooks had deployed.

"Chopper's en route to rendezvous," Zim announced.

"Let's go," Garrett called as they quick-stepped through the shadows with King bringing up the rear, monitoring their six.

Hoofing it through the city, they stayed alert, grateful for no contact. And for the helo waiting for them once they reached the beach extraction point. They slid the litter onto the deck and climbed in. The chopper lifted and whisked them away from the site.

Grateful his dizziness had faded, Garrett glanced at his swim buddy next to him. Something about the way Samwise was lying there, unmoving…"Sam!" Garrett lunged. Checked for breathing—nothing. Shoved two fingers against his buddy's throat—again, nothing! "Sam, c'mon!" He dropped to his knees and began CPR.

From the back, Brooks counted out loud to keep him steady. "Check his pulse."

Garrett did. "Nothing!" And he started CPR again.

"One man down, chemical inhalation. Unknown agent," King comm'd, shouting above the rotor noise. "Not breathing, no pulse. En route, three mikes out."

Garrett kept up the rhythmic presses on Sam's chest. "Live for Catherine, Samwise. Catherine!" he yelled over the chopper noise.

"Check pulse," Brooks said again.

"Nothing!" Despite the pronouncement, they kept working. Compressions. Breath. Compressions. Breath.

Garrett bit back a curse as they landed at Lemonnier hospital. A medical team swept forward and set Sam's litter on a gurney. A doctor climbed on and continued resuscitation efforts as they rushed into the facility. Brooks followed, providing Sam's medical status info.

Garrett pounded the side of the helo, then spotted a team loading Tsunami onto a gurney. He rushed over to her.

"Animal hospital. Now!" a corpsman barked.

Medical staff moved toward Zim.

"I'm fine," he snarled, and the woman backed away, eyes wide.

As they hurried toward a vehicle, Garrett ran his hands slowly up and down the sweet, hard-working Malinois as she was transferred to another gurney. His gut tightened as she let out a keening whimper beneath raspy, difficult breathing.

The nurse pulled out her phone and called the vet clinic as he climbed into a waiting ambulance with Tsunami.

Garrett stood on the tarmac, the team hurrying in one direction or another to take care of the injured. Didn't look good for Reicher. Iffy for Tsunami. All because of...

"The chemicals were weaponized," Zim huffed. "They didn't tell us that. I mean, it was a possibility, I guess—but..." Face sweaty and pale, the newb looked up at him. "They'd tell us if they knew that. Right?"

"Caldwell," he growled.

This was Caldwell's fault. No way the operative didn't know...

An hour later, Garrett threw open the door to the Tactical Operations Center and strode up to a CIA analyst whose hair was tied in a tight bun at the back of her head. The remnant of Charlie team gathered behind him, battle faces on.

"Where's Caldwell?" Garrett demanded.

"B-break room," she stammered, finger pointing to the rear.

Garrett pivoted toward the hall, feeling the team snake behind him. He punched open the door that reeked of burnt coffee and frozen dinners.

At their intrusion, Lieutenant Commander Taylor swiveled from the counter as he heated some food, licking his thumb. His gaze seemed to automatically slide to the far side of the room.

In that back corner, Bryan Caldwell smacked his laptop shut and rose. "Problem, Walker?"

"You could say that." Garrett stalked over and got into Caldwell's smug CIA face, and the team circled behind him. "You knew the chemicals had already been weaponized and didn't tell us! " He clenched his fists at his side. "Tsunami's sick, snapping at Hell's gates, and Reicher's dead."

The operative held his gaze as he processed the news. "My condolences." He scratched at his long nose like that itch was more important. "Sorry to hear that."

"Condolences? This is your fault! You withheld vital intel and killed Reicher."

"Now hold up." The man's face reddened. "There was no way to know they'd made a weaponized form already. And your team should have exercised more caution consid—"

Garrett's fist swung on its own. Connected with Caldwell's nose. *Crack!*

With a strangled shout, Caldwell shoved away, cupping his hands over his blood-gushing nose. "What the—" His eyes widened. "Walker, you're through!"

"Through with you? You bet your sorry six I am!" He didn't step back, hoping Caldwell would try something so he could level him.

Silence strained the air between them. Caldwell spat to the side, then stormed out.

"He'll press charges," Taylor warned from behind. "That was…dangerous—he's powerfully connected to the brass. Could get you discharged."

Behind him, Garrett felt the hot eyes of Charlie team.

"I'm not re-upping anyway."

We hope you loved the action, adventure, and romance in this riveting story. Discover more exciting romantic suspense from Sunrise Publishing!

## A BREED APART: LEGACY UNLEASHED!

Don't miss any of the high-octane thrills, danger, and romance in Ronie Kendig's A Breed Apart: Legacy series.

# GET READY . . . THINGS ARE ABOUT TO GET HOT!

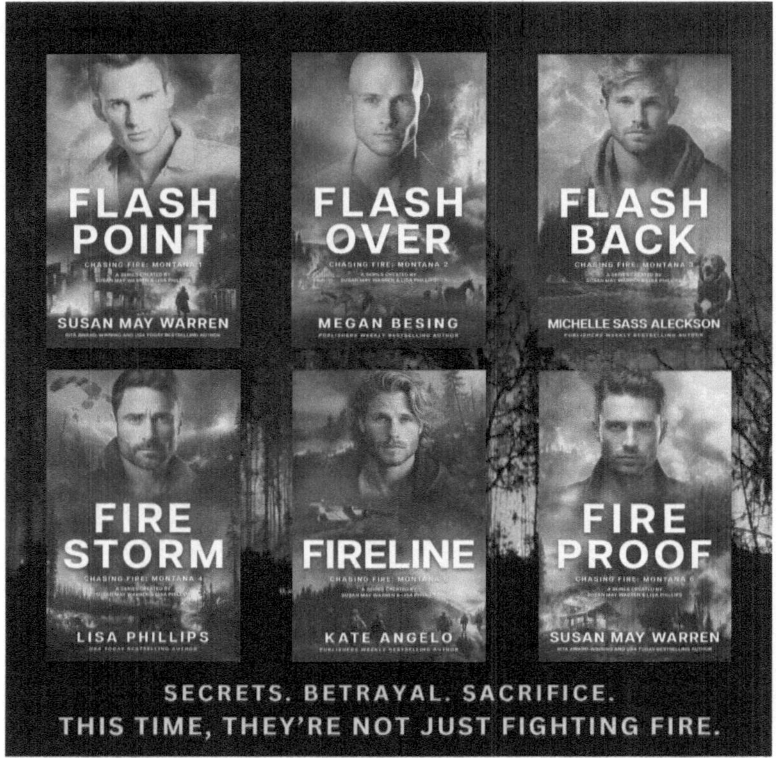


With heart-pounding excitement, gripping suspense, and sizzling (but clean!) romance, the CHASING FIRE: MONTANA series, brought to you by the incredible authors of Sunrise Publishing, including the dynamic duo of bestselling authors Susan May Warren and Lisa Phillips, is your epic summer binge read.

Immerse yourself in a world of short, captivating novels that are designed to be devoured in one sitting. Each book is a standalone masterpiece, (no story cliffhangers!) although you'll be craving the next one in the series!

Follow the Montana Hotshots and Smokejumpers as they chase a wildfire through northwest Montana. The pages ignite with clean romance and high-stakes danger—these heroes (and heroines!) will capture your heart. The biggest question is . . . who will be your summer book boyfriend?

This exciting series will be available in ebook, print, and audiobook. What are you waiting for? Pre-order the entire series now!

## FIRE. FAMILY. FAITH. LAST CHANCE FIRE AND RESCUE.

Dive into this thrilling first responder series now!

**FIND THEM ALL AT SUNRISE PUBLISHING!**

# CONNECT WITH SUNRISE

Thank you again for reading *FURY*. We hope you enjoyed the story. If you did, would you be willing to do us a favor and leave a review? It doesn't have to be long—just a few words to help other readers know what they're getting. (But no spoilers  We don't want to wreck the fun!) Thank you again for reading!

We'd love to hear from you—not only about this story, but about any characters or stories you'd like to read in the future. Contact us at www.sunrisepublishing.com/contact.

We also have a monthly update that contains sneak peeks, reviews, upcoming releases, and fun stuff for our reader friends. Sign up at www.sunrisepublishing.com or scan our QR code.

# ABOUT THE AUTHORS

**Ronie Kendig** is a bestselling, award-winning author of over thirty-five books. She grew up an Army brat, and now she and her Army-veteran husband have returned to their beloved Texas after a ten-year stint in the Northeast. They survive on Sonic runs, barbecue, and peach cobbler that they share—sometimes—with Benning the Stealth Golden and AAndromeda the MWD Washout. Ronie's degree in psychology has helped her pen novels of intense, raw characters.

To learn more about Ronie, visit www.roniekendig.com and follow her on social media.

**Steffani Webb** was born and raised in the Pacific Northwest. She is married to a wonderful husband, is a stay-at-home mom to three children, and runs a bookish Etsy shop. Fiction has always been part of her life and she was inspired to start writing her own stories at a young age. An avid reader of Romantic Suspense, Steffani loves creating relatable, character-driven stories.

# MORE A BREED APART NOVELS

**A Breed Apart: Legacy**

Havoc

Chaos

Riot

Fury

Surge

**A Breed Apart**

Trinity

Talon

Beowulf

www.ingramcontent.com/pod-product-compliance
Lightning Source LLC
Chambersburg PA
CBHW032357310726
48973CB00007B/2053